John Ramsay

The selected writings of John Ramsay, M.A.

With memoir and notes by Alexander Walker

John Ramsay

The selected writings of John Ramsay, M.A.
With memoir and notes by Alexander Walker

ISBN/EAN: 9783337276423

Printed in Europe, USA, Canada, Australia, Japan

Cover: Foto ©Andreas Hilbeck / pixelio.de

More available books at **www.hansebooks.com**

THE

SELECTED WRITINGS

OF

JOHN RAMSAY, M.A.

WITH

MEMOIR AND NOTES

BY ALEXANDER WALKER
(HIS LITERARY EXECUTOR)

PORTRAIT AND ILLUSTRATIONS

BY GEORGE REID, A.R.S.A.

JOHN RAE SMITH, ABERDEEN
WILLIAM BLACKWOOD AND SONS
EDINBURGH AND LONDON

1871

TO

THE GENTLE READER.

—◆—

A WISE man wrote some forty years ago, that "there were three difficulties in authorship—to write anything worth publishing, to find honest men to publish it, and, to get sensible men to read it. Literature has now become a game, in which the booksellers are the kings, the critics the knaves, the public the pack, and the poor author the mere table, or thing played upon."

The writer of the following papers, while in life, held some such opinion as to the gains and comforts of book-making. At his death he gave his executors the liberty to gather together into a volume such of his literary bantlings as were thought worth preserving.

For the characteristic portrait of Mr. Ramsay, and graceful artistic drawings of "bits" and "places" which he loved to look upon, the Editor has to thank the facile pencil of his friend Mr. George Reid, A.R.S.A.

CONTENTS.

CONTENTS.

LIST OF ILLUSTRATIONS.

MEMOIR.

MANY a memorial notice, pensive and graceful, did the author of the following papers write during that long life it was given him to spend in Aberdeen. To reciprocate for him this office—to sketch John Ramsay in manner as he lived,—in all his rugged independence, shrewdness, wit, with all his power of fascinating talk, telling repartee, or stinging sarcasm, is no easy task. Careless of posthumous fame—heedless of the effects of the sharp words he used—and, to many, seemingly profoundly indifferent to everything that did not minister in one way or another to his personal comfort, he had yet a depth of kindly feeling which few gave him credit for, and, the writer believes that, in spite of all his acrid utterances, he was a thoughtful Christian gentleman. No man ever suffered more from incapacity to control the expressions of a keen wit. His *perfervidum ingenium* often forced from him sayings he would have recalled as soon as uttered, and if unhappily some stinging epigram, or sharp incisive witticism, did now and again turn a kindly acquaintance into a bitter enemy, we may well lay them to rest with him in his grave.   He is no friend to the memory of John Ramsay who can repeat such sayings of his, brilliant though many of them were, apart from the circumstances of real or fancied wrong which called them forth.   Here at least they can find no place.   The selected articles which constitute the bulk of this volume indicate with sufficient clearness his position as an essayist, mathematician, poet, and wit.   Of necessity, and to a great extent, only a local interest can be felt in the subjects treated, but many of these writings, by the grace and purity of their style, merit and will receive a broader recognition of their worth.   If the Memoir fails to catch the salient points, or show the true character

> "Of that friend of mine who lives in God—
> That God who ever lives and loves,"

it will be the fault of the Editor ; for discernment, perception, force and solidity of character, every quality needed in portraiture, the subject had in abundance.

John Ramsay was born in London on the 18th September 1799.   His father, John Ramsay, was Master of a West India trader.   He died in Barbadoes.   His mother was the only daughter of Alexander M'Donald, of Calcutta, and of Elizabeth Smith, eldest daughter of the Alexander Smith, of Blairdaff, near Monymusk, whose name occurs in the list of the Commissioners of Supply for 1690. This family was one of the oldest in the county, having been settled at Blairdaff for many generations. When Ramsay was only nine months old, his mother left London for Aberdeen, taking up house in Correction Wynd, afterwards in Black's Buildings, where he was brought up. At four years of age he was initiated in reading and spelling by Miss Hogg, who taught a juvenile school in the neighbouring street, and whose good graces he fortunately gained. His two grandmothers, both women of strong sense, were at this time alive, and vied with each other in affectionate regard for him. He never had an aunt, and those elegant Cowper-like verses of his, "To my good old Aunt," the writer thinks are a creation of the poet's fancy from a study of the characters of those two gentle-women. His grandmother by the mother's side, Mrs. M'Donald, had received a liberal education, had herself been a teacher of youth, and had seen much good society. She had lived for some time in the family of Thomas Ruddiman, to whom she was related. Sir John Peter Grant of Rothie-murchus was at one period her juvenile pupil, and in the family of his father she became acquainted with the celebrated Hawkesworth, and used to amuse young Ramsay's childhood with anecdotes of him and other distinguished persons of the day, to whose society she had been introduced. This excellent lady delighted to superintend his religious, moral, and intellectual training. Before he could read with fluency, she used to read the Bible, the Spectator, and other works to him. The vision of the valley of dry bones in Ezekiel, the Vision of Mirza in the Spectator, the death of Mary Queen of Scots, were all favourite passages. After having been about two years with Miss Hogg, he entered Mr. Falconer's English and Writing School, where he continued to extend his elementary studies. Mr. Falconer was a remarkably good-tempered and able teacher, for whose memory Ramsay cherished the deepest gratitude and affection. He entered the Grammar School in November 1807, under Mr. Nicol, with whom he remained three years. He was then transferred to the Rector's care. With Mr. Nicol he had the character of being a clever, spirited little chap, who *could* when he *would.* Ramsay once, on a holiday afternoon, stopped so long at Fittie, that his mother, getting alarmed, called on Mr. Nicol. John came home, all right, late at night. Next morning, Mr. Nicol administered a long advice and a heavy thrashing to the wanderer, winding both up with the assurance that he had done it all "for the sake of his mother, Betty M'Donald."

He had no private tutor. He always enjoyed his play first, and *then* his lessons ; and sometimes in the longer summer nights, used to write his *version* outside the window, after an evening of play, for his careful mother allowed no candles at that season. He was passionately fond of reading all sorts of books, of attending the Circuit Court, the meetings of the Synod, and other public assemblies, and much given to bell-ringing, and all manner of pranks. He was a keen hand at all boyish sports, but rather given to suggesting than leading in the *ploys* of his schoolfellows, by whom he was generally liked. For story-books he would have done or given anything. He was free from vice, and never *could* tell a lie. Even when disposed to make the attempt, his face betrayed him. He did not like Mr. Cromar so well as Mr. Nicol; his progress with the former was therefore less satisfactory. In 1812 he competed for a bursary at Marischal College. Twelve were given, and he stood *fourteenth.* A son of Mr. Falconer's was thirteenth, and George Moir, afterwards distinguished at the Scotch Bar and in literature, ranked next below. They all went back to the Grammar School, of which Ramsay tired in six months. He then went to the town's Public School, at that time taught by Mr. Cruden, afterwards minister of Logie-Buchan, for arithmetic and mathematics, of which studies he became very fond. Mr. Alexander Leith Ross and Mr. Ramsay conceived about this time a great mutual friendship. Mr. Ross advised him to try his luck again at the competition, and took considerable pains with him, prescribing his versions. Ramsay's pride would not allow him to compete again at Marischal College, so he went to King's and gained the second bursary, being the youngest of ninety competitors. From Mr. Ross, and his worthy father, the Rev. Dr. Ross, of the East Kirk, he received many acts of kindness, particularly the loan of books. Ramsay's first attempt in verse was made on the occasion of the death of the amiable and lamented Mr. Ross in 1821. It was the natural expression of sincere grief.

He did not like the studies pursued during the first year at College, and therefore did not make suitable progress. He was cut off from the society of his former class-fellows, most of whom were at Marischal College. Of these, Forbes Falconer, who was formerly unsuccessful along with himself, had gained the first bursary, and George Moir, also at first unsuccessful, gained the second. Next session Ramsay entered on the study of mathematics, to which he now became greatly attached. He had begun to study astronomy by himself, and copied out a short system from a book which had been lent to him by a class-fellow. He drew the figures with a fork for want of a compass, and was reckoned the best youthful mathematician in his class. During the long vacation he prosecuted his mathematical studies with enthusiastic ardour, generally getting up at four o'clock in the morning, and many times not going abroad till nine in the evening. He could go over the whole of Euclid mentally, without the diagrams, and this used to be his employment in his walks. He loved the study for its own sake, and overcame many difficulties and discouragements in its pursuit. After this session he continued to prosecute his mathematical studies, and began an acquaintance with French mathematics. He was particularly delighted with the *Arithmetic of Sines*, and at this early age (seventeen) discovered some curious theorems in that branch.

Mr. Ramsay was never married, but in his own way defined the influences of the fits of the tender passion, to which he had been exposed. He owned to having had two—the first inspired by Annie Downie, who sat near him in the East Kirk, whose brother's battles he could fight, but to whom for three whole years he could only pay a silent worship—and the tidings of whose death, while Ramsay was deep in Lacroix, caused him not a pang; and the other by that English girl to whom he spoke his love, and was spurned. His wild rush from her father's house, out over the moor for four long miles, till he fell down exhausted, may draw a smile from those who knew Ramsay in his latter years—they laugh at wounds who never felt a scar." As regards the forming of John Ramsay's character, would not he himself have said—

> " 'Tis better to have loved and lost
> Than never to have loved at all."

Mr. Ramsay graduated in 1817, and on leaving College was for several years much engaged in teaching. Previous to this he had commenced the study of the higher calculus in the writings of Lacroix and others.

Every fresh accession of knowledge only stimulated him to acquire more. In this way he obtained a large amount of general information, which an iron memory enabled him to retain. He found no difficulty in recollecting facts and reasonings, but never had a great memory for dates, or isolated quotations. He became tutor in the family of one gentleman after another, till the late Mr. Joseph Hume, noting the capacity of the man, engaged him as his private secretary. Private secretary to Mr. Hume was not an office much in a poet's way, and accordingly we find Mr. Ramsay quickly quitting the uncongenial task of transcribing extracts from Blue Books, or following out such instructions as are contained in the following very characteristic note of the old Reformer.

"SEVEN OAKS, KENT, *2d April* 1823.

"DEAR SIR—All the letters and newspapers that come for me (except the *Times,* which must be regularly sent off to Arbroath every night), are to be sent by post to this place, until I advise you again.

"Let me know whether you have received any of the Essays from the binder, that I may give you directions respecting them.

"Open the desk at which I sit (the fir one), and in the left hand corner you will find a list of subscribers to Mill's Essays. Send that list to me in course of post.

"Put up 10 copies of the Essays in a parcel, addressed to Alex. Bannerman, Esq., Aberdeen.

"Also 20 copies addressed to Mr. James Glen, Montrose.

"Also 5 copies addressed to James Goodall, Esq., Arbroath, and put up with Mr. Glen's.

"Also 10 copies to Mr. Francis Allan, Hanover Street, Edinburgh; and on every one of them write, with Mr. Hume's compliments.

"Let the 10 copies for Mr. Allan, addressed as directed, be put up in a parcel and taken down immediately to Mr. Plow's, at Charing Cross, who will send it off immediately to Edinburgh.

"Whoever takes that parcel to Mr. Plow's, let him ask for 250 copies of the article on Government, which Mr. Plow has, take them to York Place, and keep them separate from those you have.

"Let the parcel for Mr. Glen, and the parcel

for Mr. Bannerman, be neatly put up, sealed, and directed, and you will take them down to Down's Wharf, at Wapping, where the Aberdeen and Montrose Packets lie, and give them to the captains, who will take charge of them, without the expense of entering them as parcels at the Wharf.

"If any person call, or you have anything to say, do so daily, and oblige,—Yours truly,

"JOSEPH HUME.

"Mr. Ramsay."

"Impracticable," or some such disparaging verdict, was the eminently "practical" Joe's finding on our friend. A few months after leaving Mr. Hume's employment, Mr. Ramsay became one of the teachers in Robert Gordon's Hospital, Aberdeen. In 1827 we find him contributing some mathematical questions to *The Ladies' Diary*.

It is amusing to glance over those neatly printed *Ladies' Diaries*, in which the mathematicians of those days gave each other nuts to crack. Mr. Ramsay's nuts, although hardish then are not hard now, our mathematicians having hit upon simpler forms of solution.

In the comparative quiet and ease of Gordon's Hospital, Mr. Ramsay found leisure for much else besides mathematical trifles. He contributed articles to *Blackwood's Magazine*, *The Aberdeen Magazine*, and other serials—got into correspondence with Southey, Wordsworth, Joanna Baillie, Miss Mitford, Christopher North, etc. ; in short, began the life of a man of letters. In 1834, he left the Hospital and became editorial writer for the *Aberdeen Journal,* whose leaders from this date exhibit a vigour and literary finish not common in a provincial paper.

Joseph Robertson, James Bruce, William Duncan, Thomas Spark, and Robert Brown, formed then his close companions. These wrote and spoke much, and enjoyed life with the zest which youth, sound teeth, and a good digestion, ever give. Ramsay's wit made him often cock of the company. The symposiums held in " Susie Affleck's," the squibs let off in the *Letter of Marque, Pirate,* etc., etc., were of this date. At " Susie's," high jinks were held after the manner of those immortal nights at Ambrose's, with this difference, that a racy verbal description was all that remained of the one, while a mass of glorious reading is the produce of the other. In the *Shaver, Quizzing Glass,* and *Pirate,* Ramsay indulged freely in teasing Aberdeen writers and readers. Much of it deserves to perish, but some is good and pure, and will live when the *media* through which it first saw light are utterly forgotten. The Aberdeen editors of those days delighted in humbugging each other.

Local publications were then greatly more numerous than now, and in *Aberdeen Magazines,*

Censors, Journals, Chronicles, Pirates, Shavers, Observers, etc., there was much vigorous good writing. His work upon the *Journal* did not then sit heavy on him, and many a table at that time owed its chief attraction to Ramsay's presence there. He was an exquisite mimic, and at these merry meetings, by some inimitable imitation or drollery, would set the table in a roar. His talk was always in "native Doric," and pithily could he use it. As illustrations, amongst many that occur to the writer, the following indicate the vein in which much of his conversation ran. Speaking of the frequent necessity for the rough and ready practical enforcement of principles on the young idea, he added—

> "Yer fine moral 'suasion is all humbug ;
> Naething persuades like a rap on the lug."

"I min' weel when I was scarcely five years old, how my mither taught me that. The good woman had been hearing me repeat 'The Lord's Prayer.' She had added to her other instructions that night the information that next night she wished me to say in addition 'something of my own—something that I earnestly wished God to grant me.' Ye can fancy her amazement, when from the lips of her kneeling boy there rose the petition, 'Oh Lord, gi'e my mither a better temper—mak' her—.' The 'dirl,' that instantly rang through my head, rings in't now when I'm speakin' o't." Changing the current of conversation, he would dramatise some scene which had occurred during the week, and the rendering of the manners and peculiarities of all the characters introduced was a treat such as is rarely enjoyed. One such scene may be recorded here, but without the facile imitative voice and mobile face of the little man, it loses much of its point. Robbie Brown had given an account of a political harangue of Dr. Kidd's. This report, though reproduced *verbatim et literatim*, did not please the doctor, who went from one devout admirer to another, as was his custom in such difficulties, asking, "Did I say so and so," till he got enough of "Eh na, Doctor," to satisfy himself. Then hurrying to Woolmanhill, where Brown's little shop was, he demanded of Brown's aged mother, also an admirer of the popular preacher, "Does Robert Brown live here?" "Yes, Doctor." "I want to see him." Robbie was in the cellar, and being lame, came up so far leaning on his crutch. As the head appeared above the floor level, he stopped at the shout of the irate polemic, "Are you Robert Brown?" "Yes, Doctor." "You write for the papers."— No answer. "You put words into my mouth which I never uttered." No answer. "You put a lie on the lips of a minister of the gospel." No word from Robbie, who "stood on the leg that was good," waiting the clearing of the storm. It came in the following thunder-clap. "You've done that, sir,

and I'll hunt you——I'll hunt you thro' earth——
I'll hunt you to ——." Ramsay's dramatised
version of the scene was exquisite;—" Old Mrs.
Brown, weeping and crying, " Oh, Rob, Rob, I tell't
ye nae to meddle wi' the papers. An' ye canna
thrive fin ye've interfered wi' the ministers. Oh,
Rob, Rob, ye canna brak anither mither's heart."
The Hebraist's thundering, and Robbie's calm
serenity, were all done justice to.

Mr. Ramsay was at a dinner party, in the days
when black velvet vests were held to be the correct
thing to wear, his honest black cloth one drew
down a shower of jokes upon him from Dr. D——.
till Ramsay stopped the medico's fun by naively
uttering, " Doctor, doctor, the *mort-cloth* is *not* the
insignia of my profession." " Ramsay, I'll paint
your portrait for that hit," said Mr. Giles, and
painted forthwith it was.* " Why do you let Mr.
Power of the *Aberdeen Herald* go on so?" said
some one in the course of the evening to Mr.
Ramsay : the question evoked from Ramsay the
neat quotation—

" Ah !
The pomp of *Heraldry*,
The pride of *Power*,
Alike await the inevitable hour."

Having a deep reverence for things sacred,

---

* Now the property of the writer ; Mr. Giles at his death
having bequeathed it to him.

Ramsay was yet intolerant of everything approaching to cant or formalism, and the constant protest which he felt constrained to make against the sayings and doings of the "unco guid" who drifted across his path, often led to his own feeling and practice being misunderstood. Flowing from this, or rather accompanying it, there was in Ramsay, as in many thoughtful and right-minded Scotchmen and Scotchwomen of days gone by, an audacity of thought and speech in dealing with sacred things which in a differently constituted mind would have bordered on profanity. His quaint apology for cursing a man who had done him grievous wrong —"They're guid Auld Testament curses,"—his message to an old spinster—"Tell Kirstie that she winna be comfortable in the kingdom o' heaven, for there's neither cats nor scandal there,"—his reply to a self-righteous friend, who had gratified his suppressed love for excitement by attending an oratorio, and lamented to Ramsay his having missed the singing of the Psalms, "Like eneuch, like eneuch, Geordie, listen ye to as mony o' the Psalms o' David as ye can here, for ye'll no get mony o' them faar ye're gaun."—"Your wife reminds me o' the commandments." "Why?" "Because she is exceeding broad," are specimens of the freedom with which this audacious wit touched on things which to another mind would have been hedged in and sacred.

About this time Mr. Ramsay seems to have resolved on launching a volume of his poems on the world, but he appears to have proceeded with commendable caution. He had ready beside him a quantity of MS. He had been greatly praised for what he had already published, and a laudable desire for fame led him on ; but the common-sense shrewdness of Poet-laureate Southey and Mr. Robert Chambers, as shown in the following letters, nipped the notion in the bud :—

" KESWICK.

" SIR—Your letter with its enclosed poems has this day reached me. I am sorry you have been at the trouble and expense of sending them to one who has no means of promoting your wishes, having no connection with newspapers or magazines, nor with any of the persons engaged in, or conducting them. Thirty or forty years ago your poems would have obtained the notice and the approbation which they deserve ; but it is your misfortune, like that of very many others, to live at a time when fine literature (not to mention its other diseases) is desperately sick of a surfeit. Excessive competition, which is at the root of all our national evils, affects this as it does everything else.

" From such compositions, however great their merit, it is hopeless now to look for any remuneration, unless they are published by subscription ;

and success in that way must depend wholly upon the number and activity of an author's friends. He must be a fortunate man who can count upon enough to encourage him in making the attempt.

"I wish I could have given you a more cheering reply; but this is the melancholy truth.—I remain, Sir, Yours in all good-will,

ROBERT SOUTHEY."

EXTRACT from a LETTER to GEORGE MONRO by ROBERT CHAMBERS.

"His poem came to my hands without a full signature, and it seemed to me so beautiful that I feared some one was passing off a piece of Herrick's upon us as original. Accordingly I went to a library, and painfully looked over the whole of the mingled garden and nettle-field of that man's works, to ascertain if 'My Grave' were among them. It was not, and I published it without any signature whatever. Poetry is so little in our way, that I cannot encourage your friend to write any more of that kind of thing for the *Journal*."

After this he did not cease to write poetry, as the contents of this volume show; but he never again seriously entertained the thought of collecting into a volume what he had written. In after years he burned much of it ; but enough is here given to show that "the light which never shone on sea or land—the poet's consecration and his dream"—was his.

Long extracts from *Journal* editorials on the governmental polity of the period—political party struggles, or parish politics even, are not to be worked up as "packing" for this volume. Nor, interesting though they be, will the Editor be tempted into quotations from those clear strong essays in which Mr. Ramsay fought "The Kirk's" fight against the secessionists of the day. No grander moral spectacle did the world ever see than that crowd of educated gentlemen leaving the Church of their fathers, and *their daily bread*, for a principle.

Scotland, and the Church of Scotland, gained much by their self-sacrifice. Unquestionable good has arisen out of the evil of that day,—*nec tamen consumebatur.* The reasonings and writings of the so-called Erastian party were sound and good, and Mr. Ramsay's writing was not behind the best, but it is better left where it lies. Those interested know where to find it. To the present race and to the general reader it offers no attraction. The fight is over, the feuds forgotten—"the glory dies not, and the grief is past."

In 1846-7 some influential friends made an effort to advance Mr. Ramsay's interests by securing for him the editorship of the *Edinburgh Evening Courant*, then as now the leading Conservative journal in Scotland, Lord Aberdeen—" Athenian Aberdeen," —among others doing all he could to promote his interests. " I have been a regular reader of the *Journal,*" says his Lordship, " and have always found reason to approve of the manner in which it has been conducted. . . . The ability and temper exhibited in the principal articles, I think, are incontestable. . . . I shall be glad if any favourable opinion expressed by me should be of use to you in your endeavours to obtain a more lucrative and less laborious situation, but I shall very sincerely regret the loss of your services in a quarter where I think they have been eminently useful."

While these negotiations were proceeding, an event occurred which brought them to a close. His mother died. She had been abroad at her daily walk, and was passing home somewhere about Queen Street, when a horse and cart knocked her over. She was carried home, declining to allow any one to tell her son, and giving as her reason, " It's Saturday, his busy day, an' he'll ken sune eneuch." She lingered some little time, but died of the effects of the shock on the morning of the 30th June 1847, aged eighty-two years. Deep and devoted was Mrs. Ramsay's love to her son. From her he inherited his wit and love of letters.   The keen, tidy, little gentlewoman was much respected by all who knew her, and there were many besides the Grammar-School teacher who did John Ramsay a good turn "for the sake of his mother, Betty M'Donald."   Her last advice to her son was very eminently characteristic—"*Do your duty, run no risks, and put your trust in Christ.*"   Her last articulate utterances were—"I canna bide here."

This irreparable loss crushed him.   He stopped his friends in their candidature for the editorship of the *Courant*, and shortly after gave up all connection with the *Aberdeen Journal.* The Editor cannot pass this important point in his friend's career without giving some slight sketch of what Mr. Ramsay's fourteen years' work on this excellent paper represented.   He had written all the original articles—political, ecclesiastical, literary, antiquarian, and miscellaneous, in number rather over nine thousand.   When he joined the *Journal*, its circulation, according to the Parliamentary Returns, was *Nineteen Hundred stamped copies* weekly ; when he left, it was *Three Thousand Two Hundred odd.*

The exhaustive and readable essay upon "Newspapers" was written by Mr. Ramsay a few months before leaving the *Journal.* It had been meant to be of service at the Centenary banquet, January 1848, but was not so used.   It is here printed for the first time.   Amidst much in it that is Isaac Disraeli's, there is enough of John Ramsay to make us grateful that he wrote it.

In 1851 he was an unsuccessful candidate for the Chair of Mathematics in his "Alma Mater." His fitness for this appointment, which would not have been doubted by any one who knew him intimately, was certified by such men as Dr. Olinthus Gregory, Dr. Anderson, and others. This disappointment evidently preyed upon him—"set his hair up," as he would say—"giving him no joy in man or—woman either." His own diagnosis of his case was ingenious if not scientific. "Suppressed irritation, pent up ire, ails me." "Guid keep's, Ramsay," said a friend, to whom he was telling this, "If you suppressed or keepit back ony,—you've let out plenty."

Mr. Ramsay continued in impaired health for some years, and frequently talked about quitting Aberdeen, but never could succeed in tearing himself away from the familiar places for more than a few weeks at a time. Gilcomston, the Heading Hill, Black's Buildings, Spa Street, the houses where his mother had lived, the churchyard where she slept, had irresistible power over him. He had a deep poetic reverence for the past, and a nervous dislike to change. At length this lassitude and depression wore off, and we find him again writing archæological papers, pensive notices of "friends that round him fell," energetic defences of

some time-honoured building, or ancient right
assailed.   The grand old belfry of Saint Nicholas
again asserted over him its magic power—

> " Here he found
> A sweeter paradise of sound,
> Than where the sirens take their summer stands,
> Among the breathing waters and glib sands."

In his boyhood, "Maria and Lawrence" had
drawn him, by their deep melodious tones, into many
a close communing with Carr the sexton, beneath
the dust-laden beams of the old Tower.   Carr was
dead now, but Drum's Aisle and the bells were there,
fascinating as ever, and many an hour was spent by
Mr. Ramsay in quiet meditation in the belfry and
the aisle ; while not many years elapsed before his
intimate acquaintance with the tower and its bells
became of great use.   Under the provostship of
Mr. Webster, who entered into the movement with
great spirit, a handsome equipment of bells was
presented to the Church of Saint Nicholas.   "Honorabilis Vir" is all that remains legible of the inscription on the monument of Provost William
Leyth, who presented the two great bells, Maria
and Lawrence, to the Church, in expiation of his
having slain Bailie Catnach at Barkmill in a
quarrel.   More than five centuries had passed since
that expiatory gift was made, but it was left to the
citizens and sons of Bon-Accord in distant lands to
complete, in 1857, the present peal of eight bells.

Change-ringing was then little practised, and less understood, in Aberdeen, and Mr. Ramsay, with commendable zeal and rare enthusiasm, set about learning it scientifically and thoroughly. He neither spåred himself nor his friends, but worked in the belfry, and wrote to every man of note in campanological matters. He thus accumulated a great amount of information which he worked up into a variety of papers. They have never been published, and are unsuited for this volume. Many an evening, at curfew hour, has the writer stood in the belfry, while Mr. Ramsay, with coat off, by voice and hand, taught his "sett." He had made himself a good ringer, and was proving himself a good teacher, when a studied insult drove him in disgust from the belfry.

For many years, with intervals of quiet, a keen discussion had been carried on as to the best means of shutting the door of one of the two Northern Universities. Dr. Johnson in 1773 described them—"In both" (King's and Marischal) said he, "there are professors of the same parts of learning, and the Colleges hold their sessions and confer degrees separately, with total independence one of the other." Between 1684 and 1742 the Marischal College and University of Dr. Johnson's time had arisen, and the building having (1826) become dilapidated and insufficient in size for the work it had to do, an effort was made to secure for its reconstruction part of an unappropriated government grant as supplemental aid to the liberal subscription which the citizens had raised. The application was successful (1834), and fully £20,000 were granted by Parliament for the purpose. Marischal College was then handsomely rebuilt—its professorial staff and standard of teaching raised in efficiency. The irritation left on the minds of the professors and friends of the sister University by this success— the latent dread of being still more eclipsed by such men as had been teaching in Marischal College, and such alumni as they had sent out into the world during the first quarter of the century —and the dislike to having a rival standard of efficiency so close to their door, rankled in the minds of the older corporation. The position and prospects of Marischal College were thus felt to be less a gain to education, than a loss to King's College and University. This feeling had culminated in 1835, in the introduction of a Bill into Parliament to unite the two Universities; but the measure was defeated. For twenty years Mr. Ramsay did his share of the party-writing which filled the local papers on this vexed question, and so hotly did the quarrel rage, that " Fusionist" and " Anti-Fusionist " became terms of *endearment* as powerful as " Intrusion " and "Non-Intrusion " slang had ever been. With Mr. Ramsay's voluminous writings upon this subject the writer does not mean to meddle. While, however, claiming for Mr. Ramsay his position in the front van of those who fought for the City University, he feels compelled in justice to add that Mr. Ramsay did not stand alone. We cannot say of him, "of all the faithless faithful only he." Dr. Torrie, Dr. Daun, Mr. Leslie of Powis, Dr. Mearns of Kineff, Mr. Fraser of Saint Clement's, and a host of other King's College men fought consistently for the rights of Marischal College. They fought, however, an unequal fight, as their antagonist now had a few skilful diplomatists managing her interests, while the urban University was weakened by the very incongruity of the crowd of untried defenders who, in pamphlet, speech, paper, on platform, in Town Council, or at Head Court, ventilated each his pet project. The Aberdeen demand for duplicate arts classes helped King's College most effectually. The disciplined few defeated the unskilled many, and the wishes of a great city and district were set aside to benefit the Professors, and to give to the Aberdeen Medical School a set of handsome class-rooms. And thus, *for these ends only*, was blotted out in 1860 the individuality of a noble institution, nobly used, whose very name and legend was a glory to the city. The cost of education in the north of Scotland was raised enormously, and so great is the effect of this increased cost, that at the present day, with an increased population, there are not a score more entrants at *the* University than used to present themselves at each of the Colleges when the Universities were separate and distinct.

During the fifty years that preceded the Union, the carefully-guarded chairs of Marischal College had been filled by such men as Campbell, Beattie, Brown, Hamilton, Copland, Black, Macgillivray. The Senatus-filled seats at King's during the same period had been honoured by three names of distinguished merit — Gerard, Eden Scott, and Mearns. A Professor at Marischal College told the world with the coolness of an Old Bailey lawyer, that " this fusion of the Colleges was to be for the benefit of the poor."   If, "*sotto voce*," he had added, " professors," the object has doubtless been gained, otherwise, one may look in vain for the good that has resulted from the amalgamation.

To the subject of this memoir the excitement of the discussion, and the stirring interest he took in the struggle, did more good than all the "waters of Israel."

Again his dapper little figure sunned itself in Union Street, and many a table was again joyous with his wit. Mr. Ramsay's political feelings were at no time markedly positive, and being facile with his pen, and fond of using it, the passing topics of the hour were written about in the *Herald, Free Press*, or *Journal* indiscriminately. In the pages of all these his hand may be traced during the last ten years of his life. The trial of the woman M'Lauchlan in Glasgow—the repairs and restoration of St. Machar's Cathedral—the returning Municipal Elections—the need of a new Fish Market; in short, nothing came amiss to his head and hand.

The gratitude of an old pupil, who had made a fortune in India, and, dying about this time, bequeathed a few hundred pounds to Mr. Ramsay, helped to swell the little store, which, beginning with his good thrifty mother's savings, had since her death grown steadily in her son's hands. He was very careful and economical, and lived on what many would have called a starvation pittance, saving and setting aside a little every year, giving at the same time many a thanklessly-received help to some needy one. There still live among us "lorn, forsaken brothers," who, by Mr. Ramsay's timely aid were enabled to "take heart again." In such matters he let not his right hand know what his left had done, and when discovered, his hasty remark would be "we'll get a blessin' wi' the lave, and never miss't." His tastes were simple, and in a grave and serious tone he would often denounce the extravagance of some one of the Aberdeen "Upper Ten Thousand," who for the day was foremost in the wild race of waste and dissipation.

The future, "that all haill hereafter," was never

absent from his mind, and this too close intro-
spection to which he was ever submitting himself,
had the usual hurtful result. At three previous
periods of his life, but now with greater severity
and longer continuance of mental disquiet, he was
confined to bed, almost seeming " like one that was
of sense forlorn," seeing scarcely one of the friends
of his untroubled days, and feeling an unutterable
longing for " the rest that remaineth"—" I *know*
in whom I have believed." " I neither am, nor
ever was, sceptic or free-thinker, tell him *that*," he
said, referring to one who had doubted the sincerity
of his faith. While recovering from this illness—
1865—he wrote " The Sick Chamber," and slowly
once again came back among old familiar faces
for the last time.

A couple of years of comparative health—many
little contributions thrown off—old favourite
sketches re-written and re-touched.—sparkles of
the old wit, mellowed by time—were still gladden-
ing the homes and hearts of the few friends whom
he now visited, when an attack of bronchitis laid
him down, prostrating and shattering in a few weeks
the hale and hearty little man.

An old school-fellow, a rich metropolitan
merchant, being in Aberdeen, and hearing of his
illness, called to see him at Black's Buildings. " So
ye never married, Robert." " No, Ramsay, I got a
wife and family handed to me ready made." " Oh,

yes, I recollect" (remembering that a widowed sister and her children had been taken to his friend's house). "Ye're doing the work o' yer heavenly father, takin' care o' the widow and the fatherless, and it'll no be forgotten ; it'll be a crown o' joy and rejoicing to you ae day." Returning summer brought no renewed strength ; he moved from one house to another in search of health, and found his last home on earth in Marischal Street, in the house that once was Historian Kennedy's. There for months he lingered, preparing with his own hands his last will and settlement, bequeathing to the fund for Aged and Indigent Gentlewomen the greater part of that little which it had cost him so much to accumulate. He suffered greatly during the last four months of his life ; yet ever and anon gleams of the old power flashed out. One instance, occurring a few weeks before his decease, brings the man so completely before those who knew him, that the writer does not hesitate to give it. "You are placing too much trust in medicine for relief, Mr. Ramsay," said a dear kind friend to him. "Ay, ay, that's a' very good o' you, who never had a day's illness a' yer life." "Oh, but, Mr. Ramsay, *my* time of trial and pain *will* come." "I'm nae sure o' that ; it's whom the Lord loveth that He chasteneth." Chastened sore he was, with much suffering, struggling into that brighter day, yet, leaning firmly on that *one* arm which could alone sustain him, he passed down the dark valley, and entered into his rest, on the morning of Saturday, the 4th June 1870 ; and, on the seventh day of the same month, amidst flowers that love had strewn around his grave, the friends of early years laid him beside his mother in " the Auld Kirkyard," where, " after life's fitful fever he sleeps well."

25 DEE STREET, ABERDEEN.
   1st November 1870.

SELECTED WRITINGS.

MY GOOD OLD AUNT.

Ah ! never, never, can my heart forget
My good Old Aunt—I was her infant pet !
Methinks I see her in her sober trim—
So clean—so tidy, but by no means prim—
That pointed backward to the olden time
When she, and many gone, were in their prime.
Her decent head-dress of transparent lace
A simple ribbon fastened to its place ;
Beneath the chin it formed a little knot,
Above her brow there bound it to the spot
A tiny brooch of sparkling garnet stone ;
Her chastened taste permitted that alone
To deck her forehead, where the " almond tree"
Usurped the place where auburn used to be !
Around her neck, as pure as summer dawn,
Was thrown a kerchief of unsullied lawn ;
Let not the belles within our own good town
Deride the antique fashion of her gown :
What though the sleeve just reached the elbow-joint ?
What though the train seems rather from the point ?
What though its rustling length would hardly suit
The wanton mincing of some pretty foot !
Still she'd salute me with endearing word—
Her " sweet"—her " darling"—or her " bonny bird!"
Would gently stroke my little head, the while

B

The action suited by her kindly smile !
Would make me con the hymn or simple prayer ;
From naughty thought would caution to forbear ;
Would speak of Him who loves the little child,
Who tends the lamb, and clothes the floweret wild ;
Of that most happy place where enter none
That lack the temper of the little one ;
To that thrice holy book would draw mine eye,
And lead me on, mine infant skill to try
Its sacred page to scan ; and when away
To luring print my giddy thought might stray,
Would still endeavour, with some wile of love,
To hint a lesson of the things above !
Then, from her pocket there would ever come
The pretty book—confectionary plum ;
And as I kissed my hand with beaming eyes,
More pleased than since with some far greater prize,
The mother's heart would glisten in her eye !
But her true love had died :—and when her sigh
Had caught my ready notice, then I took
Her hand, with childhood's unsuspecting look,
And asked, in lisping accent, if she ailed ?
Her quivering hand her eyes a moment veiled !
'Twas but a passing cloud—for the clear blue
Of their fair sky resumed its customed hue.
And when, at walks, I toddled in her hand
To daisied mead, or sea-begirting sand,
With ceaseless converse we beguiled the way :
Then from her side I oft would scour away,
To cull some pretty weed or shining shell
Where ocean's mimic murmurs seemed to dwell.
And she would smile to mark my childish glee,
When fleeing from the fast-pursuing sea ;

And, when I bilked the drenching of the spray,
Her feeble cheer would join my shrill huzza !
Much would I prattle of the passing sail,
When scudding fast before the favouring gale.
Much of the finny tenants of the wave,
Much of the " sinking sands," and " mermaid's cave ;"
Much of the hidden treasures of the deep,
Where many crews of gallant sailors sleep
The sleep that needs nor couch nor downy pillow !
Nor constant lulling of the rolling billow !—
And when the Sabbath brought its heavenly calm,
With chime of bell, and voice of simple psalm,
How pleased was I to seek the house of prayer,
My hand in hers !   With what a solemn air—
Precocious mannikin !—I took my seat !
Far was the flooring from my dangling feet,
Unwelcome neighbours of the muslin gown
Of buckram spinster, whose forbidding frown
And jerking jog, and eye as fierce as cat's,
Denounced both marriage and its plaguy brats !
But *my* old maid would draw me to her side,
With shoes and all, and looked so gratified
When I would note the text in holy book,
From which the man of God his counsel took,
And still would help her fading sight to trace
Th' appointed service to its proper place.
And when some pettish mood or froward pranks
Procured me something in the shape of thanks
(For some transgression of a high command),
From dreaded ferule, or the ready hand,
Bent on performance of the parent's duty,
In stern accordance with the moral beauty
Of that same proverb which seems rather odd

To all who *feel* the *fondling* of the rod ;
How she would strive to soothe my little grief,
And to my faults would still refuse belief!
Of some "bad boy" she now and then would hear,
Yet sure she was it could not be "her dear!"
And when, with coming years, I laid aside
The child—the boy—for the gay stripling's pride,
And stepp'd abroad in all the confidence
Of what I deemed my own matured sense,
Careless of counsel—of success secure—
In hope, so rich !—in caution, very poor !
With what delight she viewed my ripening years—
Myself the centre of her hopes and fears !
At length, I helped to lay her reverend head
Gently upon her last and lowly bed.
Still to her grave my pensive steps I bend,
To bless my early venerable friend !
Ah ! often 'midst the tumults of the strife
Of joys and sorrows in my after life,
Would I bethink me of my good old maid,
And e'en would fancy that her friendly shade
(If such permission to the saints were given)
Might steal a moment from the bliss of heaven
To touch my heart !—Did not the contrite tear—
My better thoughts—bespeak her presence near ?
How dear, O memory ! thy reflective power
To render back the bygone happy hour !
Too oft, alas ! thou only bringest gloom
From the dim precincts of the beacon-tomb
Of days departed !—When thou dost display
A pleasing dream of some past halcyon day,
We yearn for joys that never must return,
As fondly as we vainly clasp the cherished urn !

CRITICISM ON ADDISON.

ADDISON is justly regarded as one of the earliest and greatest improvers of the English language. During a period, which some have been pleased to consider the Augustan age of English Literature, his style was esteemed the standard of elegant composition. Although he is by no means an absolutely faultless author, and more recent usage has rendered his style in some respects antiquated, yet there are few writers whose style can be more safely recommended as a general model for imitation. The style of Addison is, generally speaking, extremely simple and unaffected. It is perspicuous and pure in a very remarkable degree ; and if occasionally it is not very precise, it is at least as much so as his subject requires. In the construction of his sentences he is distinguished by graceful ease and insinuating melody. He often displays a rich vein of figurative language, which greatly enhances the beauty of his manner. Although he was careful, even to fastidiousness, in polishing his style, yet it bears no obtrusive marks of labour, no appearance of constraint, but a happy union of elegance, simplicity, and ease.   The moral characteristics of his works are of a very high order.   All his writings are distinguished by a spirit of modesty, of urbanity, of philanthropy, and of devotion to the great interests of religion and morality, which is as creditable to his heart, as the merely intellectual excellences of his style are to his head.   If, in any respects, he is deficient, it is, as already remarked, in precision and strength ; a circumstance which renders his style more suitable to such works as the *Spectator*, than to those which require a higher and more elaborate kind of composition.   This defect, however, may have naturally arisen from the light nature of some of the subjects of which he treats, and the peculiar manner which he thought fit to adopt in order to secure a favourable reception from the public for others of a graver character. The more we consider the character of the age in which he wrote, the greater will the merit of Addison's writings appear in effecting a remarkable revolution in our literature, the beneficial effects of which have been transmitted through succeeding years, and are still conspicuous at the present day. True it is that, before his time, various writers had appeared who had exhibited unquestionable proofs of the vast capabilities of our language ; yet, while these were distinguished for originality of thought, and masculine energy of style, they were frequently deficient in that purity, harmony, simplicity, and polished grace, which Addison displayed in so re-markable a degree as mainly to contribute to the *fixation* of the English language. We shall now proceed to consider the most remarkable points, both in sentiment and style, in that paper of the *Spectator*, from the pen of Addison, which is the proper subject of this essay. In endeavouring, however imperfectly, to execute this task, we trust we shall experience that measure of indulgence to which its difficulty is entitled. The subject of the paper is Westminster Abbey. It so happens that a distinguished writer of the present day (Washington Irving) has treated the same subject in one of his essays in the *Sketch Book*. An occasional comparison of the different ways in which these two distinguished writers handle the same topic cannot fail to prove an interesting and profitable employment. The subject of this essay appears to us to have been peculiarly suited to the genius of Addison. The reflections to which a survey of this venerable cathedral naturally give rise, are of that pensive, moral, and religious character which are much akin to the subjects of many of Addison's most successful efforts. For example, the train of thought which might be supposed to be suggested by an edifice in which repose the ashes of many of the great and good of a series of ages, must be of a kindred nature with that which is so beautifully

developed in his *Vision of Mirza.* Although the
subject of the present paper is similar to those of
various others in which the master-mind of Addison
shines forth in all its strength and elegance, yet it
strikes us that he has not, on the present occasion,
displayed those transcendant qualities in an equal
degree. This is by no means an uncommon case
with distinguished writers. It sometimes happens
that in treating subjects which seem to be peculiarly adapted to their genius, they unaccountably
fall short of their usual success ; while, in handling
others of a less promising nature, they display a
measure of talent which is as great as it is, in some
respects, unexpected. We do not mean to say that
the paper which is the subject of discussion is unworthy of Addison in every respect ; we only mean
to express our conviction, and that with all due sub-
mission, that it is not, on the whole, the happiest of
his essays, and certainly inferior to various others
of the same class. We think that, in general, there
is a want of keeping in it, and that he introduces
certain reflections which do not harmonise with the
peculiar train of sentiment which we deem congenial
to the subject. Westminster Abbey is an edifice
devoted to the service of the Almighty, and a sanctuary for the gathered dust of many generations.
The thoughts, therefore, which the contemplation
of such a building inspires, must naturally be of a
solemn, elevated, and pensive complexion ; and,

consequently, reflections of a light, trivial, or sarcastic nature, appear to us to be quite unsuitable to the occasion. But to proceed to particulars. Generally speaking, the introductory sentence of an essay is the most difficult and important part of it. It ought in some measure to be a key to the whole. It ought to be perspicuous, of moderate length, and embued with the pervading character of the essay. The first sentence of this essay is as follows :—"When I am in a serious humour, I very often walk by myself in Westminster Abbey, where the gloominess of the place, and the use to which it is applied, with the solemnity of the building, and the condition of the people who lie in it, are apt to fill the mind with a kind of melancholy, or rather thoughtfulness, that is not disagreeable."

If we may be allowed to hazard an opinion on this sentence, we would say that it appears to us to be rather loose in its texture, and somewhat deficient in harmony. We consider the term "gloominess" somewhat inappropriate, as conveying ideas of a disagreeable nature, which are foreign to the subject. We think, too, that the conjunctive particles employed in enumerating the four characteristics of the building here mentioned might have been omitted, and their cumulative force thereby increased. We think that the expressions, " a kind of melancholy, or rather thoughtfulness," are perhaps a little redundant, and that the idea might

have been better conveyed by a single expression.
Let us compare this with the introductory sentence
of Irving's essay. " On one of those sober, or
rather melancholy days in the latter part of autumn,
when the shadows of morning and evening almost
mingle together, and throw a gloom over the decline of the year, I passed several hours in rambling
about Westminster Abbey." We think this introductory sentence superior to Addison's in all essen-
tial points. It surpasses it in harmony, precision,
and propriety. Nothing can be finer than its
melody; and nothing more congenial to the subject than the train of sentiment which it breathes.
In these respects it strongly reminds us of the introductory sentence of the vision of Mirza already
alluded to. Passing over the next sentence, which
does not seem to contain anything remarkable, we
would beg leave to make a few remarks on the
three sentences which follow:—" Most of them—
i.e. the inscriptions on the tombstones—recorded
nothing else of the buried person, but that he was
born upon one day, and died upon another; the
whole history of his life being comprehended in
these two circumstances, that are common to all
mankind. I could not but look upon these regis-
ters of existence, whether of brass or marble, as a
kind of satire on the departed persons, who had
left no other memorial of them, but that they were
born, and that they died. They put me in mind

of several persons mentioned in the battles of heroic poems, who have sounding names given them, for no other reason but that they may be killed, and are celebrated for nothing, but being knocked on the head." We do not think that the sentiments here expressed are in strict accordance with good taste and suitable feeling. The occasion on which they are made, is, we think, of too solemn and pensive a nature for such sarcastic remarks. The contemplation of the memorials, whether more simple, or more gorgeous, of mortality, we should think, must dispose the mind to feelings of a subdued and tender nature. In such a survey we must feel that death levels all distinctions arising from connection with the present world ; and that it is the means of introducing all mankind into a state, in which it were unwise to form too sanguine conjectures respecting the fate of those who, in this world, were apparently as faultless as is consistent with the fallen state of humanity ; or to indulge in too severe suspicions with regard to the condition of those who, in the eyes of their fellow-mortals, seemed less worthy of approbation. On such an occasion every harsher thought ought to be hushed, and every desire to be quenched to draw the frailties of the departed from their drear abode. To say that they erred, is but to say that they were mortal. The remark about the simplicity of most of the inscriptions is not generally just. The more simple that a monumental inscription is, it is always the more appropriate ; and there are some cases in which simplicity is far more striking than the most ornate eulogium. For example, could any inscription be more appropriate for a monument to Newton than the name alone, with the simple record of his birth and death ? In such a case the name alone would convey an idea of affecting sublimity, which the most laboured epitaph could not impart. The mere inscription of the persons' names, with the dates of their births and deaths, cannot be justly regarded as a kind of satire on their memories. The absence of monumental encomium is no evidence that the deceased were unworthy of praise ; and the most eulogistic epitaph may be undeserved. The remarks here, therefore, appear to us to be unworthy of the occasion, and at variance with the dictates of proper feeling and just views of human nature. The allusion to the heroes " mentioned in the battles of heroic poems," appears to us to be far-fetched and constrained ; and the phrase, "knocked on the head," savours too much of vulgarity. Let us compare this passage with a corresponding extract from the essay of Irving. " The epitaphs were entirely effaced, the names alone remained, having no doubt been renewed in latter times. I remained some little while musing over these casual reliques of antiquity, thus left like wrecks upon the distant shore of time, telling no tale but that such beings had been and had perished, teaching no moral but the futility of that pride which hopes still to exact homage in its ashes, and to live in an inscription. A little longer, and even these faint records will be obliterated, and the monument will cease to be a memorial." The sentiments, and the language in which they are conveyed, of the above extract, appear to us to be far more proper than those of Addison in the extract already quoted. A little farther on Addison says, " I entertained myself with the digging of a grave," etc. To our ears the use of the word " entertained " appears to be somewhat strange. This, however, arises from the change which its application has undergone since the days of Addison. The words " entertain " and " entertainment," according to present usage, convey the idea of diversions of a light and joyous character. We talk of the entertainment of the evening with reference to the amusements of the theatre ; but, in the common acceptation of the term, the digging of a grave is by no means an entertaining spectacle. However, all that Addison means by thus entertaining himself, is, that he interested himself in contemplating the performance of one of the sad offices of mortality. We proceed to the next sentence, which, though a long one, we are glad to quote as matter of commendation. " Upon this I began to consider with myself what innumerable multitudes of people lay confused together under the pavement of that ancient cathedral ; how men and women, friends and enemies, priests and soldiers, monks and prebendaries, were crumbled amongst one another, and blended together in the same common mass ; how beauty, strength, and youth, with old age, weakness, and deformity, lay undistinguished in the same promiscuous heap of matter." It is unnecessary to point out particularly the excellences of this sentence. It is just in sentiment, clear in expression, and harmoniously balanced throughout. In the next sentence there occurs an unfortunate expression. It runs thus:—" After having surveyed this great magazine of mortality, as it were, in the lump," etc. The phrases "as it were," and "in the lump," we consider objectionable, particularly the latter, with reference to the occasion on which it is employed. We may with propriety talk of surveying a package of goods, or any equally undignified quantity, "in the lump," but the phrase as used in the present instance is certainly out of place. In the following four sentences Addison again indulges in a strain of sarcastic remark, which, although it may be partially just, we consider, for reasons already assigned, to be somewhat unsuitable. "Some of them were covered with such extravagant epitaphs, that, if it were possible for the dead person to be acquainted with them, he would blush at the praises which his friends have bestowed upon him." The word "person" seems to be here incorrectly used. It appears to imply that the same dead person had a common right to all the extravagant epitaphs, which certainly is not the meaning which the author intended to convey. In a subsequent sentence he says, "In the poetical quarter I found there were poets who had no monuments, and monuments which had no poets." This is rather a summary way of discussing the most interesting part of the Abbey. Let us hear Irving on this point. "I passed some time in Poets' Corner, which occupies an end of one of the transepts or cross aisles of the Abbey. The monuments are generally simple, for the lives of literary men afford no striking themes for the sculptor. Shakespeare and Addison have statues erected to their memories, but the greater part have busts, medallions, and sometimes mere inscriptions. Notwithstanding the simplicity of these memorials, I have always observed that the visitors to the Abbey remain longest about them. A kinder and fonder feeling takes place of that cold curiosity and vague admiration with which they gaze on the monuments of the great and the heroic. They linger about these as about the tombs of friends and companions—for, indeed, there is something of companionship between the author and the reader. Other men are known to posterity only through the medium of history, which is continually grow-

ing faint and obscure ; but the intercourse between
the author and his fellow men is ever new, active,
and immediate.   He has lived for them more than
for himself ; he has sacrificed surrounding enjoyments, and shut himself up from the delights of
social life, that he might the more immediately
commune with distant minds and distant ages.
Well may the world cherish his renown, for it has
been purchased, not by deeds of violence and
blood, but by the diligent dispensation of pleasure.
Well may posterity be grateful to his memory, for
he has left it an inheritance, not of empty names
and sounding actions, but whole treasures of wisdom, bright gems of thought, and golden veins of
language."   The allusion to Addison in this beautiful passage we deem highly interesting.   It could
scarcely occur to the author of the *Spectator*, while
surveying the monuments of departed genius, that,
after an interval of a hundred years, a kindred spirit
from a foreign land might make a pilgrimage to
his tomb, and thus record a tribute of veneration
for his memory.   In a subsequent sentence he says,
" As a foreigner is very apt to conceive an idea of
the ignorance or politeness of a nation," etc.   Here
the word "politeness," as opposed to "ignorance,"
means an acquaintance with elegant literature and
the fine arts.   This acceptation of the term is now
obsolete.   The term "politeness," in its modern
sense, is employed to express elegance of manners

and urbanity of demeanour in social intercourse. The episode, if we may use the term, about Sir Cloudesley Shovel's monument, and the remark on the Dutch monuments which follow, have little else in them remarkable than their being rather out of place—and certainly not very complimentary to English taste—and, perhaps, not very just. The four following sentences, though sufficiently common-place in point of sentiment and expression, do not contain anything remarkably objectionable, either in the one respect or in the other. In the last three sentences, however, Addison is decidedly himself. We must quote at length this admirable passage. "When I look upon the tombs of the great, every emotion of envy dies in me; when I read the epitaphs of the beautiful, every inordinate desire goes out; when I meet with the grief of parents upon a tombstone, my heart melts with compassion; when I see the tomb of the parents themselves, I consider the vanity of grieving for those whom we must quickly follow. When I see kings lying by those who deposed them, when I consider rival wits placed side by side, or the holy men that divided the world with their contests and disputes, I reflect, with sorrow and astonishment, on the little competitions, factions, and debates of mankind. When I read the several dates of the tombs of some that died yesterday, and some six hundred years ago, I consider that great day when we shall all of us be contemporaries, and make our appearance together." The whole of this passage deserves unqualified praise. We do not think that it contains anything faulty in point of expression, and the sentiments conveyed are admirably suited to the solemnity of the occasion. Each succeeding sentence rises above that which precedes it, in elevation of thought, and the last contains the natural climax of the whole train of reflection. From reflections on the more common chances of life and death, the author ascends to such as relate to the fate of those who were prominent in the world for rank, for genius, or for learning, and at length reaches that great consummation which connects time with eternity, and the circumstances of our globe, and all who it inherit, with the unseen realities of the world beyond the grave.

ON TAKING LEAVE OF ABERDEEN.

Fair blows the wind, the lagging waves
    With murmurs seek the shore,
The flowing tide our vessel laves,
    Old ocean spreads before,

And, rolling on his sandy couch,
    Methinks, seems now to smile
To night's fair queen, and fondly crouch,
    Though lashed to rage erewhile.

But time and tide must fail at last,
    The pilot chides our stay,
The canvas wings our straining mast,
    We bound across the bay !

Sure some there are—on shore—on board—
    On whom the pilot's call
Came like the knell of all adored
    By them on earth ; 'tis gall

To mark th' embrace—all speech above—
    The scarcely breathed—" Adieu !"
The eloquence of looks which love
    Interprets—" Still be true."

And then—the fixed—the straining eye
    Bright glistening through a tear,
And, mingled with a stifled sigh,
    The oft-repeated cheer!

Though no such strong emotions shake
    My heart, it cannot well,
Of much that has been dear now take,
    Without one throb, farewell.

What though each dear familiar scene
    No more may greet mine eye!
Nor time nor place my soul shall wean
    From days long long gone by!

Those days on which fond mem'ry throws
    A soft reflective gleam,
Sweet as the smile my country shows
    All in the moon's mild beam!

Farewell! farewell! thrice-honoured land!
    Still clings my heart to thee!
Though urged my course, by fate's command,
    Far, far across the sea!

ROYAL VISITS TO ABERDEEN IN OLDEN TIMES.

AT a time when the ancient and ever loyal City of Bon-Accord is about to receive a passing visit from our most gracious and beloved Queen, it may be deemed not inappropriate to the auspicious occasion to present a few notes of the circumstances under which some of her Majesty's royal predecessors have honoured Aberdeen with their presence.

Some of our old chroniclers will have it, that Aberdeen was one of the residences of the usurper Grig, commonly called Gregory the Great, whose misty history belongs to the latter half of the ninth century. They assure us, that he had what they magniloquently call a "palace" in Aberdeen ; that he bestowed on the city its first charter ; and that he was so specially fond of it, as to speak of it as "his own city." These statements, however, are not borne out by any trustworthy evidence, and must be regarded as in a great measure, if not wholly, fabulous.

It is most likely that Aberdeen owed its first

charter, if not its origin, to the munificence and enlightened patriotism of David I., since the oldest
charters extant are partly confirmatory of privileges conferred on the citizens by that monarch,
but make no reference to earlier marks of royal
favour.

The first monarch of whose residence in Aberdeen there is authentic evidence is King William
the Lion, grandson of David I.   He appears to
have resided frequently, either in the city or county,
between the years 1179 and 1214.   The oldest extant charter of the city was granted by him, and is
believed to be of the former date.   It is still in
good preservation.   William appears to have had a
house in Aberdeen, which, about 1211, he bestowed
on the order of Trinity, Red, or Maturine Friars,
whose chief business it was to collect funds for the
redemption of Christians held in slavery by the In-
fidels in Palestine.   Of this palace nothing now remains ; the site is occupied by the Old Trades
Hall.   But there is still to be seen in the new Hall
a ponderous table, at which tradition says the leo-
nine monarch used to preside.   It is a very curious
piece of furniture, consisting of a massive slab of
artificial stone, smoothly polished, and set in a
beautiful oak frame of much later date; the style of
the ornaments showing that it belongs to the early
part of the seventeenth century.   The framework
bears the arms of Dr. Guild, who purchased and

fitted up the ruins of the monastery as an hospital for decayed burgesses of trade.

Alexander II. appears to have been frequently in Aberdeen between the years 1222 and 1235. Old Wynton says that, in the former year,

"He held his yule in Abbyrdene."

He, too, is said to have had a palace in the city, which he afterwards bestowed on the Preaching or Black Friars, an order of which he was a great patron. Its site was in what now forms the garden of Gordon's Hospital. The building was destroyed at the period of the Reformation, and not a vestige of it was visible for many years, until latterly its foundations were accidentally discovered. Between 1272 and 1369, Aberdeen was the occasional residence of Alexander III., John Baliol, Robert the Bruce, and David II. The unfortunate Baliol was taken captive here by John Comyn, Laird of Strathbogie, and delivered up to Edward I. of England at Montrose. Edward himself came to Aberdeen on the 14th of July 1296, and remained in it for five days. On the 17th he received the homage and oath of allegiance of the burgesses and community. For this act, however, the citizens afterwards made so ample an atonement to "The Bruce," that that illustrious monarch conferred on them many privileges, which are set forth in what is justly called the Great Charter of the Burgh. In some of the battles which he fought, in vindication of his title to the Crown, the citizens of Aberdeen seem to have afforded him signal assistance. We may here mention incidentally that the citizens gave undoubted proof of their loyalty and bravery at the battle of Harlaw, July 1411, when their gallant Provost, Sir Robert Davidson, and many of the burgesses, were slain in defending the rights of the Crown against the usurper Donald of the Isles.

In the month of July 1448 James II. paid his first visit to Aberdeen, when the Magistrates made him a present, under name of a "propine," of two tuns of Gascony wine, wax candles, and sweetmeats. His Queen paid a visit in January 1455, and was presented with 100 merks in money. James IV. visited Aberdeen in 1492, 1495, 1497, 1504, 1507, 1509, when he received "propines" of wine, wax, spiceries, and money. In May 1511 Aberdeen was visited by his Queen, Margaret, eldest daughter of Henry VII. of England. The occasion was afterwards celebrated in a poem written by Dunbar (who seems to have accompanied the royal party), entitled, "The Queeneis Reception at Aberdein." Great preparations were made to receive her Majesty with suitable pomp and circumstance. Commissioners were appointed to raise money to defray the expenses of the occasion; and the citizens were ordered to decorate the fronts of their houses with arras work, evergreens, and flowers.

It appears from Dunbar's poem, that the Queen was met, at some distance from the city, by the burgesses, "richelie arrayit, as became thame to be;" four of their number, "men of renoun,"

> "In gounes of velvet, young, able, and lustie,
>   To beir the pall of velvet cramasie,
>   Abone her heid, as the custome has bein."

Under this canopy the Queen took her seat, and was borne to the Shiprow Port of the city. Here she was welcomed by another procession, "in cap of gold and silk full pleasantlie," and was treated with a succession of masques and pageants. The first represented the Salutation of the Virgin—

> "The sound of menstrallis blawing to the sky."

Then came the pageant of "The Orient Kingis three;" then the expulsion of Adam and Eve from Paradise by an Angel, "with the sword of violence;" lastly came the Bruce—

> " * * * that ever was bold in stour,
>   Richt awful, strang, and large of portraitour,
>   Ane noble, dreadful, michtie champion."

Then followed a procession of "four-and-twenty maidens young," all clad in green with white hats, and "of marvellous beautie"—

> "Playand on timberallis, and singin richt sweetlie."

In fine—

> " At her coming, great was the mirth and joy ;
> For at the cross abundantly ran wine ;
> Unto her lodging the town did her convoy ;
> Her for to treat they set their haill ingine ;
> A rich present they did to her propine,
> A costlie cup that large thing would contain,
> Covered, and full of coin-ed gold richt fine :
> Be blyth and blissful, Brugh of Aberdeen ! "

The gold in the cup amounted to two hundred pounds.

In 1537 James V. visited the city, and was sumptuously entertained in it for the space of fifteen days. The unfortunate Queen Mary visited Aberdeen about August 1562, when she was received with every mark of loyalty and attachment. She was also here in the end of October that year, when the Earl of Huntly was defeated by the Earl of Murray, in the battle of Corrichie, fought in one of the glens of the Hill of Fare, in this county. The Gordon chief and many of his followers were slain ; and many prisoners were conveyed to Aberdeen, including Huntly's second son, the gallant and handsome Sir John Gordon, for whom the Queen is said to have had at one time a strong attachment. He was beheaded in Castle Street on the 2d of November, to the profound grief of the Queen, who was so situated as not to have the power of saving his life. James VI. often found a loyal reception and comfortable quarters in Aberdeen between the years 1581 and

1600. On all these occasions he received "propines" of money, and sometimes levied a needful contribution. On the occasion of his marriage with Anne of Denmark, the citizens fitted out a vessel called the *Nicholas* (after the patron saint of the city), which was commanded by one of the Bailies, and sailed from Aberdeen, to join the royal squadron bound for Denmark, on the 16th of April 1589. The vessel was completely armed, and decorated with "ensigns, flags, and streamers of war, red side-cloths, and gilded tops." It would appear that James contemplated a visit in 1617, for the Magistrates received a despatch, recommending "that lodgings be prepared in the most handsome, civil, and courtly manner; with good bedding, well-washed and well-smelled naperie; clear and clean vessels, of sufficient largeness; plenty of provisions and vivres." Suitable preparations were made, but the King came no farther north than Dunnottar Castle. In 1620, one of the citizens, Sir Thomas Menzies, presented to his Majesty a large pearl found in the brook of Kelly, which runs into the Ythan, not far from Haddo House, and which is said to be " the top pearl in the Crown of Scotland." For this gift the King bestowed on Menzies the honour of knighthood.

The next, and last, Sovereign who visited Aberdeen was the "merry monarch," Charles II.

During his first exile, the Scottish Parliament having proclaimed him King of Great Britain, Commissioners, one of whom was Provost Jaffray of Aberdeen, were despatched to bring him over from the Continent. He embarked under convoy of a Dutch fleet, and landed at Speymouth on Monday, the 4th of July 1650. After resting at Bog of Gight, now Gordon Castle, he arrived in Aberdeen on the 7th, and took up his residence in a house in Castle Street, which some conceive to have been that which is now called the " Bursars' House." His visit to the city was intimated to the Magistrates in the following letter from the Commissioners, of date 23d June 1650 :—

" Worschipfull and good friendis, we have directed thess to let you know, that the King is saiflie arryved, and intendis, if God permit, to be at Abirdein on Thursday at night ; thairfore ye will tack such cair to prowyd fitt ludgingis for him, and for the Commissioneris, and for the trayne, as may be best haid, on so short adverteismentis ; and we beseik you let nothing be wanting quhich may testifie your effectioun to the native King, quha haith fullie assured all the desyr of his people. No further, but we ar your werie assured freindis. (Signed) Cassillis, Lothiane, Brodie, Geo. Wynram, J. Smith, Al. Jaffray. Speymouth, 23d Jany. 1650. For the Richt Worschipfull the Magistratis of the toun of Abdn. Thess."

On his arrival he was received with every mark of distinction and popular attachment. He conferred the honour of knighthood on the Provost, Farquhar of Mounie, and on Mr. Leslie of Eden, who had formerly held that office. The King remained in the town but one night, proceeding next day to Dunnottar. He would appear to have been again in Aberdeen on the 25th of February 1651—the last time that our city enjoyed the honour of the presence of royalty. Now that,* after the lapse of nearly two centuries, we are about to receive a renewal of that distinguished honour, under the happiest auspices, well may we exclaim with old Dunbar—

" Be blyth and blissful, Brugh of Aberdeen ! "

---

* Her Most Gracious Majesty arrived in Aberdeen, for the first time, on the morning of Thursday the 7th September 1848, and this account of " Royal Visits to Aberdeen in Olden Times," appeared in the *Aberdeen Journal* the day before.

LINES ADDRESSED TO A LADY

*Who sent me a Watch Paper, cut in the form of
a* DART, *a* KEY, *and a* HEART.

In vain the Fair, with skilful hand,
  The polished scissors plies,
And paper any form may take
  Her fancy can devise.

Assailed by far more potent charms,
  Unconquered I remain,
For tears and smiles, and sighs and song,
  I equally disdain.

Cupid his *arrows* may exhaust—
  May aim with all his skill—
His *darts* I dread not, for my breast
  Is armed with triple steel.

If for admittance to my heart,
  The wily elf should knock,
The door is barred—the key is safe—
  And potent is the lock.

Then know the Fair, though I her gift
  In complaisance reject not,
Yet, for her *paper one, my* heart
  She really must expect not.

THE AUL'TON CROSS.

A REMNANT of this ancient and beautiful fabric, of which the original place has long ceased to know it, was recently rescued from a situation of most inglorious obscurity, and placed in a fitting asylum in King's College.

Our topographers tell us that there formerly stood in the centre of the area fronting the Town House of Old Aberdeen a cross which was formed of an upright stone, raised upon a pedestal of three steps above the level of the street. This stone was surmounted by a figure of the blessed Virgin, and underneath were the armorial bearings of Bishops Dunbar, Stewart, and Gordon. The last named succeeded to the episcopate in 1545, which serves to indicate the period about which the cross was erected.

At the era of the Reformation it was defaced by those whose indiscriminating zeal took offence at whatever even "smelt somewhat of Popery:" and, after experiencing the inclemency of many a trying season, and the rough manipulation of ruthless hands—ministers of wanton mischief—the fabric was finally removed about the time when the Town House was rebuilt.

What became of the shaft is not known; but the stone on which were cut the armorial bearings of the episcopal trio was one day discovered in a smithy in Old Aberdeen, where it had long been degraded into an utensil for holding tackets, old iron, and other odds and ends, tossed into the square cavity into which the top of the shaft had been inserted. To such vile uses had come a portion of a time-honoured fabric, which had once so proudly "cropped the causey!" This curious relic owed its more congenial quarters in King's College to the commendable care of the party who by chance discovered it.

In Spalding's *Troubles* there is a droll passage, from which it appears that this cross was pressed into a Candlemas "lark," played off by certain juveniles of 1643.

"Upon the second of Februar," saith he, with notable gravity, "being Candlemas day, the bairns of the Old Town Grammar School, at six hours, cam up the gate with candles lichtit in their hands, crying, rejoicing, and blythe eneuch; and, being six hours at nicht, cam thus up to the cross, and round about goes diverse times, climbs to the head thereof, and sets on ane burning torch thereupon. I marvellit, being at sic tyme [of the dour Covenant], and whereof myself had never seen the like. Atour, they went down from the cross, convoying John Keith, brother to the Earl Marischal, who was their [Candlemas] King, to his lodgings in the Chanonrie, with lichtit candles!"

This ebullient demonstration seems greatly to have refreshed the Episcopalian spirit of the worthy Commissary Clerk, who lets slip no opportunity of bewailing every falling-away from the observances of the good old times, through the chilling influence of Andrew Cant and his crabbed confederates.

Spalding, indeed, seems to have regarded the "ploy," which he so carefully records, as a cheering revival in a small way—a proof that there was yet some hope of young Scotland—and a pregnant sign of the times—doubtless, "afore something!" It is just probable that the merry, mad-cap rogues may have got up their "rig" in brave defiance of Cant himself, and all his tyrannical, ascetic whimsies ; for, of a surety, he appears to have been so noted a hand to "frichten bairns" in his day, that no wonder if, as O'Connell used to say, the young blood might sometimes bethink itself of the wild justice of revenge.

Spalding assures us that, on one occasion, when

some children, outside church, were rather noisy, Cant, who was within, lost all patience with them, and, instead of tipping the requisite wink to the beadle, banged out of the reader's desk—chased the young fry from the scene of their " collie-shangie" — and then returned to his seat, quite satisfied with himself, and seemingly all the easier for his explosive demonstration, but to the great " admiration" of his worshipping flock, who were exceedingly scandalised by his indecorous sally. Such severities must have rendered him no favourite with the rising race, and may have even provoked the Candlemas *crusade* which Spalding with such gusto narrateth.   The careful circumstantiality, indeed, with which the quaint annalist records the pranks of John Keith, *Rex*, as aforesaid, and his rollicking con-disciples, would almost suggest a suspicion that the " nickums" had actually coaxed the old chronicler—nothing loath—to give their " shine" a sunny nook in his *Troubles !*

NEWSPAPERS.

THE origin of periodical records of passing events, subsequently known by the general name of Newspapers, is enveloped in much obscurity, any attempt to remove which would involve not only a wide departure from my present purpose, but, I fear, a severe trial of your patience. I pause not, therefore, to inquire how far the *Acta Diurna*, said to have been published at Rome in the time of Julius Cæsar, may be placed in the same category with the newspapers of later and present times. Nor will I detain you by canvassing the rival pretensions of England, Italy, or Germany, to the establishment, during the sixteenth century, of printed newspapers, circulated by post ; although it seems to me that, on the whole, such periodicals first emanated from Augsburg and Vienna. In England, the first attempt at the establishment of newspapers, of which there is undoubted evidence, seems to have been made about the beginning of the seventeenth century. We hear of " News from

Spain," in 1611; " News out of Germany," in 1612, etc. etc. These occasional pamphlets of intelligence soon became regular periodical publications, such as Butler's "Courant, or Weekly News from Foreign Parts," published in 1621. Between this period and 1665, upwards of 350 various publications of this kind are said to have appeared, none of which, however, were long-lived. On the 7th of November of the latter year the present *London Gazette* was established. Of English *provincial* newspapers, still existing, the oldest is the *Stamford Mercury*, established in 1695. The parent of the Irish Press is the *Dublin Evening Post*, first published in 1725.

In regard to Scottish newspapers, we find that the first *published* in this country was, "A Diurnal of some Passages and Affairs," *printed* in *London*, and *reprinted* in *Leith* in the year 1652. It lived about a year. The first newspaper *written, printed*, and *published* in Scotland, was the *Mercurius Caledonius*, edited by Thomas Sydserf, son of the Bishop of Orkney. It appeared weekly, commencing on the 31st of December 1660, and expiring on 22d March 1661. In 1718 appeared the *Edinburgh Evening Courant.* In 1720 the *Caledonian Mercury.** The oldest paper published in Glasgow, is the *Glasgow Journal*, which first appeared in 1713.

* Since incorporated with the *Scotsman.*—ED.

The first Scottish newspaper published beyond the Forth was the *Aberdeen Journal,* the first number of which appeared on Tuesday, the 5th of January 1748. The paper has since regularly appeared every week, although the day of publication has been occasionally changed to suit the convenience of the time. The original printer, publisher, and proprietor of the *Journal* was Mr. James Chalmers, father of the late, and great-grandfather of the present, proprietor. Mr. Chalmers was a son of the Rev. James Chalmers, originally minister of Dyke, in Morayshire, and afterwards Professor of Divinity in Marischal College, and one of the ministers of this city. To these offices he was appointed in the year 1725, and died in 1745. His son, Mr. Chalmers, learned the art of printing under the City and University printer, Mr. James Nicol, who succeeded his father-in-law, Mr. John Forbes, in these offices, in the year 1710. Between this year and 1705, the period of Mr. Forbes's death, the business was carried on by his widow, Margaret Cuthbeard. Mr. Forbes became printer to the City and University, in the year 1662, on the death of Mr. James Brown, who had held those offices from the year 1649, being the immediate successor of Edward Raban, the first printer in Aberdeen, or the north of Scotland.

In the year 1621 a patent was obtained from King James, by Bishop Patrick Forbes, and Sir

Paul Menzies of Kinmundie, Provost of Aberdeen, for establishing printing in this city.

In consequence of this patent, Mr. Edward Raban quitted St. Andrews, and settled here in 1622, having been appointed printer to the City and University. From the specimens of his works still extant, he appears to have been no mean master of his art, although then in its comparative infancy in this country. Latterly, Raban appears to have opened a shop at the south end of Broad Street, under the quaint designation of the " Laird of Letters." He appears to have established his printing office in what was then a new house, belonging to the Corporation, situated on the north side of what was then Castle Street, its south front being a few feet in rear of the back wall of the present North of Scotland Bank. The lower part of this building is said to have been originally occupied as a meat market, the upper-floor as a dwelling-house for the printer, while in the attic-floor was his printing office. In this ancient tenement the *Journal* was printed. There was " Chalmers' stair," which the learned and ingenious Skinner celebrates as the means of conducting him to an interview with Robert Burns.

Mr. Chalmers died in 1764, and was succeeded by his son, the late Mr. James Chalmers, as printer to the City and University. An excellent scholar and a thorough master of his business, Mr. Chalmers had previously been employed at Cambridge in printing various works for the University there; and, a vacancy occurring in its printership, he was a candidate, and lost the appointment, I believe, by an adverse majority of only *one* vote. On succeeding to his father's business in Aberdeen, Mr. Chalmers continued to publish the *Journal,* and to print various classical and other works with much approbation and success for many years. He died in 1810.

About the year 1798 the printing office was removed to a building in the rear of the Town House, and which had been originally erected for the purposes of a ribbon manufactory. In 1814 the office was removed to the present premises in Adelphi Court.

The *Journal,* as I have already mentioned, was commenced in 1748 ; but it would appear that its proprietor, who had been in business as City and University printer for some years previously, had published in 1746 a broad-sheet, in some respects claiming the character of a newspaper, as it contained an account of the battle of Culloden, and other transactions of the day. Mr. Chalmers was a staunch loyalist, and had a commission in the Commissariat Department of the Royal Army. This employment, so incompatible with his professional pursuits, compelled his temporary absence from Aberdeen, and probably interrupted the publication of a periodical, which he intended to be continuous. His account, however, of the battle of Culloden, coupled, it may be presumed, with statements unfavourable to the cause of the Pretender, rendered him so offensive to the adherents of that unfortunate Prince, that a party of them, coming to Aberdeen, beleaguered the worthy *Journalist* in his own office, whence he was fortunate enough to secure his retreat by a back window, and thus escaped their vengeance !

We may here mention that the success which seems to have attended Mr. Chalmers' paper induced Mr. Francis Douglas and Mr. William Murray to establish a printing office in Aberdeen in 1752, and to publish, on the 3d of October of that year, a weekly newspaper called the *Aberdeen Intelligencer*, which ceased on the 22d of February 1757. About the year 1770 a weekly paper was established by Mr. John Boyle, and continued for a year or two. Other attempts of the same kind seem to have been made last century, but they all failed ; the truth being that the *Journal* was in pre-occupation of a field where there was then no scope for another newspaper. It was not until 1806 that the *Aberdeen Chronicle* was published by a worthy and venerable citizen, Mr. Booth. The increase of population, and various other circumstances, have induced the publication of several local newspapers in this and adjoining counties ;

proofs of the advancing spirit of enterprise which distinguishes the present times. Among these, I cannot omit particular mention of the *Aberdeen Observer*, as having made much exertion to improve the art of *reporting*, and to stimulate the literary character of the local press. To the establishment of the other existing newspapers in this quarter, it is unnecessary particularly to advert.

The first number of the *Journal* is a small folio of four pages, containing in all about 200 square inches of letterpress. The price was twopence each number. For advertisements the charge was 2s. 6d. for the first time, and 2s. for each time afterwards. It contains no introductory address other than the fashion of our times ; but at the end of the paper there is a *Nota Bene*, requesting those who may be good enough to " encourage" the undertaking, to transmit their names and places of abode. Country subscribers were to receive the paper by the first post or carrier. The first number is almost entirely occupied with foreign news, without any reference to domestic politics or local occurrences. It contains *one* advertisement, which is as follows :—
" That on the 29th of March last [*i.e.* in 1747] were amissing three promissory notes of the *Aberdeen's Company*, one for £10, and two for 20s. each ; and of the Bank of Scotland, two for 20s. Whoever brings them to the publisher of this paper shall have two guineas reward, and no questions asked."

At what precise period this bank was established I have not ascertained. The partners seem to have been Provost Mowat, Messrs. Elphinston, Osborne, and Brebner ; for, about the year '55 or '56, I find these parties advertising the winding up of the concern.

At the conclusion of the first year of the *Journal*, the proprietor seems to have been very well pleased with its success—a feeling to which he gives expression in the following address to his " encouragers :"—

> " My grateful thanks for all your favours past,
> Which, pray, continue, this year as the last,
> From every post, *impartially* I'll cull,
> Whatever is not trifling, false, or dull ;
> And tho' no more you must expect to hear
> Of Cities stormed, and Castles blown in air ·
> The fruits of peace, of concord, and of joy,
> And happier events shall the press employ."

Taking a saunter through the columns of the earlier numbers, we discover the following among the most interesting of the *notabilia.*

On the 1st December 1748 we find an advertisement by Mr. David Dalrymple, Sheriff-depute of Aberdeen, and afterwards Lord Westhall, prohibiting the wearing of the Highland dress, under the penalty of imprisonment for six months. Nevertheless, among the domestic occurrences are several, stating that so many parties had been brought from this or that quarter and lodged in gaol for this offence.

In another part of the volume we find the announcement of the *first* great and beneficial change which was introduced by the Senatus of Marischal College into the curriculum of study in that seminary.

In connection with this institution, it is interesting to find the record of the *first* literary triumph of the Author of the " Minstrel" :—" On Tuesday, April 10th, 1750, the Premium given by Principal Blackwell towards the end of the session to the best scholar of his first class, was, after a severe trial, adjudged to *James Beattie*, from Laurencekirk.* The trial was an analysis of part of the 4th Book of the Odyssey, and the students were close locked up while they wrote it.

There seems to have been at all times a *Poet's Corner* in the Journal.   In No. 58 is a piece on the death of the famous Lochiel, who, on the defeat of the Pretender, retired to France, accepted a commission in the French army, but soon died.   The poet, after lauding his character, and mildly relating his politics, thus concludes :—

> " Compelled by hard necessity to bear
>   In Gallia's bands a mercenary spear !
>   Yet heaven, in pity to his honest heart,
>   Resolved to snatch him from so poor a part.

---

* Beattie must have been then only fourteen.

> To cure, at once, his spirit and his mind,
> With exile wretched, and with error blind,
> 'The mighty mandate unto death was given,
> And good Lochiel is now—a Whig in heaven."
>
> *Dr. Johnson's Opinion.*

We find some intimation of the sort of education young ladies used to receive, in an advertisement from Miss Isobel Garioch, in which she announces her having opened a boarding school for young ladies, "where they are to be trained to all accomplishments, including the first principles of genteel behaviour and good address, white and coloured seam, and *washing* and *dressing* after the best manner." Some of these accomplishments would be reckoned rather homely now-a-days, but they seem not in the least to have impaired the charms of the young ladies a century ago, repeated proof of which is seen in the announcements of their marriages. Thus we find that such a one married "a young lady of great beauty, and possessed of all the amiable virtues that can render happy the nuptial state." Another gentleman is fortunate enough to make himself the husband of "a young lady of distinguished beauty, virtue, and merit." Even of old folks entering the married state most honourable mention is made. Thus, "a venerable couple were married at Old Deer; the man was 76 and the woman 73, having only five teeth betwixt them both, yet they re-entered the connubial state with as much vigour and warmth as the decline of life could possibly admit of." More-over, "a venerable, well-meaning couple in the parish of Bellie, warmed with a feeble ray of their declining sun, in spite of old age and its attend-ants, boldly ventured on lawful wedlock—the man 96, and the woman 70, years of age. The same week the contagion spread to the neighbourhood, where a man and woman, each aged 89, followed the laudable and pious example."

It would appear that the art of matrimonial advertising was not unknown in old times. In the twenty-eighth number of the *Journal* we find that "any well-behaved young woman, between thirty and fifty years of age, and having £100 at her own disposal, may hear of an affable and agreeable husband, aged thirty-three," provided she will only name where she is to be "spoken with." Well, a reply appears from Ketty Willing, Nairn, to the effect that said Ketty is a young unmarried woman, eighteen years of age, fit to be a wife, of good com-plexion, for a nurse, and not deformed in any part, and having also in her custody £2000 pounds 41 Scots. But she demurs as to further negotiation until she shall obtain the *male* advertiser's real address, that she may send a friend to commune with him.

In those days infanticide and child-exposure seem to have been very common, and no wonder, for the kirk-sessions bore not their sword in vain.

Thus, we find the kirk-session of Rathen hounding the whole country after a frail pair who had stolen away from the lash of their discipline. After particularly describing the parties and the circumstances of their elopement, the kirk-session express a fervent hope " that wherever they are seen they will not be permitted to cohabit as man and wife!" Another advertisement of this sort seems to have been nearly the cause of the murder of the frail parties after whom it was launched.

In the times to which we refer, the principles of religious toleration were not much understood, for we find that William Grant was arraigned before the Aberdeen Circuit Court in September 1750 " as being habit and repute a priest, Jesuit, or trafficing papist." He pled guilty, and was sentenced to banishment from Scotland, under pain of death in case of his return—the soldier who apprehended him having been allowed a reward of 500 merks according to Act of Parliament.

But while our fellow-creatures were thus badly dealt with, the canine race seem to have been held in high consideration. Thus, we read that " a favourite dog belonging to a lady near Grosvenor Square was put into a coffin, and, being carried by her two chairmen on a horse, was interred behind Primrose Hill and Hampstead. The footmen walked before, and the dog-doctor, who had attended him all night, behind."

This leads us to notice another story about a dog which belonged to Mr. James Rait, tanner, brother of Professor Rait of King's College. Rait had a farm at Hilton, where he was much annoyed by a fox. He contrived to set the fox and his watch-dog *Tyger* by the ears, about a leg of mutton, when *Tyger* proved too many for the fox. It is particularly mentioned that this dog *Tyger* was nephew to the famous *Tyger* given by Mr. Rait (in testimony of his loyalty) to *the* Duke (of Cumberland) in a present, in the year 1747, and the son of *Old Dublin*, the Irish bitch who fought an Irish grenadier of Fleming's Regiment in 1747.

But, to come to serious matters, we find that, in 1751, a proposal was in agitation, which we would specially recommend to the notice of our temperance societies. "We hear that a learned argument is preparing, and will shortly be exhibited, to show that the only effectual means of preventing the pernicious use of distilled spirituous liquors will be to inflict a corporal punishment, instead of a fine, upon the retailers and vendors of them. Some are of the opinion that the most certain way to prevent the decrease of his Majesty's subjects, so much and so justly complained of, will be to hang, or transport for life, any one who shall be found guilty of serving his neighbour with a quarterin. Others think that perpetual imprison-

ment, and a public whipping once a quarter, may
be sufficient punishment in this case."

The political articles in the *Journal*, as in
other provincial papers of the time, are all extracts
from the *London Evening Post*, and some of them
are great curiosities in their way—perfect riddles,
which *could not*, as they were perhaps never *meant*
to be solved.   Here is a specimen in 1750—"Our
correspondent at Paris assures us that something
of very great importance is upon the carpet there,
and that, notwithstanding the greatest secrecy is
observed at Court, yet some of the members have
intimated that it will not be long before a great
event will happen, extremely acceptable to the
nation—but of what nature is entirely left to
conjecture !"

Strange notions seem to have prevailed on the
subjects of political economy. We find a fierce
argument against the transportation of corn to
starving France, thus put forward. "Whether, as
Providence has thought fit to afflict the French
with so dreadful a scourge, the running counter
to this benevolent dispensation with regard to *this*
island, may not turn that blessing into a curse
upon ourselves ?"

In 1752 we have the first report from the
infirmary. It appears that for the year ending
August '43, the number of patients admitted was
21 ; cured, 9 ; dismissed, 10 ; dead, 2. We sup-

pose there were not eight doctors. In '45-'46 the house was filled with sick and wounded soldiers.

So early as the beginning of 1749 we find a society of honest farmers in Aberdeen and Banff-shires, established for the purpose of taking into consideration the proper methods for improving difficult soils.

The first Whale Fishing Company signed their contract of copartnery on 27th June 1751, the subscribed capital being then nearly £7000.

Boy hurt by falling from the joggs in Castle Street—(Pety Vault)—Woman had her eye severely injured by the creels of a man riding on horseback —William Wast accommodated with a *neat suit* of irons, etc. etc.

THE PAPISTS.

CHAPTER I.

"O my soul, come not thou into their secret ; unto their assembly,
mine honour, be not thou united."—GEN. xlix. 6.

WE intend to address a few words to those Protestants who are in the habit of frequenting the
Papist chapel for the seemingly laudable purpose
of hearing the errors of Unitarianism exposed. We
cannot but regard the conduct of such individuals
as inconsistent. Is it wise in them to run the risk
of spiritual contamination of one kind, as a pre-
ventive against spiritual contagion of another description ? If they scout the doctrines of Unitarians
as being contrary to their creed, why lend their
countenance to the worship of the Papists, which is
as much at variance with the principles of their
faith ? Would they, to avoid the chance of being
scorched by the flames of a conflagration, which
they need not approach, rashly expose themselves,
in a crazy boat, to the dangers of the wintry wave ?
Would they, as an antidote against a poisoned cup,

which they might at will pass from their lips, needlessly court the deadly sting of the rattlesnake? What monstrous absurdity! what heaven-tempting folly! What have they to do with Papists or Unitarians? Have they not the Bible as an infallible rule of faith? The Papists are anxious to make proselytes. They are industrious, artful, persevering, insatiable, and alas! too often successful in this trade of spiritual kidnapping! We deem it the more necessary to warn Protestants against the wiles of the Papists, since, in the harangues delivered in St. Peter's on Sunday evening, due care is taken to *sink* the more startling dogmas of the Church of Rome. When a simple Protestant hears the divinity of the Son so earnestly advocated from a Papist pulpit, he is disposed to think that the doctrines of the Romish Church are perhaps, after all, not so very absurd as he has been accustomed to regard them. He begins to fancy that there is not so very wide a difference between the creeds of Protestant and Papist as he had been taught to believe that there was. This is the first step towards the unsettlement of his faith. This is the great, the primary point, at which the Papists aim. They wish to impress on the minds of Protestants that the discrepancy between the Papist and Protestant creeds is but slight—mere *distinction* without *difference*. They thus endeavour to smooth the passage from the one to the other. But Protestants will never know thoroughly what Papist doctrine is, until they are once fairly entrapped into an adoption of the Papist creed. When once within the mysterious inquisitional walls of the *Confessional,* then, and then only, will they know the wide gulf which separates the creed which they have adopted from that which they have renounced. If the Papists affect to honour the Son by maintaining his divinity against the Unitarians, they dishonour him in many other ways. They may declaim against Unitarianism as they will; we think it far more consistent to deny the divinity of the Son altogether, than to support it on one hand, in form, but to belie it on the other, in effect. It is not our intention *at present* to enter into any lengthened discussion of the doctrines of the Papists. Let any Protestant of common sense only look into their *Book of Vespers,* or their " New Testament," and say, whether he does not there find the formal avowal of principles the most glaringly contrary to reason, and to the word of God. It is no very easy matter for Protestants to get hold of these books ; they are generally carefully smuggled out of sight, as if the owners of them were conscious of the contraband nature of their contents. In these institutes of superstition, these travesties of the genuine word, Protestants will find the broad declaration of doctrines which strike at the very roots of the Gospel. Those who wish to enter the lists of controversy with the Papists, ought to be well acquainted with their official and accredited manuals of doctrine and discipline. We were grieved at the sorry figure which some of our Protestant clergy and laymen made at their public discussions of the Roman Catholic creed. They showed an unfortunate ignorance of the doctrines of the Papists. On some points of their faith the Papists have a plausible show of reason on their side, but it is all mere show when thoroughly examined. Let Protestants beware of thoughtlessly imputing to Papists doctrines which these do not maintain. By disavowing, as they justly may, such doctrines, they obtain a triumph over their opponents, and thus derive borrowed credit for the really objectional dogmas of their creed. We deem it the more necessary thus boldly to state our opinions on this momentous subject, and to warn Protestants of their danger from the craftiness of Papists, because in the present day there are some who, under the affectation of charity, are offended, forsooth! at what they are pleased to stigmatise as bigoted zeal! We shall be told that these are not times for reviving the antiquated trivial controversies of divines about Popery and Protestantism; that all creeds are becoming gradually assimilated; that it is quite unseemly to be zealous about a mere difference of opinion. That there is nothing like a *gentlemanly* impartiality in such matters. The Papists, we are told, are very different persons from their fore-fathers. There are no such things now-a-days as—crowds of racked, or burning, or bleeding martyrs for the Protestant faith ; many pious and holy men perishing in dungeons and deserts ; soldiers stimulated by priests to merit heaven by revelling in the torments of helpless women and innocent babes ; midnight spies and domestics wiled or tortured into informers ; the annihilation of the knowledge of the truth by severe punishments for reading the Bible ; swarms of lazy, bigoted, and vicious ecclesiastics.

CHAPTER II.

IN our last chapter we exposed the folly and inconsistency of the conduct of those professing Protestants who frequent the Papist chapel on Sunday evenings. We are happy to find that our observations on this subject have given satisfaction to not a few—Papists, of course, excepted. Confident of the justness of our sentiments, we were convinced that they only required to be plainly stated in order to command ready acquiescence in their propriety. We were fully satisfied that no rational Protestant could, on mature consideration, deny the *inconsistency*, at least, of lending his countenance to the Papists, who hold doctrines so widely different from his own, and who cautiously avoid giving *his* religion the slightest shadow of support in return. How much at variance soever the opinions of different sects of professing Christians on some points of doctrine and discipline, we think it well becomes them to be on terms of good fellowship one with another, and only to vie in promoting, each in the way of its own approval, the diffusion of religious knowledge. This, however, the Papists will not do. *Their* system is quite exclusive. Their great aim is to promote, not the grand principles of Christianity, but the peculiar dogmas of the Church of Rome. Very eager are they to propagate their own creed,— very willing are they to *receive* support from Protestants,—but do they ever, in any single instance, make the slightest return of countenance to the Protestant faith? Do they not, on the contrary, do everything *for* themselves, and everything, directly or indirectly, *against* the Protestants? If they contributed occasionally their mite towards the support of Protestantism, then might they justly claim a mite in return, on the grounds of the interchange of good offices; but since they will not on any account *give*, what business have they to *get?* To Protestants we would say—"If you *will* haunt St. Peter's Chapel in defiance of common sense and regard for the faith of your fathers, be not so silly as to allow the Papists to *extort* a single farthing from you. What you do give, give of your own good will, if you cannot make a better use of it. If the Papists will not treat *you* as they would themselves be treated should they enter a Protestant place of worship, let them have their seats to themselves! Is there *one Protestant* place of worship in our city, at the gates of which the *smallest coin* is *demanded* before accommodation is afforded to the stranger? Sorry should we be to see the humblest Protestant church or chapel thus degraded into a level with the theatre, or an exhibition of wild beasts! Will Papists say that they do not *insist* on something for the plate? Try them. Is the knowledge of the Protestant faith so very widely different that there is no necessity for endeavouring to extend it farther? Does it abound in the uttermost parts of the earth—in the distant isles of the Gentiles? Is there no room for spreading it in our own island—in our own native land—in our own city? Alas! alas! those who visit the abodes of ignorance and its inseparable concomitant, vice, can tell but too truly how much there is yet to be done, even in our own city, to extend the benefits of our faith to many within its bounds. Is it then right to give the children's "bread" to "dogs," while many of them are starving for want of the very "crumbs?"

We intend to make a few simple remarks on

some of the peculiar doctrines of the Church of Rome. We shall take for our guides the Word of God and common sense, avoiding all scholastic quibbling as unprofitable in itself, and unsuitable to our purpose. We write for plain people, who take the Bible into their hands in simplicity of heart, and not to gratify the cravings of a controversial spirit. In making our observations on Papist doctrine, we shall quote their own accredited and official manuals of faith and discipline. In *The Ordinary of the Mass*, laid down in their Book of Vespers, is the following *Oblation of the Host :—*

" Accept, O holy Father, almighty and eternal God, this unspotted Host, which I thy unworthy servant (the priest) *offer unto thee, my living and true God, for my innumerable sins, offences, and negligences, and for all present ;* as also for all faithful Christians (Papists of course), both living and *dead* (!); that it may avail both me and them unto life everlasting."

Next comes the *Oblation of the Chalice :—*

" We offer unto thee, O Lord, the chalice of salvation, beseeching thy clemency, that it may ascend before thy divine Majesty, as a sweet odour, *for our salvation* (!), and for that of the whole world."

Now, even admitting, for the time, the absurd doctrine of *Transubstantiation,* to what purpose did Christ suffer on Mount Calvary, if this constant repetition of sacrifice is to be made? Did he not offer himself up, a willing sacrifice, once for all? If this Papist sacrifice is necessary, then was the sacrifice of Christ ineffectual. Is not this striking at the very roots of the gospel? A little farther on we find—

"May the Lord, by the *intercession* of *blessed* Michael the archangel, standing at the right hand of the Altar of Incense, and of all the elect, (*Michael* and the *elect*, all Papists of course!) vouchsafe to bless this incense, and receive it as an odour of sweetness."

Here Christ is set aside by Michael in the office of intercessor with the Father. This is but consistent. If his office as Mediator is infringed, it is but consistent to rob him of the glory due unto him as our *Intercessor*. A little farther on we find—

"Receive, O holy Trinity, this oblation which we make to thee, in memory of the Passion, Resurrection, and Ascension of our Lord Jesus Christ, *and in honour of the blessed Mary, ever a virgin, of blessed John Baptist, the holy Apostles Peter and Paul, and of all the Saints, that it may be available to their honour and our salvation.*"

Chapter III.

In our last chapter we attempted to prove, from the Book of Vespers, one of the accredited manuals of Papist doctrine and discipline, that that creed is at variance with the distinguishing feature of Christianity—the Atonement of Christ. This we conceive to be a mode of controversy to which no Papist can reasonably object. We take up their doctrines just as we find them laid down in their books, which have the seal of their own authority. If these doctrines are absurd, then are we not to blame for exposing them? Their absurdity is not merely *constructive ;* it is inseparable from the doctrines, and requires only to be barely enunciated, without any laboured comment of ours, to expose it in its true colours. The Papists cannot thus find a temporary refuge in the bold disavowal of doctrines which are falsely imputed to them. We ascribe to them no other creed than that which they themselves believe, and would palm on unwary Protestants. We have heard it affirmed that the creed of Papists is of a very plastic and accommodating nature—that their catechisms are suited to time and place—that doctrines which are maintained in Spain are found unsuitable to the meridian of Britain—and that certain points of faith pass current in Ireland which would be rather too much for the credence of our " north countrie." Be this as it may, the Book of Vespers, now before us, we make our text at present, and from it we think it will be no difficult matter to condemn the Papists.

The doctrine of the Atonement is the chief corner-stone of Christianity. Any system of belief which contains doctrines incompatible with this is *not* Christianity, although it may falsely assume that name. We think that a great deal of unnecessary trouble may be often spared by calling things by their proper names. What can be more absurd than to concede the title of Christians to those who refuse the distinctive marks of the true disciples of Christ ? These pseudo-Christians thus derive a degree of credit and advantage to which they have no shadow of claim. Now-a-days, a man who professes himself a disbeliever in Christianity is not by any means regarded as a *very* respectable character. The consequence is, that many *profess* to believe, more to obtain the praise of men than the praise of God. Under the name of Christianity, too, various sects of religionists obtain a more ready reception for their dogmas, how much soever at variance with the Gospel scheme. But to return to the *Vespers*. At page 23 we find the following prayer to the Virgin :—

" O Holy Mary, succour the miserable, assist

the dejected, comfort those that mourn ; pray for the people, intercede for the clergy, plead for the devout female sex. Let all be sensible of thy aid who celebrate thy holy memory."

Now, where is it said in Scripture that the Virgin Mary has power to answer the prayer thus offered up to her? Where are we required to celebrate her memory? Where is she set forth as a proper object of adoration? A little farther on, at page 24, we find—

"Grant, we beseech thee, O Lord God, that we, thy servants, may enjoy constant health of mind and body, and, *by the glorious intercession of the ever blessed Virgin Mary, be delivered from present sorrow, and possess eternal joy.*"

Now, in what stronger terms could one plead with Christ? Here our eternal happiness is represented as depending on the Virgin Mary. If this is not setting aside Christ in his mediatorial office, what is it? The absurdity of this must be manifest to any person of common sense. At page 25 we find—

"Grant, we beseech thee, that we may experience her intercession for us *by whom we deserved* to receive the author of life, our Lord Jesus Christ."

Here Christ is called the author of life, *but* this life we derive not from him of his own free grace : no! the *merits* of the Virgin must entitle us to this ! In the whole compass of sacred writ, nay, in the Papist *Bible* itself, is there one word about the *mediatorial merits* of the Virgin Mary? At page 29, we find—

"I confess to Almighty God, to blessed Mary, ever a Virgin, to blessed Michael the Archangel, to blessed John Baptist, to the holy Apostles Peter and Paul, to all the saints, and you Father (the priest), that I have grievously sinned, therefore I beseech the blessed Mary, ever a Virgin (and the rest before-mentioned), to pray to the Lord our God for me."

Who constituted the Virgin Mary, and the rest, our confessors? For what purpose is confession of sin made? To whom ought it to be made but to Him who has power to forgive? Can Michael forgive our sins? At page 39, we have a hymn in praise of the Virgin—

> " Hail, Mary ! Queen of heavenly spheres,
>   Hail, whom the angelic host reveres !
>   Hail, fruitful root !   Hail, sacred gate !
>   Whence the world's light derives its date ! " etc. etc.

" Vouchsafe, O *sacred* Virgin, to accept my praises, give me strength against mine enemies."

At page 41 we find—

" Grant, we beseech thee, that through the Virgin Mary, Christ's mother, *we may receive the joys of eternal life.*"

At page 110 we have another hymn to the Virgin, which says—

> "The sinner's bonds unbind,
> Our evils drive away."

So much for the office of the Virgin Mary. Here we find her regarded as an object of adoration, prayed to as our intercessor with God, and as being able to confer on us those blessings which Christ died to purchase for us. No one who is acquainted with the Word of God can have the effrontery to maintain that such doctrines have any foundation *there.* They are the cunning inventions of man to answer the basest of purposes—to arrogate a tyrannical sway over the conscience—to support the cause of spiritual ignorance—to aggrandise an artful priesthood, and to prop an ambitious hierarchy. Well may the priests refuse to their flocks the rights of exercising their judgment in perusing their books of devotion ? The man who can believe such monstrous contradictions must first completely surrender his right of exercising the measure of common sense with which God has gifted him. Darkness is the proper element of the true sons of the Romish Church ; *and if the light that is in them be darkness, how great is that darkness !* In making our observations on this subject, we have no personal quarrel with Papists. In the various relations of life, we take *them* just as we take Protestants—as we find them. Their *creed* is a fair subject of free discussion.

CONCLUSION.

WE intend now to close our remarks on some points of the creed of the Romish Church. The peculiar dogmas of this Church have given rise to numberless controversies, of which not a few have been conducted, on both sides, in a spirit but too much at variance with that divine message which proclaims " peace on earth, and good will to the children of men." While the supporters of the Protestant faith have sometimes denounced the Romish creed, *in toto*, as containing *nothing* whatever which had the slightest claim on the adoption of rational beings ; on the other hand, the advocates of Catholicism have not been slack to retort on their opponents charges of a similar nature, with at least an equal intensity of acrimonious feeling. In the present imperfect state of human nature, such consequences are more or less unavoidable in all disputes ; but in controversies concerning subjects which, like religion, so deeply affect the present and future state of the contending parties, rousing every latent passion of the soul, and engaging the most stubborn prepossessions of moral and religious education, the spirit of overbearing zeal for a particular system of belief, operates with peculiar force. It were well if controversialists on *all* subjects would bear in mind that every speculative error which boasts a multitude of advocates, has its golden as well as dark side ; that there is always some truth connected with it, the exclusive attention to which has given it charms for the heart. In the remarks which we have ventured to offer on some points of Romish doctrine, we have endeavoured to avoid as much as possible any personal reference to those by whom such doctrines are held. We have been careful not to impute to Catholics other doctrines than such as we conceive to be contained in their own books.   To enter into any elaborate discussion of these doctrines was quite foreign to our present purpose.   We are far from indulging the vain hope of gaining over Catholics to the Protestant faith, but we do not despair of our success in warning unwary Protestants against being entrapped into a hasty adoption of the Romish creed.   This is our principal object.   The Catholics in this place have of late manifested an eager spirit of proselytising, and their efforts to make converts have been, in too many instances, crowned with success.   This has been greatly owing to the interest excited by the musical part of the Catholic worship, and by the popular talents of one of the priests.   If those Protestants who are so fond of frequenting St. Peter's are really dissatisfied with their own creed, we hope that, for their own sakes, this dissatisfaction is the result of a patient and candid examination of the doctrines of the Protestant faith. We hope that before they shall inquire into the soundness of the Romish creed they shall have good reason for condemning that in which they have been brought up. But, if they are satisfied with their own faith, let them stand fast by it, and, in this particular, at any rate, learn a lesson from the votaries of the Catholic Church. We proceed to make one or two extracts from the Romish "Vespers," as its title page bears. At page 215 we find the following :—

"O Cross! brighter than all the stars, renowned throughout the world; more holy and lovely to men than all things; who alone wast worthy to bear the price of the world! *Sweet wood! sweet nails*, that bore so sweet a burthen! *Save us* here assembled to celebrate thy praises, *Allel.*"

Now, let any person of common sense say what the above means, if words have any meaning at all. Is it not a prayer addressed to the *wood* of the cross which bore the Saviour, in terms as plain as can be devised? Could any stronger petition be offered up, *mutatis mutandis*, to the Saviour himself? Is not this *very like* the worshipping of *stocks?* What virtue can there be in a piece of wood? Do Papists say—"It was the instrument of crucifying Jesus for the sins of the world?" Why, on a similar principle, we might adore *Judas Iscariot*, and with much better reason, for *he* was an *active* agent in the death of Christ, whereas the cross was a mere passive instrument. We are forbidden to do evil that good may come, and is it likely that we should be required to pay homage to an evil agent which may have produced contingent good? At page 226 we find—

" O God, who didst translate blessed *Dunstan*, thy Bishop, to heavenly kingdoms, grant by his glorious merits, that we may pass from hence to endless joys. Thro'," etc.

What *assurance* is there that this same *Dunstan* is in heaven? How can his presence there be ascertained, except by revelation? Admitting him to be there, what authority have we for praying to him in particular? Is such authority to be found in Scripture? Here again we are to be saved *partly* by his *glorious merits*. Who was this Dunstan? We hope he was not the *wretch* of the same name who figures in the early period of English history. The mercy of God is doubtless unbounded, and is displayed in the salvation of the chief of sinners, but wé should as soon think, humanly speaking, of canonising the great enemy of mankind himself as the infamous *Dunstan*. At page 299 we find—

" O God! who hast crowned blessed King *Edward*, thy Confessor, grant, we beseech thee, that we may so honour him on earth as to reign with him hereafter in heaven."

Here there is no *Thro'*, *etc.* brought in as a saving clause at the end. We leave this, and, indeed all our extracts, with the common sense of Protestant readers. They may compare our extracts with the original whenever they please. We are not conscious of our having wilfully misquoted from the "Vespers;" indeed, had we been so disposed, we trust we had prudence enough to refrain from a species of fraud which could be so easily detected. We have no wish unnecessarily to wound the feelings, or to offer violence to the prejudices of Catholics, and we are convinced that such of them as are disposed to think for themselves must at once admit that "a disputable point is no man's ground." One principal object of our remarks has been, as we said before, to warn Protestants against what we conceive to be the errors of Papists. They ought not to throw themselves in the way of hearing Catholic doctrine until they have good reason for rejecting their own. But we are confident that those Protestants who are able to give a reason of the hope that is in them, are in no danger from Catholic contagion. To suppose that our opposition to Papists proceeds from any dread that in this country they should gain an ascendency, is the height of folly. Theirs is, and long has been, a falling cause. Need we prove this? Think what the creed of this country was three centuries ago, compared with the prevailing faith of the present times. The palmy days of the Romish Church have passed away like a dream of the night. Its spirit is truly congenial only with an unenlightened age. Where are now the days when the Popes not only usurped the authority of supreme arbiters in disputes about religion or church discipline, but assumed the character of lords of the universe, arbiters of the fate of kingdoms and empires, and supreme rulers of the kings and princes of the earth ? Where are now the authority, the opulence, and splendour of the Papal See? Need we wonder at its reverse of fortune ? Its kingdom was of *this* world, and it has therefore shared the vicissitudes of every power which is not founded on the "rock of ages !"

BE HEAVEN MY STAY.

In all the changes, here below,
Of transient weal—of common woe,
It may be given me to know;
        Be Heaven my stay!

When my poor heart would fail for fear,
Without the hand of pity near,
Gently to wipe the unseen tear;
        Be Heaven my stay!

When I must bear the worldling's scorn,
Derided for my lot forlorn,
E'en of itself, but hardly borne;
        Be heaven my stay!

When many friends, whom once I knew,
Have waxed, in number, very few,
And doubts arise if *these* be true;
        Be Heaven my stay!

When one with whom I'd link my fate
Forsakes—like silly bird its mate—
And leaves my heart all desolate;
        Be Heaven my stay!

When days of health and youth are flown,
My path with faded roses strewn ;
The *thorns* are all I find my own ;
      Be Heaven my stay !

When full of tossings on my bed,
I cannot—cannot rest my head,
Scared with dim visions of the dead !
      Be Heaven my stay !

When sorely chastened for my sins,
And pleasure ends, while grief begins,
And suffering no guerdon wins ;
      Be Heaven my stay !

When all in vain, I strive to brave
The gloom of Jordan's swelling wave,
And hand of mortal cannot save !
      Be Heaven my stay !

When faith itself begins to fail,
When prayer seems of no avail,
And when, for praise, I find but wail ;
      Be Heaven my stay !

FASCICULUS FACETIARUM
ABREDONENSIUM.

" A word in season—how good is it ?"—SOLOMON.

A TALE OF THE BROADGATE.—A member of
that proverbially loquacious craft, who are particularly hostile to the distinguishing mark of the disciples of Joanna Southcote, which they denounce
as a barbarism, was one night " working with sinu-
osities" along the Broadgate, with several bottles in
his pate, making sundry hair-breadth escapes of a
broken nose, ever and anon coining soap-suds,
encountering a brush with a Charley, a dry-shave
from a quizzical crony, a cut from every strapping
wench he chanced to meet, when he was thus accosted by a douce woman of his acquaintance :
" Ah ! George, George, ye're i' the Braidgate." Unwilling to be thus bearded, George, with a con-
temptuous curl of the lip, replied, " I ken that ; but
for as braid as it is, I need it a' !"

A FRIEND IN NEED.—Our townsman, Captain

Cushnie, whose simple characteristic monument in the West Church records his charitable bequeathment of a fortune found in the lottery, with the heart, possessed also the humour, of a genuine son of Neptune. After the accidental acquisition of his prize-money he cast anchor on his native shore, where he spent his time and fortune in relieving the necessities of the poor. He was a great walker, and would naturally often steer his course towards the sea-beach. During one of his visits thither, while he was viewing a fleet of fishing-boats in the offing, suddenly the sky became overcast, the wind blew with fitful and increasing violence, until the sea into a storm it roused. The bents were soon covered with the relatives of the fishermen, who were in great jeopardy. Amid the roar of the waves, and the howling of the wind, nought was heard save loud lament, and the most extravagant expressions of despair. One luckie, on whose lungs frequent practice in crying " caller haddocks " had conferred stentorian strength, was particularly exclamatory, and seemed determined to arrogate a monopoly of woe. Amongst other ravings which she bellowed, she exclaimed, "O gin I had but a knife, I wad cut my ain throat!" Whereupon the captain, who was standing alongside of her, thinking it a hard case that the honest woman should be prevented, for lack of the needful, from carrying into immediate execution so rational a resolve, took from his pocket a large *jocteleg*, which he presented, unclasped, to the forlorn matron.   But, instead of availing herself of the proferred aid, she ungratefully exclaimed, " Ah ! you villain ! wad ye gie a knife to a mad woman ?"

THE REV. MR. ABERCROMBIE AND THE REV. MR. FULLERTON, MINISTERS OF ABERDEEN.—The former of these gentlemen possessed great natural shrewdness, was an orthodox and popular preacher, a stern disciplinarian, " given to hospitality," but a somewhat overbearing · disputant in the church courts, and, for reasons best known to himself, bitterly and personally hostile to Mr. F., whose character in some points as much excelled, as in others it differed from his own. Mr. F. was a pious, a learned, and a most modest man. On some question which was being discussed in the Presbytery, Mr. F. made a motion, which Mr. A., according to use and wont, opposed with tooth and nail, although it was evident to all except himself, that his opposition militated against his own interest. After Mr. F. had endured with patience and imperturbable good humour, a torrent of scurrilous invective from Mr. A., he said, " Well, Mr. A., have it your own way ; but will you hear a story ?"   Mr. A. gruffly assented. " A man and his wife," said Mr. F., " who led a cat-and-doggish sort of life (his better half, like you, Mr. A., wishing to have everything her own way, whether right or wrong), were once walking together by the side of a river. The wife, slipping a foot, fell into the stream ; but, in her fall, caught hold of a bush, by which she contrived to keep her head above water until her husband, to whom she bawled for help, should come to her assistance. Her husband, however, took from his pocket a knife, with which he cut her forlorn hope, while he coolly said, " Many a thing have I allowed to go with you, and I shall let this go too."

A PAT REMONSTRANCE.—Our townsmen, notwithstanding their proverbial acuteness, and keen sense of the ridiculous, sometimes betray a disposition to emulate the sons of the Emerald Isle, in that species of colloquial " dulcia vitia" commonly called bulls. The late Bailie Farquharson once afforded a notable instance of this. He was a captain in the volunteer corps during the war ; and finding that his company did not on some occasion dress so well as he could wish, he remonstrated in these terms :—" O fie ! gentlemen ; ye're crooked like an ousen bow. Only come out and look at yoursel's !"

THE WEAKER VESSEL.—The many excellent qualities of the late venerable Dr. C— will long preserve his memory in the parish of Nigg, where he officiated for some threescore years or so. By

all his parishioners he was justly regarded as a
father, and was constantly referred to as umpire
in all their differences. An honest fisherman in
the Cove happened to be cursed with a termagant
of a wife. His frequent disputations with this
Xantippe were not always conducted according to
the Socratic method. At length, after finding that
his wife and he could not by any means row in the
same boat ; that he could not manage her either by
hook or by crook ; that they were daily and hourly
making a sad kettle of fish of it ; after in vain
attempting to manage her on the " claw me, claw
thee" plan, he resolved to lay all oars in the water,
and tell the Doctor how he was baited. He described his wife as being a perfect *pictarnty ;* that
he was quite upset by her jaw ; that her conduct
cost him " mony a saut-tear ;" that, for all his
dauting of her, he could not steer her by any means.
The Doctor, after remarking that he believed his
tale, although it was somewhat confused, recommended patience and forbearance, observing, that
his wife was the weaker vessel. " Weel, stir," replied the man, " gin she be the weaker vesshel, she
sud carry the laigher sail."

AN ATTENTIVE HEARER.—A member of a certain seceder kirk (*not very far from St. Nicholas
Street*), on one occasion took along with him to a
prayer meeting one of his sons, a boy about nine

years of age. The boy appeared very attentive to a very long prayer which one of the *lay* members was making—a circumstance which was remarked with no small satisfaction by the father, who, on arriving at home, asked his son whether he could give some *notes* of the prayer. " Weel, father," replied the observant younker, " d'ye ken, yon man said *Oh !* jist *seventy-three* times in his prayer, for I keepit an exact coont o' them !"

A PROBATIONER of the kirk, who died here not many years ago, was once preaching in the church of Banff. In prayer he used the following expression : " Bless thy servants in the magistracy—*such as they are!*"—*N.B.* The *magistrates* were sitting in the front of the gallery right opposite to the pulpit.

THE late Mr. L—th of the Grammar School was once questioned about the progress of one of his pupils, who was by no means a bright genius. Mr. L. replied, " O ! he'll *improve* as he *mends !*"

A DOUBLE-ENTENDRE.—Let not this equivocal Gallicism startle our fair readers. The story we are about to tell contains nothing but what they may safely peruse. The late Colonel T—r, although an Aberdonian, was by no means very far north. During a residence on the Continent he received, while in Brussels, a card of invitation to a ball. In the corner of the card were written the letters R. S. V. P. (*Reponse s'il vous plait*, An answer, if you please.) The meaning of these letters was to the Colonel a perfect mystery. He did not like to ask any one ; vanity forbade such an exposure of his ignorance of the formulary of *bon ton*. On his return to Aberdeen, being at a dinner party given by the late Mr. Y— of C—, he mentioned the circumstance, affecting to know the meaning of the letters, and propounding them, with towering confidence, as a riddle which he defied any one in the company to solve. The host well knew the meaning of the letters, but, pretending ignorance and wonder, determined to amuse himself at the Colonel's expense. After affecting to ponder the meaning of the letters with intense and anxious interest, he suddenly exclaimed, with counterfeited glee,—"I have it : I have it !" "Well," said the Colonel, "I shall call you clever fellow if you have." "The letters," said Mr. Y., " are evidently the initials of the words, ' *Rien sans votre presence,*' "without your company there will be no ball." " Egad," wheezed the Colonel, delighted with an interpretation which his vanity and ignorance united in pronouncing the true one, " the very thing. Well, now, I thought I had puzzled you ; but I see I was mistaken for once in my life."

DR. JOHN CHALMERS, formerly Principal of King's College (an office which he held during an ordinary life-time), had a country-house at Sclattie, to which he used to retire during the summer months. On one of his journeys thither, he fell from his horse and received a severe contusion on the shoulder. The report of the accident soon spread, and it was confidently asserted in Aberdeen that the Principal was lying at the point of death. Two of the professors, each an aspirant to the expected vacancy, set out, post haste, to inquire after their friend's health, and arrived simultaneously at Sclattie. They were ushered into the silent and darkened bed-chamber of the wounded man, and on stealthy tiptoe, with countenances arranged into suitable demureness, took their stations on opposite sides of what they believed (hoped ?) was his death-bed. A solemn silence of some minutes was at length abruptly broken by the Principal thrusting out his cap-enveloped head, and putting the dumb-founding question, " Well, gentlemen, which of you is to be Principal ?" The Professors looked first at the Doctor and then at each other, and, after a hearty laugh, in which the Principal's voice was " ready chorus," sincerely congratulated him on his state, which was by no means so dangerous as they had been induced to suppose it. The Principal lived a good many years after the accident.

A LEFT-HANDED COMPLIMENT.—The Rev. Mr. Thomas D— was employed for some time as assistant to the Rev. Mr. Forbes. Mr. D. was not a very popular preacher, but nevertheless he steered on, independent of the *aura popularis*, " neither dreading the censure nor courting the applause of of his hearers," as the late Rev. Mr. D—g used to say. He would even tell, with a good deal of humour, some stories about himself, which most people, under similar circumstances, would have prudently kept for private rumination. One of these was the following : — One Sunday, after divine service, as Mr. D. was returning homewards, he was accosted by an old woman, who said, " Oh, Sir, weel div I like whan ye preach." " Ou yea, my wifie," replied the astonished preacher ; " I wat ye're nae like mony ane. Fat for do you like whan I preach ?" " Ou, sir," quoth the wifie, "whan ye preach I get a guid seat !" The same gentleman was distantly related to the Earl of A—. Being on a visit at H— House, soon after obtaining a situation as a teacher in an institution in Aberdeen, he mentioned the circumstance to Lord A., and at the same time hinted that he hoped his lordship might perhaps be able to get him a kirk. His lordship observed, that he " should be satisfied in the meantime ; and that his present situation, although humble, was yet bread." " True," rejoined Mr. D., " but it is written, man cannot live by bread alone." " Well," said his Lordship, humouring the joke, " we must see to get you some *kitchen* for it."

A NEW SETT.—Our political readers will be disappointed if they imagine that we mean to give them a story about a New Sett of the Burgh ; that is so old a story that we are quite set with it, and shall therefore allow them to settle it as they please. Nor is our story about a sett of milk, although it is necessary that our readers should know the meaning of the word sett as thus applied, in order to understand the fun of it. Lest, in these " march of intellect days," there should be any so learnedly ignorant as not to know what is meant by so familiar a " household word" as " sett-o'-milk ;" for the information of such milksops in philology, such literary sucklings, we beg leave to premise, that a sett of milk means a regular daily allowance of that beverage which is paid for weekly. Now for our story :—One of the masters of a certain " seminary *op* learning" (those who were there when we were will appreciate our variorum reading of *op* for *of*), belonged to that class whom Horace had in his eye in the lines—

> " Est qui nec veteris pocula Massici,
>   Nec partem solido demere de die,
>   Spernit."

His progress to his daily task was uniformly retarded by a certain shop, where he used to get his " morning." On one occasion he came in as usual, while there was a customer in the shop, and " taking off his dram," went out without saying a word

The customer observing this, remarked that the dominie had gone away without paying. " Oh !" replied the shopman, " he has a sett."

THE learned *Blackwell*, formerly Principal of Marischal College, was remarkably *stingy*. While the workmen were employed in building his house at *Pulmuir*, where it is still to be seen, he sometimes gave them a *gaudeamus* of particularly small *small-beer*, which was commonly carried in a *water-bucket*. On these festive occasions he used to honour the masons with his company, and drink to their health, always remarking—" Ah ! my lads ! this will *put marrow in your bones !*" On one occasion a mason, of particularly *dry* turn, observed, " Aye, aye, *water-buckets bear nae ale !*"

JEAN CARR.—The late Rev. Mr. F., minister of F—vie, used to tell a story about one of Jean Carr's queer pranks, which well nigh upset his gravity while he was preaching one Sunday in the Kirk of Tarves. In a back pew in the gallery, right oppo-site to the pulpit, sat a young clodhopper who went by the name of the *buck of the parish*. He wore his hair tied in a long *queue*, and the dust of the *meal-pock* had not been spared on his nob. In tripped *Jean*, during sermon, frisking about here and there, until she halted immediately behind the youth. Suddenly seizing him by the *tye*, she twisted round his phiz, and fairly kissed him! The time, the place, the parties, not to mention Jean's *mouth*, which was none of the most *tempting*, were almost too much for the composure of Mr. F., who was at all times a grave man.

Mr. W——, formerly minister of Echt, was often obliged to employ assistants during the latter years of his life. One of these was rather vain of his qualifications as a preacher, but affected to be quite embarrassed by any compliments, which he received on that score. Mr. W——, after the sermon, went up to the probationer, and was going to shake hands with him. The young man anticipating nothing short of some high-flown compliment, exclaimed, "My good sir, no compliments— no compliments!" "Na, na," replied the parson, "now-a-days I'm glad o' ony body!"

THE Rev. Mr. Forbes, formerly one of the ministers of Aberdeen, was equally celebrated for the purity of his doctrine, the integrity of his life, and a Nathaniel-like simplicity of character, which endeared him to all who knew him. He was one of those few who let not their left hand know what their right doeth. His better half was a not-able woman in her way—

"To thrift and parsimony much inclined,"

and considered that her spouse "dealt with too

slack a hand," in his almsgiving; in short, she had a "saving knowledge."　Mr. F. was a studious and rather absent man.　One day, his lady having occasion to go abroad, locked the minister in; during her absence a beggar came to the door; Mr. F. finding it locked, took up a large loaf and handed it out at the window to the grateful mendicant.　Mrs. F. on her return made a sad fuss about the loaf, marvelling greatly at its disappearance, and charged the minister with having made away with it.　Mr. F. mildly observed, "My dear, what is kept in at the door, sometimes goes out at the window."

TIMMER TO TIMMER.—A reverend gentleman in the presbytery of A——, who has the misfortune to require crutches, assisting at the ordination of one whom he not unjustly regarded as a lame brother, when the "laying on of hands" was being performed, instead of coming forward from his seat, which was rather distant from the noviciate, and laying on his hand, deputed his staff to perform that important office.　One of his brethren remonstrating with him on such an indecorous departure from the usual ceremonial, he coolly observed, " There is naething like timmer to timmer."

A DEAD HIT.—A gentleman who holds a responsible situation in a banking establishment in our "guid town," was travelling in one of our northern stages along with a respectable house-builder of "that ilk." The builder, although a plain man, and not disposed to say a great deal, nevertheless attempted a shaving of the banker, and, looking as mysteriously piercing as an augur, observed that such and such a banker in the North was dead, with a screwing of the mouth, which plainly said, "I suppose you are looking after his place." The banker was not so green as the man of jeests ; according to current account, he replied "Well, sir, I hope you have got his coffin to make."

THE late Rev. Mr. G—d-n, formerly minister of Banff, used to let part of his glebe in grass to some persons who kept cows in the neighbourhood. One *honest 'oman* happened to *march* (not in the *intellect* way) with a field of grass which the worthy divine kept in his own hands, to his no small annoy-ance, as the said *honest 'oman* appeared to have rather indistinct notions of the relations of *meum* and *tuum*, often allowing her cows to *sorn* on his grass. The minister frequently remonstrated, when obedience was readily *promised* by the *guidwife*, but *performed* only while he was in sight. Finding the cows, one day, as usual, at free quarters in his grass, he says to the *'oman*, "You must keep your cows off my grass." "Ou aye, sir," was the reply, followed up by instant obedience. Coming soon after, he found the cows *as they were*, whereupon the minister says, " If you don't keep your cows off my grass, *I'll prosecute you.*"   Next time, finding even this threat in vain, he says, " I'll give you *five shillings*, if you'll keep your cows off my grass." " Troth, sir," replied the *honest* 'oman, " I wadna de't for *twenty !*"

AN ACCOMMODATING SERVANT.—A boy who had been some time in the employment of W——r and Y——, was informed by their clerk that he could be no longer retained in their employment, as there was no work for him.   " O !" said the loun, " lat's only stay, an' *we sanna cast oot about the wark !*"

" SINE DIE."—A certain Dr. S—— O——, very popular with the old ladies as a preacher, was before his fathers and brethren 'of the Presbytery, on a charge of being in a certain house, on a certain morning, and there conducting himself in a manner unbecoming the character of a clergyman and a gentleman.   Around the kirk door an eager crowd of gossips waited to learn their favourite's fate.   " What have they done ?"   " Oh," said the first bringer of the unwelcome news, " heard ye ever the like o't, they've suspen'it him till they *see in he dee !*"

SONNETS.

The Planet Venus.

Bright star ! thy name is Beauty, justly thine,
Daughter of Morning and of Evening, thou
Dost wear a lasting radiance on thy brow,
And, 'mong thy sisters that around thee shine
In softest glory, thou art queen divine !
Beautiful ! canst thou tell me whence we trace·
That more than earthly brightness on thy face ?
Art thou that distant speck which thou dost seem,
A thing of light to deck our evening sky,
Thou, with the myriads of thy shining train,
That wing, with thee, their course in harmony ?
Or art thou what our hoary sages deem,—
A world,—perchance inhabited by men
Even like ourselves, who now would scan thee but in
    vain ?

Moonlight.

Oh ! how delightful 'tis to gaze on thee,
Transcendent empress of the starry night,
Thou mildest, softest, loveliest, heavenly light,
Shining and sailing in chaste majesty !

See how the little clouds, all fringed with white,
Drunk with thy beauty, come to kiss thy beam,
And melt away like rain-drops in the stream,
And all the thousands of the starry throng
Twinkling like diamonds in the sun's bright ray,
Around thee move in loveliness along,
Till lost to the admirer's dazzled gaze.
Creation's God! how wondrous are thy ways!
Thy greatness framed this glorious canopy,
Thy goodness spread it out for creatures such as we!

OUR CATHEDRAL.

OF the Cathedral of Saint Machar the history is rather obscure. If we may trust authority more or less worthy of credit, it occupies the site of a primitive place of worship established by a missionary sent forth by Columba, with instructions to plant his preaching station fast by a river which pursued its course towards the neighbouring sea in windings like the crook of a bishop's staff. The holy man trudged along the coast until he came to the place where rose the future Cathedral, and there he took his station. As this must have occurred some thirteen centuries ago, it might be an inquiry for the geologist whether the Don at that time pursued its present course, or ran right in front of Seaton House, then crossing into the hollow north of the brickwork, and turning down the links into the estuary common to it with the river Dee, opposite to the Broad Hill? Be this as it may, however, in process of time—some five hundred years afterwards—mention is made of an episcopate having been founded at Mortlach, where are said to have ruled three bishops, whose names prove them to have been of native origin, Beyn, Cormack, and Nectan, the last of whom is said to have been translated along with his See to Aberdeen, where he ruled for several years. These particulars rest rather on tradition (somewhat hazy, although not perhaps entirely constructive), than on documents which antiquarians have considered unexceptionably genuine. The earliest document of satisfactory character dates 1157, when Edward was certainly Bishop, whoever his predecessors may have been. Beyn is said to have been Bishop from 1010 to 1047.

What we must accept as the history of the Cathedral tells us, that the first which was built on the present site was reared by Bishop Mathew Kininmonth, 1163-1197, and was, as we may well believe, a very humble building. We are told, that " Alexander Kininmonth, second of that name, who became Bishop in 1357, caused demolish said old church, esteeming it not beautiful enough for a Cathedral, and laid the foundation of another more magnificent [the present], but died before the work was raised six cubits high, in the year 1381." Another account says that " he finished only the bell-tower." Was this the great central tower which held all the bells gifted by Bishop Elphinstone? or was it the south-western tower, which was the only bell-tower during the chronicler's time? The other building prelates were—Leighton, 1424-41 ; Lindsay, 1441-59; Spence, 1459-80; Elphinstone, 1484-1514 ; Dunbar, 1518-32.

This most munificent and excellent prelate, the worthy successor of the illustrious Elphinstone, built the south aisle of the transept, in which, with an allowable feeling, he constructed a tomb for the reception of his remains, little thinking that, within a few and evil years thereafter, the sanctuary of his rest would be invaded and rifled by felon troopers of the Cromwellian domination. Among other impressive mementoes of the humiliating vicissitudes of time, it is most touching to note how completely, save to the antiquarian, the monument of this great and good man has long ceased to be memorial.

Some years ago, during the opening of a grave contiguous to the Bishop's tomb, the wall of the vault in which his remains had been placed was discovered, and (at the suggestion of the writer) the whole having been cleared out, it showed a receptacle some eight feet square and five deep, beautifully built of freestone ashlar. It presented but too palpable proofs of having been desecrated, being completely filled with rubbish like a dust-hole. There were some mouldering remains of an oak coffin, lozenge-shaped pieces of tinselled tin, oyster shells, a fragment of a skull, and part of a backbone.   All that remained of the Bishop's statue of black marble, which had lain under the arch of the tomb was one foot, trampling a dragon, all executed with great spirit and precision. There was also found the head of the effigy of a Canon, of much older date, which was restored to its trunk, which had long lain, and now lies, on the Bishop's tomb.   As for the foot, that too was carefully placed there, and remained for some weeks, *when it was stolen.*

What now remains, and has been so long used as a parish church, is only the nave of the original Cathedral.   The ruin of the transept, of the choir, and of the central tower and steeple, was begun by

" Hands, more rude than wintry sky."

The portion left is the oldest part of the fabric; and it is in this respect unique, that it is built of granite, but of a softer kind than that now used. It is somewhat singular that the less ancient portions are built of freestone.

Viewed as it now stands, although sadly shorn of its original glory, the Cathedral is a highly picturesque and interesting object.   The aspect of its western end, with its noble window of seven lights, flanked by lofty towers capped by those quaint old steeples, is singularly beautiful and striking—more especially when glowing in the mellowed ray of the western sun, and partly shaded by the venerable trees, which so beautify and solemnise the scene, redeeming the dreariness of the graveyard, and, by their obedience to the law of the seasons, so instructively symbolising the change from mortal to immortal life. None but the veriest clod of the valley can be uninfluenced by the spell which binds one in the rapt contemplation of so fair a scene, of which the fascination is crowned by the swelling music of the Don—"unseen, but not remote." Of a surety, other homilies there are than those delivered from the pulpit by which the heart is made better.

ABERDONIANS.

"Far fowls are fair feathered."

IN the character of Aberdonians there is, as in all others, somewhat to commend and somewhat to condemn. Let us not be deemed censorious if we select for the subject of a short essay a trait of character which all allow to be unworthy of *Bon Accord*. The trait of public character to which we allude is—*the propensity of Aberdonians to prefer strangers to public offices, to the prejudice of their fellow citizens.*

We mean not to assert that in no instance are our own people preferred to the stranger; but we do affirm that an *undue* preference has too frequently been shown to the latter in appointments to public offices. The truth of our assertion must be manifest to every one who bestows a moment's consideration on the subject. Survey our public institutions; have they not been too often filled by those who were not born and bred in Aberdeen? Is not this a common topic of self-reproach amongst us? when a vacancy occurs in any of our public situations, does it not too frequently happen that a stranger is preferred to it? When such a one is, at length, discovered to have been unworthy of the trust too unthinkingly reposed in him, immediately a hue and cry is raised against him, and after everything has been said against him which can be said, the vituperation is generally wound up with the remark—"Well, we always prefer strangers to our own folks, and see what we get!" The fact is beyond dispute; we are naturally led to the consideration of its causes. Surely it is not unreasonable to expect that we should prefer our own children to the sons of the alien. Is it not natural for the parent to prefer his own to the child of another? The bonds of affection are indeed less firmly knit in proportion as relationship is more remote; but still, in every case where there subsists the slightest connection, the correspondent obligations are indispensable. One of the causes of our preferring strangers is that proneness, common to all, to admire what is *novel.* We overlook qualities of transcendent excellence in those with whom we hold daily intercourse; while we fancy that we can discover peculiar virtues in those whom we behold for the first time.

Another cause of our preference—surely no very rational one—is our *ignorance* of strangers. We are disposed to give them credit for the possession of all the good qualities which they are *certified* to have, or which they boldly claim for themselves.

We seldom reflect that they *must* have their *defects*, which are discretely thrown into the shade when they appear as candidates for a situation. In our familiarity with the imperfections of our own people, we unfairly overlook their just claims on our patronage.

Another cause of our undue preference of a stranger is, mutual jealousy and party spirit. In filling up public offices we are too apt to separate into parties, each with a favourite candidate of his own. It thus happens that a stranger, unconnected with any party, steps in, and is successful, owing to the unwillingness of one party to yield to another. Another effect is the *discouragement of native talent*.

This effect is most deeply to be deplored ; its tendency is to eradicate from the minds of deserving young men those natural sentiments of attachment to *home* which might one day induce them to confer important benefits on their native city, as a return for the fostering care which they had once enjoyed. Few, compared with those which other places have experienced, are those proofs of grateful remembrance for *Bon Accord*, bequeathed by her sons that have breathed their last in the land of the stranger. Instead of regarding their native city as a kind parent, many of these have had but too just reason to look upon her as a cruel stepmother, whom they could neither love nor respect.

EXCURSIVE EDUCATION.

FYTTE FIRST—ICHTHYOLOGY.

" Dulce est desipere in loco.—Hor.

THE public are aware that our system of education is about to undergo certain changes of a peculiar character, which have been strongly recommended in the interim reports of our "committees," to whose legislative care this important matter has been intrusted. This is the more necessary in the Grammar School, as the first report states, with confidence, that the system of education which has hitherto been pursued at that seminary, with acknowledged success, "does not give satisfaction to the public." That system has been chiefly pursued with a view to qualify our youth for their studies at the universities, an object which must appear to every "right-thinking mind" of very little importance. Besides, the system tends "to establish one of the worst habits *for* the human mind—that of reading without comprehending." True it is, indeed, that at the last visitation the boys not only translated and parsed the classic authors, but " were also required to give an account of the proper names of places or persons which occurred, and of any other word which might convey a knowledge of ancient manners, customs, or laws,"—true it is that Dr. Melvin states that " in every department the pupils are most carefully instructed not only in facts but principles, and taught to exercise their *judgment* as well as their memory,"—true it is that he further states, " it is presumed that those who have gone through the curriculum of our school, and have profited fully by the training, must, besides everything else, have acquired such habits of industry, attention, and accuracy, as cannot fail to be highly advantageous,"—yes, all this may be very true—but " that's nothing !"　No ! the committee boldly state it as *their* opinion that, " *however* diligently and anxiously for the mental improvement of their scholars the teachers in the Grammar School may have studied to convey their instruction, *it is not to be believed* that a profitable use *can* be made of five hours a-day of the life of youths of eight to fourteen studying the Latin language, and that, too, on a plan having chiefly for aim expertness in an *almost* mechanical task."　" A habit of attention, which may be considered the mark of a promising youth, cannot *possibly* be cultivated or preserved by demanding five hours' application in a dry pedantic study." "The task must be *tiresome* and *insipid*, unless, indeed [*in order to enliven it and give it a zest*], a remedy be called into *play* [*which, however, is no joke, as we can testify !*] which has been considered and used as the only specific for the cure of inapplication in many of the famous English classical schools [*to say nothing of Solomon's recommendation*]—viz. the liberal use of a degrading punishment [*pandies !*], which ministers at the same time [*how convenient !*] in many cases a cure to the master's bad humour." No! no! a new order of things must prevail. A system of education must be introduced "better fitted for the tender mind"—a mode of discipline must be adopted "better fitted for the tender" skin! The schoolmaster, under the new system, "will be found teaching the meaning of the prepositions—the most abstract terms in our language, with *bits of wood*, and making the import of *to, towards, from, with*, and *by*, as clear to the urchin as the shape of *its* top." Nay, more, "manufactories of earthen, stone, and iron ware, and of cotton, linen, and woollen yarns and cloths, will not be in operation around him from year to year *unvisited*, and all the means they furnish for exercising the powers of observation, judgment, and reflection, and composition lost! No! he will take parties of his pupils by turns to examine some neighbouring manufactory, or to roam over the green fields of nature [*say the Links*], and imbibe *her* instructions, *aided* by his living and affectionate voice; he will require them to give a written account of what they have seen [*by way of trial version*], correct their exercises and point out their defects with a parent's care and tenderness; and, above all, he will *persevere* till he makes them what he wishes them to be." This—this is the plan of intellectual—of *Pestalozzian*—instruction which will be pursued not only in the above-mentioned departments, but also in another " to be afterwards mentioned ;" for " the means that may be employed to meet the capacities of *tender* youth, are endless as the resources of an able and enthusiastic teacher who is thoroughly *inoculated* with the Pestalozzian idea !"

Such are the principles of the new system of education, a specimen of its practical operation which we lately had the happiness to behold we now proceed to detail. We were accidentally informed that it was in contemplation to take a " party" of the Grammar School boys to a Pestalozzian excursion to the Fish Market, for the purpose of instructing them in the elements of *ichthyology*, or the philosophy of fish. We had learned that the " movement" was to be conducted by a councillor who is " thoroughly inoculated

with the Pestalozzian idea," and who had made
voluntary tender of his services on the occasion in
the absence of the Pestalozzian professor of
ichthyology, who was daily expected from the
Sketraw. As we promised ourselves some instruction and no small amusement from this expedition,
we contrived to give our bodily presence at the
time and place appointed in the Grammar School
on Friday, which was judiciously selected as
the most convenient day. When we approached
the seminary of classic lore, our ears were greeted
by certain sounds of youthful mirth and jollity, in
which it was once our delight to join in our
"tender age." The happy rogues were beating
time with their feet, not to the "march of intellect," but to the good old rhyme—

> " *O for the play, boys !*
> *Friday is the day, boys !*"

At the well-known sounds our heart leaped within
us for very joy ! We entered the class-room in a
flurry of delight, and squeezed ourselves into a
faction near the door, although with some difficulty,
as the seat and our corporation appeared to have
changed their relative proportions since the period
of our boyhood. At first we were taken for the
professor, and there was temporary silence and
expectation among the "laddies ;" but we were
soon stripped of our transitory importance by

being unluckily recognised by some of the young dogs, who simultaneously squalled out, "It's nae him—it's nae him. It's *only* —— come to see the shine!" This announcement was received with a tremendous *ruff*, and most uproarious cheering, which might have perchance been 'followed up by other tokens of recognition more free than welcome, when the riotous "demonstration" was interrupted by the *bona fide* entrance of the professor, who forthwith established himself in the *maister's* desk, when

> " There was silence deep as death,
> And the boldest held his breath
> *For a time !*"

Several of the youngsters looked round to see how *we* were affected by the presence. Poor little fellows! they might have saved themselves the trouble; we were prepared for the worst. We were not recognised by the professor, however; and, indeed, were probably by him taken for one of his disciples, for we have long relinquished the vain wish that a cubit were added unto our stature.

The professor, after a few preliminary hems, addressed his pupils as follows :—

Professor.—My dear boys ! the long wished-for period has at length arrived when you are to be disenthralled from the worse than Egyptian bondage under which you have hitherto groaned ; when you are to be emancipated from the iron fetters of antiquated forms, manumitted from the slavery of pedantic studies, and entered as free denizens of the kingdom of nature. (*A ruff.*) A new era has arrived in the moral, intellectual, political, and physical organisation of society, in which the rising generation are particularly interested. Instead of being necessitated to get by rote dry rules of grammar, and to con over lessons in a dead language, you are now to be initiated into the mysteries of the "green field, the manufactory, and the dockyard;" and, instead of being lacerated by the hateful engines of corporal punishment, you are to be cheered on in your delightful tasks by the "affectionate voice" of your teacher. (*Tremendous cheers. Cries of "Burn the tards!" "No flogging!"*)

My dear boys, it affords me heartfelt satisfaction to hear these spontaneous demonstrations of your unsophisticated feelings. (*A ruff.*) Rest assured that the period is rapidly approximating when *a tards* will be reckoned among the number of things that were, and only preserved in the cabinets of the curious. (*Thunders.*) Instead of being obliged, as formerly, to pursue your dry studies caged-up in "pitiful class-rooms," you will have the never-dying delectation of prosecuting your utilitarian researches under the open canopy of the sky! The true—the Pestalozzian—the intellectual principle of education is to convey instruction through the "medium of the senses," by familiar manipulation, and by ocular demonstration. (*One cheer more.*) Nor will your interests alone be attended to, but arrangements will be entered into for promoting the intellectual education of those whom a reverend friend of mine has emphatically denominated "the finer sex." In the new system no place will be found for coercive measures—all will be carried on by the immortal *voluntary* principle. (*Ruffing.*) To submit to be educated on any other principle is to forfeit the birthright of free-born Britons—nay, of ratiocinative beings! Such an order of things opens up a delightful vista to the Pestalozzian philanthropist. He sees in it the bloodless triumphs of intellectual manifestations, when universal peace shall reign, and we shall hear no more the sounds of what has been falsely termed "the pomp and circumstance of glorious war." (*Drums in Gordon's Hospital beat to arms—answered by a volley of ruffing.*) No! my dear boys! let *others* "follow to the field their martial lord," *we* shall turn a deaf ear alike to the "spirit-stirring drum," "the shrill fife," or "soft recorders!" Even music will have no charms for us, unless it be brought to bear on the elucidation of the useful arts. (*Band strikes up—" The rock an' th' wee pickle tow."*) The object of our present meeting is to study that branch of natural science called *Ichthyology*. This word, as I have been informed by my reverend friend to whom I have already alluded, and who is celebrated for quoting *original* Greek, is derived from two Greek vocables, the one meaning a *fish*, and the other *method*. Under the former term are comprehended not only the finny tenants of the deep, but also *lobsters*, *partans*, *oysters*, and *mussels*, and, as my *reverend* friend deems highly probable, and extremely proper, *Finnan haddies* also. But, as my friend well observes, " whatever discrepancy may exist among commentators as to the classification of the latter, there can be but one opinion as to the pre-eminent place which they occupy among the ' good things ' of this world."

The waters which cover the surface of this earth, whether they be oceans, seas, rivers, lakes, or *burns*, or ponds, or dams, or canals, are filled with innumerable living creatures, whose instincts are as different as their forms and colours are beautiful ; among these various tribes the fishes are by far the most valuable. They are found alike under the dreary skies of the poles, and in the burning latitudes of the tropics. They supply us with wholesome and nutritious food, with *oil*, and various other matters of convenience "to be afterwards mentioned." Well has Dr. Franklin observed, that "he who takes a fish out of the water, finds a piece of money." This is a saying which could not have emanated from any one except the citizen of a free country like America.

But to come to particulars. There is the herring, which, although a small fish, is nevertheless king of the sea. Herrings are said to attack the whale, whose gigantic size might well entitle him to the despotism of the deep, yet they overpower him by numbers. Hence we may learn that union among themselves must render the friends of liberty omnipotent. It was this principle which rendered complete the triumph of the memorable Bill. You have probably heard of that dreadful fish called the shark, or what sailors term *sea-lawyers*. It is a most voracious fish, and ought to be speedily extirpated from the ocean. From its other name, in conjunction with its devouring propensities, we may naturally deduce as a corollary the necessity of a speedy law-reform. From this, again, we may readily infer the urgency of reform in every department of Church and State. Ah! my dear boys, of how extensive application is the Pestalozzian principle, which teaches us to connect together causes and effects the most remote! But why should we sit here, when we ought to listen to the instructions of Nature in the Fish Market, where the unsophisticated matrons of *Collieston* and the sturdy damsels of the *Cove* may be considered as her handmaidens? This — this is our schoolroom ; here shall we best study ichthyology through "the medium of the senses." Thrice happy your fate to live in times like these, when the "Pestalozzian idea," germinated and reared beneath the genial skies of the south, is destined to bloom and bourgeon in this "our northern city cold !" Before we set out, allow me to say that we will pursue our route by the *Mutton Brae*, in the neighbourhood of which were formerly held numerous meetings of the supporters of the Bill, and where an eloquent *triumvirate* were wont to lend their oratorical talents to forward the good cause. Then we shall wend our way along the banks of the meandering *Denburn*, whence we shall steer our course through the *Green* to the arena of our Pestalozzian exercitations.

Agreeably to this resolution, the professor left the class-room, followed by a tail of a score of boys. The "party" excited considerable interest as they passed along. Bakers, grocers, shoe-makers in Kilmarnocks and leathern aprons, etc. etc., turned out to behold the passing spectacle. Various were the conjectures formed about the object of the expedition. The boys were in high glee, and cut manifold capers. The professor seemed to be absorbed in his "pursuit of know-ledge," and was all-unconscious of a long paper *queue* with which one of the rogues had kindly accommodated him. Some of them had purchased "crackers" in a neighbouring shop, which combustibles they distributed among sundry *bourocks* of auld wives in the *Mutton Brae* who had turned out with their *shanks* to see what was the matter. These proceedings excited the wrath of the aged females, who speedily withdrew within their domiciles, from the doors and windows of which, as from loop-holes in a garrison, they discharged certain "winged words" with dire intent, which it was impossible to mistake. Little remarkable occurred at the *Denburn* till their arrival at the *Bridge*, under which some of the boys discharged small-arms as a practical illustration of the *Pistol*-ozzian manner of "teaching the young idea how to shoot!" When they were opposite the head of *Carmelite Street* they were attentively surveyed by a member of the *pestle*-lozzian profession, who was engaged in superintending the beautifying of the *Correction Wynd Bridge*, agreeably to the latest *Parisian* fashion. Arrived at the *Malt-mill Bridge*, they narrowly escaped a "breeze" with certain junior members of the fifth estate, who are generally stationed in that quarter on the out-look for squalls. They at length reached the market, which presented an animated scene of buyers and sellers of all denominations, among whom we recognised a *reverend*-looking gentleman in black, with spectacles on nose, and cane in hand, who bore himself with somewhat of a martial air, as he cheapened a dozen of *haddies.* We over-heard the following :—

Gent.—I do like 'em, to be sure, and so does missus, but you ask too much.

Eppie.—Weel, my chiel, fat wull ye gie? your bode's welcome. There is na better fish i' th' market. They wad dee a sieck heart guid. They're as sweet's a nit.

Gent.—I'll tell you what, I'll give you six-pence.

Eppie.—Saxpence! Bawbees the piece! Na, na, my chiel, they're nae mine at the siller. Guid safe's, only wacht them! D'ye think I sta' them?

Here the professor came up, when greetings in the market-place were exchanged between him and the gent, who, being apprised of the professor's errand, said—

Gent.—Well, I do admire this system, and, indeed, I have always acted on it myself; it is the best way to let boys know what's what, and besides they learn to make market. Charming fish here! but deucedly dear. But we can't have our "good things" without paying for 'em, you know. What a set of fine little fellows you've got!

Here they were joined by some others who were " inoculated with the Pestalozzian idea," one of whom, *a councillor* of portly figure and good-humoured physiognomy, was instantly recognised by *Eppie, Meggie, Nannie, Kirstie,* etc. etc., who simultaneously exclaimed—

" Come awa', sir, and buy a caller haddock or a fine cod. There's a skatie nae twa hours oot o' th' water !" By her fair speaking *Meggie* prevails on the *merchant* to look at a prime skate, for which she demands aughtpence.

Mercht.—Auchtpence, ye jaud ! an' that's the deil an auchtpence ! I'se gie ye a groat an' ye like to tak it.

Meggie.—A groat ! Troth, sir, ye wad hae a muckle conscience to tak' it for that, if I were feel aneuch to gie ye't.

Mercht.—Wisht, ye limmer ! fa d'ye think is to staun here an' get your ill jaw. I'll jist gie you a saxpence for the skate, and deil a bawbee mair, tak' it or wint it.

Meggie.—Weel, weel, my chiel, you maun get it ; ye're nae that ill set after a', an a guid bread-gier. I neer took up a bit fish that I didna get a drap to weet my mou' fae the mistress.

Here the merchant is thus accosted by a broad-skirted urchin among the boys—

Boy.—Fader, gie's a penny to buy a partan ?

Mercht.—Hoot, ye rascal, are ye speakin o' partans, fan ye sud be mindin' your eddication ?

Boy.—Weel, gie's a bawbee to buy dulse.

Mercht.—An' that's the deil ane ? Ye cam na

herc to fill your wames. Ou, professor, ye dinna lat the louns eat here ?

Prof.—My dear boys, here we shall get food for the mind, which is of greater importance.

Gent. in specs.—With your leave, professor, I must say that the " good things " of this life are not to be despised. Even I am by no means indifferent to them, for without 'em I couldn't get on at all.

Mercht.—By my faith, baith you and me tee look as if we were at hame at diet time o' day. But I'm nae for bairns crammin themsels wi' trash atween hauns ; at meal-time I lat them tak their sairin, for I dinna like to be scrimpit mysel.

Prof.—Meggie ! will you allow me to show these boys that small fish ?

Meggie.—Wi' a' my heart, my chiel ! wull ye lat me tak hame this coddie to the Mistress ?

Nannie.—Guid's cause, fat's the man dein here wi' sae mony laddies ? They're seerely nae a' his ain ?

Kirstie.—He's a dominie come here to spy ferlies amo' the fisher fouk.

Prof.—This, my dear boys, if I mistake not, is a whiting.

Mercht.—Deil a bit o' that is't, for it's a codlin.

Meggie.—Ye'r richt my chiel, it's jist a codlinie.

Kirstie.—Eppie ! the dominie's nae richt, peer man ! he disna ken a fiten by a codlin.

Eppie.—The mair's the pity! guid help them that has the charge o' him. An yet, he's weel pitten on. But fat signifies brawness?

Here a squall arises in consequence of the overt act of counting the fish-wives, committed by one of the boys.

Kirstie, etc.—Deil coont ye! ye smatchets! fat's the use o' your dominie, if he dinna learn ye better fashions?

A regular row commences; the boys persevere in their *census* of the wives; talk of "baud's feet" in their creels; the wives retaliate; the Professor, Merchant, and Gentleman mediate in vain. One of the boys discharges a pistol behind the Merchant's ear, who, in the quandary of the moment, slipping his foot on an extensive skate, suddenly tumbles into a *murlin* of partans, one of which, of gigantic size, and all alive, not relishing such an invasion of his neighbourhood, fixes with slow but sure effect on the Merchant! to the grievous annoyance of the latter, who roars out most lustily. The row thickens; crackers and codlins fly about in all directions. The gentleman in the specs is seen clearing his way in the direction of the Ship-row, dragging after him a skate which has been affixed by a string to his upper garment. The wives follow in full cry, but the gentleman seems bent on securing his retreat, and never looks back. The *Professor* is seen endeavouring to escape by the entrance from the quay, after having been somewhat unceremoniously crowned with an empty *murlin*, so as to justify the remark of a bystander, that "his head was surely in a creel." He succeeded in effecting his escape by the *Back Traps*. The Merchant recovered from the claw of the crab, and trudged homewards, exclaiming, "Deil tak your partan taes, muckle mischief hae they played amo' councillors first and last, but naething like this. It was a mercy that we wisna like 'the pigs!'"

So here ended "Fytte the First," which abundantly proved that—wherever the schoolmaster might be "abroad,"—in the Fish Market he was certainly "NOT AT HOME!"

A "jeu d'esprit," on Councillors Phillip, Dunn, etc., and their intermeddling with education then. Wisdom sits enthroned in the councils of the city now. *We* have no meddling or muddling to lament over, each returning competition for bursaries at the University proving how valuable and effective for gaining these is our present Grammar School curriculum. For "the spread of letters," this same locality—the Fish Market site—is again in favour with the Aberdeen Town-Council.

PADDY WEEKS' ADDRESS.

DEAR Ladies and Gentlemen—all !
  Behold me once more in your city ;
Since I left you, my luck's been but small ;
  Och ! sure you'll say—more is the pity !

Soon after I left Aberdeen,
  I droop'd like a lone weeping willow ;
I have been quite a prey to the spleen,
  And sleep's cut his stick from my pillow.

Just look at my chop-fallen cheeks !
  I suspect I am in for consumption ;
If you know your ould friend Paddy Weeks—
  I confess I'm surprised at your gumption.

A crony I met, and says he
  You look very ill, my dear fellow !
Your liver is bad, for I see,
  Your complexion is turning quite yellow !

In dust I must very soon moulder,
  My appetite's so very bad !—Oh !
I don't like to look over my shoulder,
  For fear I should miss my own shadow !

Now, the reason of all this distress,
   You cannot with reason suppose ;
I'll tell it you all—more or less ;
   But, of course, it is under the rose !

I hope there is none within hearin'—
   (Just let me get over my spittle !)
I have been to see ould mother Erin—
   But—by J——— !—she's bad off for victual !

Says I—" Is your money all spent ?"
   What, think ye, replied the poor cratur ?
Och ! I pinch back and belly for " rint "
   To give to the " great liberator !"

Sure I found that the " Sign o' the *Fork* "
   Was no longer a sign of a Hotel ;
Bottle-stopping there must be in *Cork*,
   When there's devil a drop in the bottle !

To teach in your new *Grammar School*,
   The *Ex*-cur-sio-*nal* Education
On the system of *Dr. O' Toole*,
   Would tally with my inclination !

Or if you should rather incline
   To nestle me in your new College ;
Why—'tis quite in an Irishman's line
   To promote the confusion of knowledge !

Since I'm just like the famed *Brig o' Don*,
   Being turned rather ouldish and crazy ;
When the *best* of us both is quite gone,
   'Twere but fair that the *worst* should be aisy !

Our cases do so correspond,
   That, without any more botheration,
I'd consider a slice o' th' *fond*,
   An agreeable mortification !

Should I pluck up my old phisiog
   By the help of good eating and drinking,
I'd be liker to—" go the whole hog,"
   So I'll just tell you what I've been thinking.

What if you should make me M.P.,
   I'm sure you won't think me ambitious ;
For you know that *my* speeches would be
   All " sensible, clear, and judicious !"

Mr. Weeks, comedian, was at this time figuring on the Aberdeen stage with the Crisps, Williams', and—Tom Ryder. Dan O'Connell, " the great liberator " was levying " rint," and Lord Brougham designating the then Aberdeen M.P.'s speeches, as "sensible, clear, and judicious." One of the Aberdeen Mortifications is called " The Brig o' Don Fund."

MATHEMATICS.

THE importance of the study of Mathematics, whether with a view to mental discipline, the gratification of enlightened curiosity, or the employment of its practical results in the exigencies of professional life, has never been questioned except by those to whose crude and mistaken opinions on the subject little deference is due. By means of this powerful engine of inventive thought, we are enabled to scan the most mysterious phenomena of nature, and to perform the most striking achievements of art. It has been applied to detect the subtle agency of magnetic, electric, and capillary attraction, and to discover the laws of the forces which urge the heavenly bodies along courses traced by the finger of Omnipotence! It has been employed to assist the feeble hand of man to rear his towers of strength, the proud palace, and the consecrated fane ; and to navigate the stately vessel through the pathless deep. In every, even the most remote age, and among all nations, in any degree famed for civilisation, it has ever been prosecuted with an ardour worthy of its practical utility, and of its dignity as an abstract science. Some scanty and scattered fragments of Algebra and Geometry, and the colossal ruins of an observatory, prove that it was not unknown to primeval nations of the East, of whose existence few other traces now remain ; and, in later times, it has flourished in the countries which produced an Archimedes, a Newton, an Euler, and a Laplace. The precise *origin* of this science is involved in obscurity which baffles research. Some maintain that it dawned in the East, while others contend that Egypt gave it birth. The truth probably is, that it had a separate and nearly simultaneous origin in both regions. At a subsequent and better-known period, it was successfully cultivated in Greece and some neighbouring countries, when the particular branch of *Geometry* was brought to a state of perfection, unrivalled by the efforts of modern ingenuity. On the decay of learning in those quarters, the sciences found an asylum in the schools of Alexandria, where they were long cherished under the munificent sway of the Ptolemies, by some of whom they were studied with considerable success. To the Ancients we owe an almost immaculate elementary system of Geometry—the various branches of Geometrical Analysis—Conic Sections—Solid Geometry—and the geometrical construction of some of the higher curves, such as the Conchoid of Nicomedes, and the Cissoid of Diocles. We are also indebted to them for the *Method of Exhaustions*, by means of which they were enabled to compare the straight line with the curve—the rectilineal with the curve-bounded superficies — and the solid, which is terminated by planes, with that which is limited by a curved surface. The manner of treating the doctrine of Proportion, which is given in the fifth book of Euclid's Elements of Geometry, is the only accurate and comprehensive system of that important branch which has yet appeared. Much, however, of the ancient Geometry is lost; and not a little of what we now possess has been restored by the ingenuity of modern geometers, of whom Simson is the chief. During the darkness of posterior ages, rendered still more appalling by the flames of exterminating wars, and the jarring elements of polemical theology, the Mathematics maintained a precarious existence in Arabia, where they were too frequently enslaved by a dark superstition, and forced into a preposterous alliance with the absurdities of Astrology and other branches of occult science. At the remarkable era of the revival of letters in Europe, the science of Mathematics was not forgotten. Some of its earliest cultivators and patrons were merchants of Italy and adjacent states, who imported manuscripts on its various branches, along with the less-refined but more gainful products of the East. We soon arrive at the age which produced Ferrari, and Cardan, by whom the solution of some of the higher equations was carried to a limit beyond which it has not been far advanced by the superior resources of more recent algebraists. During this period, however, the science was cultivated rather with a view to foster the selfish vanity of the few to whom it was confined, than with that humble and liberal spirit which ought ever to distinguish its worthy votaries. The seventeenth century was distinguished by an illustrious band of discoverers in Mathematical and Physical science. Of these, one of the most remarkable was the versatile, yet often fanciful, Descartes, who, by the application of Algebra to Geometry, established an epoch in the history of science. He is also distinguished for his discoveries in the theory of equations, being the first who noticed the remarkable relation which subsists between the signs of their roots and those of their terms. He was the first who expressed roots by means of fractional indices—an important extension of the exponential notation. He also carried the general resolution of equations as far as biquadratics. Vieta is likewise to be recorded as an early inventor of an improved mode of notation, which led to results of no small moment. The name of Wallis stands conspicuous as the author of the new mode of treating the doctrine of *Conic Sections*, *in plano*—as the first who developed a fraction into a series—and as a deviser of an improved manner of explaining the *Method of Indivisibles.* Harriot first resolved an equation into as many simple binomial factors as there are units in the number denoting its degree—a property which has not yet been *demonstrated a priori*, although its reality admits not of a doubt. Nor ought we to omit the name of the profound and eloquent Barrow, who trenched on the discovery of the rich vein of mathematical science which was reserved for the searching hand of one even greater than himself.

Scotland claims the honour of producing the celebrated Napier, not more distinguished by the accidental circumstance of his noble birth, than by the invention of *Logarithms*—which have not only abridged the labour and improved the methods of mere calculation, but have also been employed as a most efficient element in the processes of the most recondite analysis. The inquirer into the progress of scientific knowledge connected with this period, must pause to pay a passing tribute of admiration to the romantic genius of Kepler—the sober sagacity of Copernicus— and the commanding talents of the persecuted Galileo. All these, however, were but the brilliant harbingers of the noon-day radiance, unknown to wane, which beamed on the most retired sanctuaries of science, from the seraphic intellect of Newton. How vain to attempt to celebrate the praise of one whose genius was as bright, as diffusive, and as benign as the sunbeam from which he charmed the secret of its birth — whose fame is an echo to the harmonious hymn, first caught by *his* heaven-instructed ear, which nature ever breathes through all her works! At the early age of twenty-four, Newton had made discoveries in science which far outshone those of all former generations, and far exceeded what the most sanguine expectations could have anticipated from many a succeeding age. To enumerate *all* his discoveries would exceed our limits, our ability, and our design. To him we owe the discovery of the *Binomial Theorem*—the sheet anchor of the analyst—improved methods of solving equations, and determining the properties of curves—and above all the *Method of Fluxions.* Contemporary with Newton was Halley—a restorer of ancient geometry, and discoverer of new modes of solving equations; Maclaurin, who first established the principles of Fluxions on the solid basis of geometrical demonstration; Taylor—whose *Theorem* for the development of a function was afterwards employed, by Lagrange, as the foundation of the Differential Calculus; and the Bernouillis—who contributed greatly to improve the various branches of Analysis, but whose contentions were disgraceful to them, both as brothers and as philosophers. During this

period, the question regarding the first discovery of
Fluxions was keenly agitated by the partisans of
Newton and Leibnitz. After all which has been
written on the subject, it is now generally admitted,
that the claim of *prior discovery* belongs exclusively
to Newton ; while, at the same time, it is not denied
that Leibnitz *may* have also found out his Infini-
tesimal Method without having borrowed the idea
of it from the English philosopher. Notwithstanding his great and diversified talents, Leibnitz
seems to have been a man of a vain-glorious and
envious disposition, forming, in these respects, a
striking contrast to the humble and unobtrusive
character of Newton. This great man, who valued
nothing, not even his own discoveries, so much as
peace of mind, was more than once involved in
disputes with certain ambitious pretenders to
science. Genius such as his never fails to provoke
the envious attacks of those who pine at the thought
of excellence in others which they vainly strive to
emulate, as the songster of the woodlands allures
by its melody the bird of prey! After the time of
Newton, the science of Mathematics could boast of
a greater number of successful votaries on the Continent than in Britain. This has been ascribed to
various causes, of which some were purely accidental, while others were of a less contingent
nature. Of these last, one of the principal seems
to have been the pertinacious adherence of the

British mathematicians to the *synthetic method*, in imitation of Newton, who chose it as the more dignified mode of presenting his discoveries to the world.   On the other hand, the Continental mathematicians would appear to have early appreciated the superiority of the *analytic method* as the more efficient instrument of investigation.   England, indeed, may justly boast of her Thomas Simson, and Landen, who was the first who proposed, instead of fluxions, a purely analytic, although not unobjectionable theory, in his *Residual Analysis ;—* Scotland may justly be proud of Simson, Maclaurin, and Stewart ; but it is not the general opinion that any of these, with the exception of Maclaurin, can be ranked with Clairaut, D'Alembert, Euler, and Daniel Bernouilli, with regard to the number and importance of their discoveries.   At a yet later period, the comparison is even still more in favour of the Continental mathematicians.   It will be difficult to find names in Britain so deservedly celebrated as those of Lagrange, Legendre, Lacroix, and Laplace.   To the ingenuity of Continental mathematicians, we are indebted for the Calculus of Sines —of Partial Differences—of Variations of Functions—of Finite Differences—and a multitude of useful discoveries in every branch of Analysis.   Of late years, the works of Continental mathematicians, after a long struggle with our national prejudices, and blind attachment to established forms, have at length found their way into some of our Universities, where their value is held in due estimation. The Calculus of Sines has superseded the Geometrical Trigonometry ; the *application of Algebra to Geometry* is no longer confined to the particular branch of the resolution of insulated problems ; and the superiority, in point of notation, principle, and facility of application, of the *Differential Calculus* over the method of Fluxions, is almost universally admitted. Several excellent elementary treatises on these subjects have lately proceeded from the pens of Wallace, Woodhouse, Peacock, Herschel, and Babbage, who are besides distinguished as the authors of original works on some of the more abstruse branches of the science.

DR. HAMILTON.

DR. HAMILTON, formerly professor of Mathematics in Marischal College, was the eighth son of Gavin Hamilton, a bookseller and publisher in Edinburgh, whose father was at one time, Professor of Divinity in the university of that city, and subsequently its Principal. In his youth, Dr. Hamilton was distinguished for the zeal and success with which he prosecuted his studies, both at school and college. At the latter he was a pupil of the celebrated Matthew Stewart, who soon discovered, with pleasure, the genius of his scholar for the mathematics, and delighted to direct the energies of his expanding talents in the paths of science. Strong as was the attachment of young Hamilton to the pursuits of literature and science, yet he was compelled, by circumstances, partially to forego his studies, for the less refined, yet more gainful occupation of a mercantile life. With this view he spent some time in the banking establishment of Messrs. William Hogg and Son—a circumstance which may have at first imbued him with a taste for those financial speculations, which in after life he prosecuted with equal credit to himself and advantage to the community. About this time he became a member of a literary club, composed of young men of rising talents, which formed a germ of the Speculative Society. At this period, too, he fortunately recommended himself to the notice of Lord Kaimes, by an anonymous criticism on some of his Lordship's works, which Mr. Hamilton had published in some of the periodicals of the day. In 1766, Mr. Hamilton then only twenty-three years of age, was prevailed on to offer himself as a candidate for the Chair of Mathematics in Marischal College, vacant by the death of Professor John Stewart, who had filled it with distinguished ability for nearly forty years. The candidates on this occasion were, besides Mr. Hamilton—Mr. Trail, Mr. Playfair, Mr. Fullerton, Mr. Douglas, and Mr. Stewart. The examination was of the most extensive, rigorous, and judicious character. The examinators were, Professor Vilant of St. Andrews ; Professor Gordon of King's College ; and Professor Skene of Marischal College. The sums of the merits of the candidates were respectively as follow :—Trail, 126 ; Hamilton, 119; Playfair, 90 ; Fullerton, 58 ; Stewart, 47 ; Douglas 16. The successful competition of Mr. Hamilton with such men as Trail and Playfair, proves that he possessed at his early age no common measure of skill in the mathematical sciences. After this Mr. Hamilton became a partner in a paper manufactory estab-

lished by his father, which he consigned to the care of
a manager, on his being appointed Rector of the
Perth Academy, in 1769.   In 1771, he married
Miss Ann Mitchell of Ladath, from whom he had
the misfortune of being separated by death seven
years afterwards.   In 1779 Mr. Hamilton was
chosen professor of Natural Philosophy in the
Marischal College, in consequence of the distinguished figure which he had made at the competition
for the Mathematical chair.   Mr. Copland, then
Professor of Mathematics, was by no means an
adept in that science, and Mr. Hamilton, owing to
his habits of mental absence, was far from being an
expert experimentalist.   They therefore exchanged
classes, but not *professorships*—Dr. Hamilton not
being elected professor of Mathematics till 1817.
About this time Dr. Hamilton published that
useful practical work, so well known by the title
of *Hamilton's Merchandise*, which he seems to
have formed on the model of a similar work by
Mair his predecessor in the Perth Academy.   In
1790 appeared his essay on Peace and War ; in
1796 his Arithmetic ; and in 1800, his *Heads of
a Course of Mathematics*.   When now in the
seventieth year of his age, he published in Edinburgh,
1813, his great work, entitled *An Inquiry concerning the Rise and Progress, the Redemption and
Present State of the National Debt of Great
Britain*.   This admirable work created a great

sensation. It clearly demonstrated the folly of the reigning system of finance, but it was not till afterwards, when his discoveries had found a general and powerful echo in public opinion, that they were gradually adopted in the management of the national income. Our limits prevent us from exhibiting a summary of Dr. Hamilton's views on this subject ; suffice it to say that he fully exposed the fallacy of a borrowed sinking fund, and of continuing its operation during war, or when the expenditure of the nation overbalances its income. The doctrines of Dr. Hamilton on this important subject have been supported by the Edinburgh Reviewers, by Ricardo, Say, and all the eminent Political Economists of the age ; while the venerable Lord Grenville, a member of the Administration which devised the sinking Fund, and for some time First Lord of the Treasury, has admitted that the treatise of Dr. Hamilton opened his eyes to the fallacy of his once favourite measure. A year after the publication of the *Inquiry*, Dr. Hamilton's declining health rendered an assistant necessary, and Mr. (now Dr.) Cruickshank was appointed for that purpose. In 1825 death deprived him of his second wife, a daughter of Mr. Morrison of Elsick, whom he had married in 1782. During his latter years Dr. Hamilton had laboured under the infirmities that usually wait on advanced age ; but his progress to the grave was gradual, and he at length reached that "bourne whence no traveller returns," on the 14th day of July 1828.

In the character of this excellent man, in what light soever it may be viewed, there is much to admire; much that rendered him a blessing to society—an ornament to the country which gave him birth. Far from being a mere frigid speculatist in philosophy, Dr. Hamilton was an enthusiastic and judicious philanthropist, in the highest sense of that honourable appellation. On more than one occasion, he left the retirement to which his native modesty as much as his studious habits so deeply attached him, and stood forth the powerful and fearless advocate of truth, warning the state against impending danger, and pointing out the path of safety. Nor were his patriotic exertions solely directed to the weightier matters of national concern; often was his benevolent spirit at work, in promoting the best interests of our municipality, in maturing schemes for the aid of the widows and children of the clergy, and in devising plans for the relief of the friendless poor. Great as were his talents, and they were of the first order, his moral qualities presented a still stronger claim on admiration. His active benevolence, guileless modesty, sterling worth, and unaffected piety, entitled him to rank as one of "the excellent of the earth," in every relation, whether public or private. Of his intellectual character, his various writings afford an unquestionably high testimony. They are evidently the productions of an acute, a well-regulated, and highly-cultivated understanding, that values the weapons of argumentative skill only as instruments of defending or establishing the cause of useful truth.

His acquirements in science and general literature were both varied and profound. At an early age we have seen him successfully coping with Playfair, who afterwards stood in the first class of British mathematicians. Dr. Hamilton's natural bias for the *useful*, induced him to quit the *flowery* yet comparatively fruitless paths of abstract science, for the important subject of Political Economy. In this department he made discoveries which exerted a beneficial influence over the affairs of the nation, and which, while they entitle him to rank with the first in philosophical ingenuity and argumentative skill, confer on him the still higher distinction of being classed with those who have done good service to the state. As a teacher, the instructions of Dr. Hamilton were invaluable to those who had discernment to prize them as they deserved ; but in the thoughtless bands of the youthful myrmidons of which his class was composed, it had been vain to look for much respect for learning—much veneration for transcendent talent. The outward demeanour of the good Professor was marked by certain unaffected peculiarities, which, while they only invested him with a charm of endearing *naïveté* to those who rightly knew him, yet would sometimes excite the irreverent notice of his giddy charge. Yet was their frolicsome recognition of his little eccentricities unmarked by malice or by petulence ; it was the mere overflowing of exuberant spirits (as yet untamed by disappointed hope), which, in the absence of real, is ever fertile in contriving imaginary sources of harmless mirth. Sure we are, that those who were most ready to smile at the peculiarities in dress or manner of their venerable teacher, cannot reflect, without a feeling of self-disapprobation, on their partial insensibility to the excellences of a character which, when years had matured their judgment, they could not but regard with the deepest veneration.

We have been informed, by those who knew him in his younger days, that Dr. Hamilton was a person of a florid, open, comely countenance, and erect carriage. *We* were only familiar with the time-worn frame which his latter years presented to the view, when " the strong men had already bowed themselves," and " the almond-tree had long been flourishing." We still delight to conjure up before the eye of fancy his long-remembered form ; —the childlike, guileless expression of his countenance, in which the discerning observer might mark the while, traces of deep thought amid the more obtrusive furrows of age ;—the bustling diligence of his shuffling gait, impeded as much as aided by his staff, now planted, in careless haste, in front ; and anon trailing, at length, in rear, the left arm generally resting behind ;—his eyes, in which intelligence twinkled through the dimness of age, sometimes fixed on the ground, and again peering straightforward from beneath his grey eyebrows ! In the arrangement of his dress the good Doctor seemed to lose sight of his mathematical precision, and truly the *fashions* would appear to have never once occurred to his mind.   Our readers must excuse this attempt at graphic reminiscence of one whose memory is associated in our mind with all that is great in talent, excellent in morality, and amiable in private character.   Long may there be found in our land those who are able to appreciate, and zealous to emulate, his sterling worth !

The late Mr. Thomson of Banchory, in his article " Hamilton," *Encyclopædia Britannica*, seventh edition, mentions a fine instance of the genuine honesty of Dr. Hamilton :—In the year 1807 fifty essays were given in for competition for the Burnet of Den's Prize, and Dr. Hamilton, one of the judges, wrote abstracts of the *whole* fifty, " in order to enable him to come to a decision on their respective merits."

DR. CHALMERS.

Oɴ the 4th June 1847 the remains of our illustrious countryman were consigned to their final
resting-place, in the New Cemetery at Grange, in
the neighbourhood of Edinburgh. The occasion
called forth a demonstration of public mourning
which bore most impressive testimony to the profound and universal feeling of veneration with
which the memory of the departed is justly regarded. It is calculated that the number of those
who either mingled in the funeral procession, or
were solemnised spectators of its progress, amounted
to not fewer than a hundred thousand ; including
individuals of all ranks and denominations, from
the highest officials in the land to the humblest
artizans — clergy of every Christian church, and
some of the most distinguished representatives of
literature and science. It was a truly sublime spectacle—a demonstration of national sorrow for a national loss.

But the number, great as it was, of those privileged to be present on this melancholy occasion,

was small indeed when compared with the aggregate of those in every corner of the Christian world, who will receive, with unfeigned regret, the tidings of the irreparable loss which the removal of our countryman has inflicted on the dearest interests of religion and philanthropy. Already are all the leading journals of the country roused from the routine of professional duty into eloquent eulogiums on the life and labours of the deceased ; while the pulpit, of which he was so long one of the brightest ornaments, has resounded with heartfelt tributes to his memory. No jarring note has been heard over the grave of one who was a faithful servant of God, and a fast friend of the human race.

The biography* of Dr. Chalmers will doubtless, in due time, appear in a form worthy of the subject. Meanwhile, a brief summary of the leading events in his illustrious career cannot fail to be interesting :—

Born at Anstruther, in Fifeshire, on the 17th of March 1780, of respectable parentage, he received his academic education at the University of St. Andrews, where he was eminently distinguished by his talents and assiduity. Devoting himself to the clerical profession, his first appointment in the Church was that of assistant to the late minister of Cavers, a parish on the Borders. On the 12th of May 1803 he was ordained minister of the parish

* By his accomplished son-in-law, Dr. Hanna.

of Kilmany in Fifeshire ; the proximity of which to St. Andrews permitted him to renew his intimacy with the friends of his academic career. The pastoral duties of a rural parish were insufficient for the full employment of his active and vigorous mind ; but he kept its faculties in healthful play by devoting his hours of leisure to the study of mathematics, chemistry, geology, and political economy. Thus, for a few years, he went on storing up the treasures of knowledge, but without perhaps being aware of the high uses to which he was destined to consecrate them.

In 1808 appeared his celebrated *Inquiry into the Extent and Stability of our National Resources,* the object of which was to prove our independence of foreign trade. The peculiar circumstances in which the country was then placed, while they must excuse his economics, bear testimony to the warmth of his patriotism. But, up to this era, he may be said to have been only imping the wings of his versatile genius. Conscious of energy for a flight far above all " middle height," accident determined his course to the sublime region in which he was thenceforward to move. He was employed by Dr. (now Sir David) Brewster to write the article " Christianity" for the *Edinburgh Encyclopædia.* This task involved a more earnest attention to the evidences of the truth of our religion than the inquirer had perhaps previously given. In his desire to enforce those evidences on others, he became the more profoundly impressed with them himself. The impression was as lasting as it was deep. Nay, with all the high ardour peculiar to his enthusiastic and truly sincere spirit, he deemed the evidences of revealed religion so overwhelming, that, with what some might think a too daring chivalry, he declined, in his battle with the unbeliever, recourse to the weapons furnished by natural religion, albeit our own Campbell, and others who had " fought the good fight," had proved them to be of ethereal temper ! But although, in regard to this particular, he found a searching and sagacious critic* in a profound theologian still spared for the unobtrusive discharge of his duties as a teacher of the young aspirants to the ministry of our Church; and although it is understood that reconsideration recommended a modification of his early impressions, still, Dr. Chalmers' " Evidences" will ever be regarded as containing pregnant proofs of a most powerful and most original mind.

Meanwhile, his fame as a pulpit orator, despite the drawbacks of a strongly provincial accent and

* Dr. Duncan Mearns of King's College, in *Principles of Christian Evidence*, illustrated by an examination of arguments subversive of natural theology, and the internal evidence of Christianity, advanced by Dr. T. Chalmers in his *Evidences and Authority of the Christian Revelation.* Edin., 1818.

an untutored manner, spread apace, and led to his
appointment, in 1815, to the ministry of the. Tron
Church of Glasgow. Here he seems to have felt
that a new and important field of usefulness was
before him. He was placed in the very vortex of
the trade, and commerce, and wealth, and, too probably, of the worldly-mindedness of his country.
He felt that he had a high message. But who was
to believe his " report ?" On the one hand were
ranged the merchant princes, strong in the faith of
their own sagacity, and not over-sensitive to ap-
peals from a source declaring the wisdom of this
world to be foolishness ; on the other was the placid,
humble, self-abjuring missionary of the truth, drawn
forth from the obscurity of a rural parish, yet
radiant with the prestige of triumphs won on an
arena which the mere votaries of Mammon regarded
with comparative indifference. Suddenly he burst
upon them in his magnificent *Astronomical Discourses.* At once he compelled them to admit that
there was more in " things unseen and eternal" than
they had ever dreamt of in their worldly philosophy.
They felt that they were under the spell of a master-
spirit. He knew that he had struck home, and he
followed up the blow. His desire was, that they
who had admired the preacher should be led to
think of what he preached. This feeling is remarkably illustrated, if we mistake not, in the last of his
Astronomical Discourses. Then he came home to

the business and bosoms of his Glasgow hearers, in his *Sermons on the application of Christianity to the Commercial and Ordinary Affairs of Life*, in which he touched the consciences of the worldly-minded to the quick. He had first awakened his hearers to a sense of the general importance of things spiritual ; now he proved their startling connection with the issues of things temporal! His versatile and vigorous genius seemed to rejoice in its expansive sympathy with the elements of the new sphere in which it had been recently placed. He sounded all the social depths of a great commercial city. He had rebuked the overweening pride of its wealth ; he undertook the mission of an angel of mercy to its abodes of wretchedness! He stirred up the rich to more consideration of the poor man's case. He was the originator of many educational and benevolent schemes in Glasgow, which still remain as monuments of his Christian philanthropy, and hallow his name in the grateful aspirations of the poor.

Engrossed with these philanthropic labours, in which his only desire was " to spend and be spent," Providence presented to him a calmer but not less important sphere of usefulness in his appointment to the chair of Moral Philosophy of St. Andrews University, in 1823. In this new situation the versatility and vigour of his genius were still conspicuous. He squared his prelections, not according to the antiquated rule, but the requirements of the day—a course of lectures on Political Economy forming a novel feature in his academic instructions.

More important duties still awaited him. In 1828 he was unanimously elected Professor of Divinity in the University of Edinburgh. Here he was the presiding genius of those fountains whence issue the streams which irrigate the land with the living waters of divine truth. Again he was a centre of attraction. He threw, as was his wont, his heart into his duties. He was adored by his pupils ; and his success as a teacher of theology was commensurate with the enthusiasm which he enkindled in the minds of his pupils. Time would fail us to enumerate all the benevolent schemes for which Dr. Chalmers' active mind found occupancy, in addition to the calls of official duty. Who can forget the leading part which he took in the highest Court of our Church—his labours in the cause of the poor—of education—and of Church Extension ?

And when that mighty controversy arose, which rent the office-bearers of the Church asunder, was he not universally regarded as the most formidable opponent of one party, and the most powerful champion of the other ? But in this notice we resile from such debatable ground. Contemplating the character of Dr. Chalmers in all its length and breadth, we feel that we should detract from his memory by viewing, in connection with any party whatever, one whose life proclaimed him to be the friend of mankind. His noble nature was not to be measured by the petty conventionalisms and curt standards of any mere party. His fame is national property, no more to be yielded up to exclusive claim than is the light of day!

As a pulpit orator there were confessedly none to be compared with Dr. Chalmers, except the late Robert Hall of Leicester, and the still living Ralph Wardlaw of Glasgow. We cannot pretend here to characterise Dr. Chalmers' pulpit merits. Suffice it to say, that earnestness and effect were distinguishing marks of his eloquence. How trite soever the theme, he invested it with interest when touched by the talismanic power of his genius. To be a listless hearer was impossible. His eloquence kindled a flame even in the hearts of the most inert. As a writer he displayed kindred power—always original, eloquent, imaginative, and generally logical. His very shortcomings were as nothing in comparison with the overpowering evidences of head and heart which he threw into all his writings. And yet, with all his imaginative turn, he was a wonderfully practical man. The author of the *Astronomical Discourses* could make himself at home with the humble economics of the poor, friendless boys of the West Port school! *There* was proof of a mighty mind;

nothing too vast for its comprehension—nothing too minute for its care!

Of the personal and private character of Dr. Chalmers we feel that we are but imperfectly qualified to speak. But they who were honoured with his familiar acquaintance, report of it in terms that cannot be otherwise than just, when tried by the standard of his public career. We cannot but *credit* their estimate of his humility, simplicity, and kind-heartedness, when we *know* him, by his public doings, to have been a man of transcendent genius and of high principle. There was nothing little, nothing sinister in his character. Even his errors were the infirmities of a noble nature. He was no self-seeker; on the contrary, did delicacy permit, signal instances of his disinterestedness might be mentioned. Who ever found him, directly or indirectly, the trumpeter of his own fame? Bitterly as he was often withstood, it was not his wont to return railing for railing. He affected not the front of battle. If he was found there, it was because none other was deemed so worthy of the post.

Some may question his judgment as to later transactions; but not one of his staunchest opponents has ventured to impugn his motives. On the contrary, those who were his strongest antagonists in the battle of principle, have been the foremost to pay their tribute of respect to his memory!

Apart, then, from all those considerations which

have so imbittered the recollection of later years, let us cherish the memory of Dr. Chalmers, as a fellow-countryman who elevated the pulpit oratory of Scotland to a standard not surpassed by a Bossuet or a Massillon ; and with whose philanthropic exertions even the names of Howard and Wilberforce may find honoured association ! Needless it is to say, that Dr. Chalmers was a man of unaffected personal piety. For some time he had wisely retired from the turmoil of active life, feeling, as it is believed, that the hour of his departure was at hand. At last it came—suddenly, but not unexpectedly. His passing spirit scarce tasted the bitterness of death—" and he was not, for God took him."

The foregoing Memoir was written and appeared in the pages of the *Aberdeen Banner* just *five days* after the death of the great and good Dr. Chalmers.

THE REV. DR. BLACK.

Pulveris exigui munus.—HOR.

THE life, just closed, of this remarkable fellow-townsman deserves notice far more adequate than it is likely to obtain. In his case are wanting some of those materials with which, in some cases, the biographer labours in a

> Vain attempt to give a deathless lot
> To names ignoble—born to be forgot.

Dr. Black has not, it is believed, left any substantive work in evidence of his vast and varied learning, and his powerful grasp of mind. It is from other sources that some idea of the man is to be gathered.

The subject of notice was born in Aberdeen, in the year 1789. His father was a market gardener, and occupied a small, old fashioned wooden tenement of his own, near the point where Justice Street joins Castle Street. Here, his only son, the future Professor, first saw the light. The father died during the son's boyhood, but the mother survived for many years. She was a very shrewd, managing person, and presented in this respect a remarkable contrast to her " Sandy," who was neither then, nor ever afterwards, an adept in the ordinary ways of the world.   From his earliest years he showed a turn for book-learning and a remarkably tenacious memory.   The competent means of his parents, and the cheapness of local education, secured for him the elements of classical learning ; and a bursary introduced him as a student at Marischal College.   He was one of several who competed for the "Silver Pen," a prize for proficiency in Greek; but the successful candidate was Mr. William Morren.

After graduating, Black resolved to adopt the medical profession, and with this view he became apprentice to Dr. George French, Professor of Chemistry, and one of the Physicians of our Infirmary.   But the surgical operations were too much for his sensitive nerves, and he exchanged the study of medicine for that of divinity.   About this time he seems to have become immersed in a very extensive and systematic course of study.   With the whole range of classic literature he cultivated a most profound and critical acquaintance.   In all the writings of the Christian Fathers he was deeply versed.   Such was the familiarity which he attained with Latin and Greek, that he could converse and correspond in both languages with ease and elegance. As subsidiary to his theological studies, he became master of Hebrew, Arabic, and the cognate Eastern languages. With French, German, Italian, Spanish, and Modern Greek, he acquired entire familiarity. He was well skilled in all the systems of mental philosophy. As a matter of course, he had studied all the branches of theology, and was so well read in the Scriptures as to be talked of as a living concordance. He was well acquainted with the whole range of English literature, and with the history of all nations. He was a good chemist, and a proficient in botany. In fact, with the exception of the exact sciences, there were few subjects not within the cyclopædical range of his acquirements. All were the fruit of incessant study by day and night. Even at meal times he had ever one of his beloved books. He learned with great facility, and never forgot what he had learnt. The uniform course of his study was never interrupted by feeble health, a touchy temperament, adverse fortune, or the distractions of society.

In due time he was licensed as a probationer of the church. From the very first he proved an acceptable preacher, more especially to the congregation of the old East Kirk. His sermons were all written fully out, and were composed with great care. They were strictly evangelical, but embraced a variety of subject and disquisition commensurate with the extensive learning and mental power of the preacher. His manner and delivery were modest, plain, primitive, and impressive, notwithstanding a

certain quaint exactitude of elocution, and somewhat of a burr.

He had not been long licensed when the Rev.
Dr. Ross, then senior minister of the East Church,
engaged him as his assistant. All the worthy
Doctor's assistants were domiciliated with himself,
and his amiable son, Alexander, in his hospitable
residence in Skene Terrace, at present occupied by
Dr. Harvey. Here Black was supremely happy.
He had a tranquil and comfortable home, congenial
society, ample opportunity for study, and occupation
in which the best principles and feelings of his
nature were deeply interested. His host was a man
of superior acquirements, a most popular preacher,
and adored by his flock. None could listen to his
earnest and affectionate addresses from the pulpit,
without being thereby deeply impressed. At the
same time, the doctrine which he so faithfully
preached was in all respects adorned by a suitable
life and conversation. Ample means enabled him
to exercise an extensive private charity, as well as
a hearty hospitality towards his brethren of all
evangelical denominations. His only son, Alexander, was then a young man of twenty or thereby
—amiable, pious, and of much literary promise. He
was an enthusiast in the study of the Eastern languages, particularly Persian ; and in Mr. Black he
found an agreeable and able companion in his
favourite pursuits. As soon as the settled state of

Europe permitted, the two set out on a continental tour. At Leyden they were introduced to the illustrious scholar, Wyttenbach, editor of the works of Plato. Mr. Ross used to tell that, although he was well aware of the great classic acquirements of his friend Black, yet the learning which he displayed on this occasion altogether astonished him. Wyttenbach and Black launched into a long and critical discussion (carried on in Latin), on some of the knottiest passages in the "divine" philosopher's works ; Black proving himself quite *au fait* on the subject, to the great delight of the erudite professor.

While Black was thus occupied, a vacancy occurred in the Divinity Professorship of King's College by the death of Dr. Gilbert Gerard. This was in 1816, when Mr. Black was only twenty-seven years of age. The appointment is always made by comparative trial, conducted by a Committee of the Synod of Aberdeen. Two candidates presented themselves — the Rev. Duncan Mearns, minister of Tarves, and the Rev. Mr. Love, of Glasgow. Mr. Black's singular, modest, and retiring character would have kept him back from such a contest ; but his scruples were overcome by the Rev. Dr. Ross and the Rev. Principal Brown, of whom the latter—a most accomplished scholar and divine, and a truly Christian gentleman—appreciated and admired the character and attainments of his quondam pupil. ' Accordingly, Mr. Black was persuaded to enter the lists with the other candidates, each being his senior by a good many years. At the examination, all the candidates gave singular proof of learning and talent. More especially, the philological erudition displayed by Mr. Black took the examiners quite a-back. Their votes were eventually in favour of Mr. Mearns, on this account—an important part of the divinity professor's duty being an off-hand criticism on the discourses delivered by students before the whole class. Of course the professor knows beforehand the student's subject, but he cannot know how the latter has treated it until the discourse is delivered. At the competition referred to, a printed sermon was read to each candidate, which he was required to criticise off-hand, *viva voce.* In this exercise Mr. Mearns was considered more expert, on the whole, than the other candidates.

The church of Tarves thus became vacant by Mr. Mearns' accession to the chair of divinity. The living was in the gift of the late Lord Aberdeen, who, without any solicitation (but, as was believed at the time, at the suggestion of Mr. Mearns), bestowed it on Mr. Black. About the same time King's College conferred on him the degree of D.D., a mark of estimation also bestowed on Mr. Love.

Mr. Black addressed himself to the duties of a

parish minister with characteristic zeal and conscientiousness. He considered a less elaborate style of sermon than he had delivered in town as more suitable for his rural congregation. Accordingly, he preached extemporaneously from a few notes. But his vast information, never-failing memory, and ever-ready expression, betrayed him into a diffuse style of preaching, with too frequent divergencies from the main line of discourse. Having considerable leisure, it was of course all devoted to study, for which his appetite seemed insatiable. Of all domestic and secular matters he was equally ignorant and careless. His good old mother took charge of the affairs of the manse and glebe, in the overseeing of which she found congenial occupation for her active and frugal turn. Greatly was she scandalised by "Sandy's" (as she still called him) serene apathy to all these worldly matters, and the bland smile with which he would receive all her lecturing on the subject. To a friend, who inquired how the doctor got on with his glebe, she declared :—" Troth, oor Sandy wadna ken his ain cow, tho' he met her on the loan !" In visiting his parish, the doctor found it would be convenient that he should perform his longer journeys on horseback. Accordingly, after diligent search, a pony was procured, with unexceptionable testimonials as to steadiness and gravity of character and conduct. The doctor's first lessons in equita-

tion were taken under the superintendence of the
" minister's man," who led the animal, while the
" loon" moved on considerably in the van to " hish
awa' the birds !"

By and by, however, the doctor astonished all
who knew him by appearing in a new character.
Sure,

> " Love will venture in
> Where it daurna weel be seen."

and, in the fulness of time, the doctor was united
to a beautiful and accomplished young lady (Miss
Rachel Booth), who predeceased him by many
years.

In the year 1831, Dr. Black was drawn from
the comparative obscurity of a country parish, by a
vacancy in the Divinity Chair of Marischal College,
occasioned by the death of the Rev. Principal
Brown, who had filled it with the highest distinction and success from the time when it was left, in
consequence of advanced age, by the celebrated
Principal George Campbell. It was with the full
approval of his illustrious predecessor that Dr.
Brown was appointed to the office ; and how well
and faithfully he discharged all the duties of his
important position as professor, preacher, and head
of Marischal College, has long been on permanent
record, and is ineffaceable from the grateful and
reverential memory of all who knew him personally
in any or all of those capacities.

The Chair of Divinity was in the gift of the Town-Council of Aberdeen. To Dr. Black's appointment there was no opposition worthy of notice. In a pecuniary point of view it involved a very considerable sacrifice on the Doctor's part. The salary was very small, but he sought not to supplement it by that of any other appointment. He had some private means, and with these he was content. Never, like some smaller men, did he clamour for more money. He probably considered his new sphere more congenial than that which he had quitted.

The Doctor continued to discharge his professorial duties in his usual serene, punctual, and methodical way, commanding universal respect, although not mixing much in society. At the Disruption conscientious conviction pointed out a certain path of duty on which he readily entered and calmly pursued; his placid and primitive spirit passing unruffled and unscathed by the heats and animosities of the stormy crisis. The record of his further labours is left for others.

People who think there is nothing of what they call fame without more or less of book-making, will probably set down Dr. Black as one of the *viri obscuriores*. They seem to hold with the Dutchman, that a man is nobody, unless he has written " a book as thick as all that !" To chasten this fond fancy, let them only step over the way to the library of King's College, and there meditate on the fate of many a ponderous tome, clad in armour of leather, vellum, and brass, which the painful and overweening author considered panoply of proof against all the attacks of time. But oblivion has fallen upon them. One would just as soon think of disturbing the dust of the authors as that which covers their works. Yet were they mighty men in their day; but that day has passed away for ever. How much better had their lives been devoted to the useful duties of active life than to the fabrication of all that useless lumber! A like fate, indeed, seems to involve many works of the most incontestible merit—the fashion of this world ever passing away.

That our erudite Doctor, therefore, never wrote a book, impairs not the credit which is justly his due on the score of his having devoted himself to the faithful discharge of the duties of life. He was naturally more acquisitive than communicative; he was modest, shy, and retiring. He was too learned to think much of anything he could do himself. He had no notion of making money by literature or anything else; and there was that in his character which fixed his ambition on the immortality secured by the inscription of his name in a BOOK where " neither moth nor rust doth corrupt."

DR. FALCONER.

TO the memory of this distinguished Oriental
scholar a more extended reference seems due than
that which was briefly made in our last obituary,*
although our materials for this purpose are by no
means so ample as we could wish.

Dr. Falconer was born in this city in the year
1805. He was the youngest, and latterly the only
surviving, son of the late Mr. Gilbert Falconer, for
many years the much-esteemed master of the
English Burgh School. Having completed his
studies at our Grammar School, under the care of
Messrs. Forbes and Cromar, he became first competition bursar at Marischal College, gained the
silver pen in the Greek class, and all but divided
the honour of mathematical bursar. On leaving
College he prosecuted the study of Latin and
Greek with great assiduity and success. The former language he wrote with much ease and elegance. Of his skill in the latter he gave a few
specimens in some metrical translations from the

* Vide *Aberdeen Herald*, 19th November 1853.

Greek Anthology, which appeared, but without his name, in one of our leading periodicals.

Before he had attained his twentieth year, he evinced a strong predilection for the study of the languages of the East. He attended the Hebrew classes of the late Professor Bentley, but owed his progress chiefly to indomitable perseverance in private study. In this way he acquired an extensive and accurate knowledge of Hebrew and its cognate dialects; and, although entirely self-taught, made considerable progress in Persian, Arabic, and Hindustani. His enthusiasm for these studies increasing with his advancement in them, he resolved to avail himself of the instructions of the most able Continental Orientalists. With this view he proceeded to Paris, where, for nearly two years, he attended the prelections of the celebrated Baron de Sacy, of M. Garçin de Tassy, and of M. Caussin de Perceval. Under those able teachers he made rapid progress ; and so high was de Sacy's opinion of his acquirements, that, before he had completed his twenty-fifth year, he was elected a member of the Asiatic Society of Paris, on the special recommendation of that illustrious scholar. At a subsequent period, Mr. Falconer attended the classes of some of the great German Orientalists.

Returning to his native city, he made it his residence for a short time ; but ultimately left it for London about the end of 1832. In the metro-

polis he established himself as a teacher of Persian
and Hindustani ; prosecuted the critical study of
these and of other Eastern languages ; and gradually secured the intimacy and friendship of all the
leading Orientalists of the day. He was speedily
elected a member of the Royal Asiatic Society,
and from time to time published in its Transactions
translations from the Persian poets. On the establishment of the London University, he presented
an application for the chair of Oriental Languages.
On this occasion he trusted entirely to his testimonials and to the proofs he had given of his fitness
for the office aspired to ; for, bashful even to a
weakness, he recoiled from all personal canvassing
with an intensity of nervous horror, which, to his
intimate friends, was perhaps as much a source of
amusement as of regret. To use a homely but
expressive phrase, the Oriental Chair did not *take;*
it was found impossible to form a public class, and
endowment there was none. So, finding that he
could be of no use as a Professor, and his increasing
reputation gaining him numerous private pupils—
besides employment as a translator of official documents for the East India Company—he retired from
the College. Latterly, the Directors of the Company assigned to him apartments in the India
House for the reception of such pupils as found it
most convenient to attend there. In the year 1839,
when he had just completed his thirty-fourth year,

he was a candidate for the Professorship of Oriental Languages in the University of Glasgow. On this occasion, the omission of personal canvassing, to which he was neither to be led nor driven, whatever the interests at stake, was understood to have materially militated against his advancement to an office for which he was pre-eminently qualified, and to which he was strongly recommended by Sir Gore Ouseley, Sir G. C. Haughton, General Briggs, Professor Shakspear of Addiscombe, Professor Johnson of the East India College, M. Garçin de Tassy, M. Caussin de Perceval, Professor Forbes of King's College, London, Dr. Gilchrist, the Earl of Munster, and other Oriental scholars. To quote some of their opinions is, perhaps, the best means of conveying an idea of Falconer's merits. Sir Gore Ouseley, V. P. Royal Asiatic Society, is of opinion that "Mr. Falconer is one of the most eminent Oriental scholars now in Europe." Professor Shakspear says—" In Persian and Hindustani I have had frequent occasion to read difficult manuscripts and authors with Mr. Falconer; and the various translations of abstruse poetical compositions, which he has from time to time executed with rare taste, correctness, and judgment, at once evince his thorough acquaintance with the language of the originals." De Tassy writes—" Vous savez parfaitement les principales langues Orientales l'Hébreu, que vous avez enseigné autrefois, l'Arabe, le Persan, l'Hindoustani." Professor Johnson states that Mr. Falconer's translations from the Bostân of the Persian poet Sadi " gave the world a sure pledge that he could readily supply that great desideratum among Oriental scholars—an accurate translation of the whole—a work which has hitherto, from its peculiar difficulties, baffled the efforts of our Orientalists to present it in an English dress."

Such are a few specimens of the tributes paid by most competent judges to the extent and accuracy of Dr. Falconer's Oriental lore. To his own talents and industry alone did he owe all this distinction. His disposition, as already mentioned, was singularly modest and retiring. To those arts by which patronage is sometimes most successfully wooed, his quiet but independent spirit was an utter stranger. In fact, if ever deserving man had distinction thrust upon him in spite of himself, it was Falconer. Had he been spared a few years longer, he would have probably attained a position, not more honourable, but less laborious than that from which death removed him in the prime of life.

We have already referred to Dr. Falconer's high classical attainments ; we have also to mention that he was familiar with the French, German, and Italian languages and literature. Among other accomplishments, he had acquired the art of writing in the characters of the Eastern languages with unrivalled beauty and precision. In fine, as an Oriental scholar, the name of Falconer will be worthily associated with those of Lumsden and of Nicoll, both, like himself, natives of Aberdeenshire.

The personal character of Dr. Falconer was most exemplary in every relation of life. To know him was to love and esteem him. Mild, unassuming, kindly, and eminently single-hearted, it were difficult, indeed, to express how deeply he was endeared to his old familiar friends, or how sincerely they deplore his premature decease. The superiority of his talents and learning seemed known to all save himself. Humble as ever, in the brighter hour of well-deserved success, the meekness of his spirit was never overcome, even under circumstances which might have justified indignant feeling.

Dr. Falconer died at his residence, 6 Edwardes Square, Kensington, London, on the 7th November 1853.

MR. ARCHIBALD SIMPSON, ARCHITECT.

" Genius, and taste, and talent gone—
For ever tombed beneath the stone !"—SCOTT.

THE unexpected and premature decease of one whose professional talents have contributed so conspicuously to the improvement and adornment of this, his native city, imposes upon us the duty of paying some tribute, how inadequate soever, to his memory, and of giving expression to the general feeling of regret which that melancholy event has occasioned.

In the beginning of March 1847, Mr. Simpson paid a visit to Edinburgh, and afterwards to Derby, on professional business. Returning to Aberdeen, he was seized with symptoms of fever, the probable consequences of cold and over-fatigue. In this state he reached home on Tuesday, and was seemingly rather better on the day following ; but, on the Thursday, he became very much indisposed, erysipelas appearing in the right side. In vain was professional skill exerted to arrest the progress of this dangerous disease, or to support the powers of

M

nature rapidly sinking under its virulence. On Sunday his medical attendants were compelled to intimate to the sufferer that his recovery was all but hopeless; and on Tuesday, 23d March 1847, between ten and eleven o'clock at night, their mournful anticipations were realised. The latter stages of the malady were comparatively painless; and their close was met in a spirit of calm resignation.

Mr. Simpson was born in Aberdeen in the year 1790, and, at the period of his decease, had nearly completed his fifty-seventh year. His father, a respectable merchant, gave him the benefit of a liberal education at the Grammar School and Marischal College. Evincing a decided partiality for the profession of an architect, he was apprenticed to the late Mr. Massie, builder, in this city, and was afterwards, for some time, under the tuition of Mr. Lugar, architect in London. He subsequently visited Italy, where he spent some time in the study of the monuments of classic art, whether ancient or modern. These studies were accompanied by the careful perusal of the best writers on architecture. His preparatory studies completed, Mr. Simpson resolved to establish himself as an architect in his native city. Although latterly eminently successful, his professional career was by no means unknown to early struggles; but from the time he obtained an opportunity of displaying his taste and talents, his business progressively increased, and he at length reached the highest status of his profession. His genius was as versatile as it was refined. He succeeded in all styles of architecture—the Classic and Gothic; the Ecclesiastical, the Institutional, Baronial, and Domestic. Of these, numerous and splendid specimens are to be found in this city and county, and in various other parts of the kingdom. To enumerate them all is impracticable; we give a list of the principal:—In the city of Aberdeen: Marischal College; the Public Rooms; Royal Infirmary; Market, and Market Street, which gives an easy access to the heart of the city from the Quays, so long a *desideratum;* the Post Office; Mechanics Hall; East Church; Orphan Asylum at Albyn Place; St. Andrew's Chapel; Free Churches in Belmont Street; Athenæum; North of Scotland Bank; Town and County Bank ;* Medical Society Hall; Lunatic Asylum; North of Scotland Assurance Office; Old Machar Free Church; Bell's Schools, Frederick Street, etc. He also planned Bon-Accord Square and Terrace. Mr. Simpson, too, was the first to give an outline of the recently-contemplated city improvements; and his ideas will doubtless be found of great value when circumstances favour that important undertaking.

Mr. Simpson was also the architect of the beau-

* Now the offices of the Scottish Provincial Assurance Company.

tiful Church of Elgin ; General Anderson's Institution there ; the Duchess of Gordon's Schools at Huntly ; the re-building of part of Gordon Castle ; and the Chapel attached to it. He planned and executed, either in whole or in part, the Mansion-houses of Boath and Glenferness, Morayshire ; Newe, Murtle, Meldrum, Heathcot, Park, Durris, Druminnor, Putachie, Crimonmogate, Scotstown, Haddo, Lessendrum, Thainston, Carnousie, Craig, Pittodrie, and Tullos, Aberdeenshire ; Stracathro and Letham, Forfarshire. Latterly, he planned the beautiful Free Church at Rothesay ; the additions to Skene House ; and, at the period of his death, he was occupied with plans for the Railway Terminus in this city. In addition to the works above enumerated, we must not forget to mention Mr. Simpson's rebuilding of the Bridge across the Spey at Fochabers, which is a signal proof of his skill in engineering.

The extensive business which Mr. Simpson thus enjoyed was entirely the reward of his undoubted genius and taste. He was imbued with the warmest enthusiasm, and the finest feeling for art. He had great tact in the adaptation of his designs to any given circumstances ; and where difficulties occurred, no man could display more adroitness in surmounting them. He was particularly happy in accommodating the style of his works to the purposes for which they were intended, and to the character of the situation in which they were placed. Thus, when at one time it was proposed to place the new Marischal College on the site now occupied by the Free Churches in Belmont Street, he designed a magnificent classical building, with an expansive and imposing front, and lofty dome, admirably calculated to bring out the greatest artistic effect of which the situation was susceptible. But when this site was afterwards abandoned for that on which Marischal College now stands, his design was altogether different. Then he chose the cloistral or monastic style, which was unquestionably the best adapted to the peculiarities of the retired site of the building, while it harmonised with the character of an academic institution. In process of time, however, the old site in Belmont Street was again to be occupied by a public building — comprising three of the Free Churches. In this case the funds were rather limited. An erection in the Classic style was impracticable. Such a building as Marischal College would have been sadly misplaced. But true to the *genius loci*, Mr. Simpson adopted the style of the Ecclesiastical Gothic, so moulding it to circumstances as to take advantage of the very same peculiarities of situation which would have given so much effect to a building in the Classic style. There was still the long-drawn horizontal line, while the effect which would have been secured by the lofty dome was sustained by the tapering spire. These remarks will, perhaps, serve to convey some idea of the peculiar character of Mr. Simpson's professional genius and skill. Of both he has left many enduring monuments, which make us proud to claim him as a native of Aberdeen. We feel that we scarcely exaggerate his merits, when we say, that some of his best works, all circumstances considered, will not suffer by a comparison with those of another architect, also a son of Bon-Accord, the distinguished Gibbs. The work of both, although by no means the happiest of either, happens to be conjoined in our East and West Churches.

The esteem in which Mr. Simpson was held as a man, is best attested by the deep regret with which his death has been regarded by all who had the pleasure of his more intimate acquaintance. His character was marked by all those peculiarities, not to say eccentricities, which are usually found in men of quick and keen perception and susceptible temperament. But throughout his whole character there ran a vein of good sense, kindly feeling, and honourable principle. They who were privileged to enjoy his liberal and tasteful hospitality, when he drew around him friends of congenial sociality— appreciating his real merits, and liking him all the better for occasional eccentricities, traceable to genuine simplicity of heart—will not soon forget the many happy hours, alas! how fled!—when none more apt than he to circulate the round of wit and humour and whim, which, however prolonged, left his guests, even those of most domestic mind, still chiding the stealthy rapidity of time! On those occasions, when he was in the vein, he would delight his friends with specimens of his exquisite taste and masterly skill in music. In his hands, his favourite instrument (the violin) attuned to some of our inimitable national airs, would charm forth the whole spirit of their touching melody. Anon, he would break away into some extempore *fantasia*—leaving the delighted listeners puzzled as to adjustment of the rival claims of the capabilities of the instrument, and of the genius and skill of the performer! But the memory of Mr. Simpson's social qualities and personal worth will fade with the mortal being of those who must soon follow him to that bourne whence there is no return. The monuments of his genius, skill, and taste, will long survive both him and them! To these may the testimony of his professional merits be well entrusted: our own intentions will have been realised if what is writ shall gratify desire, or enkindle emulation, when, haply in after times, "some kindred spirit may inquire his fate!"

MR. DUNCAN, EX-TREASURER OF POLICE.

WILLIAM DUNCAN was born in 1796, of very worthy and respectable parents. He received a good classical education at our Grammar School; and, through life, he retained creditable familiarity with the Latin language. He was a good French scholar, and well versed in the literature of that language. He attended the classes of Natural History and Natural Philosophy in Marischal College, then taught by Dr. Knight and Professor Copland. With history, especially that of his own country, he had extensive and exact acquaintance. He had a fondness, almost passionate, for Scottish antiquities; and in familiarity with those of his native city, he had few, if any equals. This was singularly proved by the large share which he had in the publication of the Book of Bon-Accord, in conjunction with his friend Mr. Robertson, of the Register House, Edinburgh. Mr. Duncan was also the author of a *Description of the Coast between Aberdeen and Leith;* of a paper on *Witchcraft in the North*, read before the Society of Scottish Antiquaries, of which he was a Corresponding Member; and of various occasional essays illustrative of olden times. Indeed, Mr. Duncan had shown a strong turn for literature from his early youth. Some fifty years ago, in conjunction with several young men, he established a sort of club, styled "The Aberdeen Literary Society," which used to meet in the schoolroom of one of the members (Mr. Robert Wilson), at the head of Broad Street. Of this Society, the noted, not to say notorious, James Gordon Bennett, now of the *New York Herald*, was an active member. Another member survives in the dapper person of a worthy burgess,* whose lively chirruping about days of yore might almost beguile us into the fancy that

> " Youth and he were house-mates still."

As Mr. Duncan advanced in life he took an unceasing interest in public matters, particularly in burgh Reform. In 1829, to promote this object, he

---

* Mr. James Burgess, a well-known merchant, who pre-deceased Mr. Ramsay two years. Mr. Burgess's taste for literature remained with him to the last. One calm evening in mid-summer he was walking up Union Street with the writer, when, stopping at the façade as the jangle from the belfry met our ears, he said with mock pathos—

> " Those evening bells, those evening bells,
> How many a tale their music tells
> Of drunken ringers without art,
> Ringing to break John Ramsay's heart."

His " Sett " were at the time giving Mr. Ramsay much trouble to train.

took an active part, along with the late Mr. Spark, in establishing and conducting the *Aberdeen Observer.* It showed much information, shrewdness, and not a little piquancy, occasionally aggravated into a good deal of acrimony. The subjects chiefly discussed were of a local nature, such as the affairs of the Guildry, Police, Harbour, etc. Along with these subjects, matters of local antiquity, drollery, customs, and manners were introduced, and treated with ability and spirit. The columns of the paper were enlivened by a band of clever contributors, among whom may be mentioned — Mr. Joseph Robertson, Mr. Cooke, the late Messrs. R. Brown, J. Bruce, F. Clerihew, Deacon Robb, and others. In general politics, the paper inclined to what would now be called Liberal Conservatism ; but, as the Reform era advanced, its tone became decidedly that of uncompromising Toryism. This change proved unfortunate for its commercial position ; and those who had stoutly, and to their personal loss, fought the battle of local Toryism, found that gratitude was not to be reckoned among the virtues of the leaders of the party. The *honorarium* which conventional usage ought to bestow in the deserving quarter is too often filched by sneaking toadies and unprincipled panders !

The *Observer* was ultimately bought up by a joint stock company, and was thus merged in the *Constitutional,* professing Conservative politics. Mr. Duncan was retained as cashier and general manager. It had a good business connection, but was unfortunate in some of its editors, who proved to have been most trusted where they were least known. Besides, there was really no room for the paper. After a dwining existence, which all the coddling of its supporters could not protract, it puffed out—*tennes recessit in auras !*

Fortunately for Mr. Duncan, although a loser, he was not ruined, as some have been, by his newspaper connection. He still had his own business, in which he had reasonable success, although, as may be supposed, it was not very congenial to his tastes. He all along continued to take an active and intelligent part in the affairs of his native city. At length his talents and knowledge of local matters pointed him out as being beyond question the fittest man for the office of treasurer of police, to which he was appointed in 1844 by the Commissioners, with a felicity of judgment which has not invariably distinguished that body.

In his public capacity he was a sagacious and honest counsellor, and averse to carrying matters with a high hand, or causing unnecessary trouble and expense; and he had the address to lead his principals to a right conclusion without making them aware of it, and thus he often kept them out of difficulties. He had great sagacity in appreciating the nature and extent of the prospective wants of the community, and, in endeavouring to meet them, he was actuated by a quiet but indomitable perseverance.

In his ordinary life and conduct, Mr. Duncan was placid, unassuming, cheerful, and friendly. His conversation, like his writing, was racy, full of useful and curious information and anecdote. When well set and in the vein, he was not only witty himself but the cause of wit in others. His memory is indissolubly entwined with the recollection of many happy hours, and of the genial beaming of many "old familiar faces." Alas! how well may the few survivors of our all but vanished circle of friendship, each take up the poet's pensive strain:—

> " When I remember all
>   The friends so linked together,
> I've seen around me fall,
> Like leaves in wintry weather ;
>   I seem like one
>   Who treads, alone,
> Some banquet-hall deserted,
>   Whose lights are fled,
>   And garlands—dead,
> And all but he departed !"

Mr. Duncan died at Morque, near Cults, on Sunday the 4th November 1866. Mr. Ramsay, on being praised for the neatness and truth of the above notice of his friend, said, " Duncan was far too good a fellow for me to let the awkward squad fire o'er his grave."

HYMN.

MIDST all this strife of hopes and fears,
This shifting scene of smiles and tears,
In all I hear, in all I see,
How few, O God ! my thoughts of thee !

In all my good, in all my ill,
Father of mercy thou art still ;
The darkest day that can arise
Is fraught with blessings in disguise !

Upon mine head doth sunshine rest ?
Still let thy truth illume my breast ?
Or do I hold my darkling way ?
Be thou my guide !   Be thou my stay !

Do foes abound when friends are few ?
Then may I prove that thou art true !
When every earthly good is flown,
Still may I call thy grace mine own !

THE LAMENT OF DAVID FOR SAUL AND JONATHAN.

2 SAMUEL, Chap. i.

THE mighty is fallen, like the oak of the forest !
He fell in the strife of the battle when sorest ;
Woe ! woe ! to the son of Philistia that pointed
A shaft to the breast of Jehovah's anointed !

Ah ! was not the holy oil poured on his head,—
And on him the hand of God's own Prophet laid ?
And o'er him the words of God's own blessing spoken,
By God's own command, for a sign and a token ?

Ye mountains of Gilboa ! let not the dew
Or the rain, late or early, descend upon you !
No firstlings—the fold, no offerings—the field,—
No heart-cheering wine let the vineyard e'er yield !

For there was the mighty one's shield cast away,—
The shield of our Saul—like a potsherd of clay !
Ye daughters of Israel, weep for your King !
Who, now, your fine gold or your scarlet shall bring ?

Alas ! is it nought that the tower which graces
The bulwarks of Zion should fall in high places ?
To the Philistine's hand is there given another ?—
My Jonathan is it ?—my brother ! my brother !

Thee, Jonathan! Jonathan! less can I mourn
Than a mother her only son, even her first-born?
My heart yearns for thee!—Thy love—was it common?
Oh! stronger it was than the deep love of woman!

In Gath shall the tale of their slaughter be told?
At the news shall the heart of the alien wax bold?—
Shall the daughters of Askelon sing their strange hymn
To their gods,—when the glory of Israel is dim?

With wing of the eagle, with heart of the lion,
They pursued and they fought in the cause of our Zion!
Was the bright sword of Saul ever baulk'd of its prey?—
From the foe turn'd my brother's bow empty away?

How the mighty are fallen! and their weapons of war
On the mountains of Gilboa scattered afar!
In the gate—in the battle—like them there were none!
In their lives they were lovely! in death they were one!

"RANDOM RHYMES."

THE wise man said—some thousand years ago—
" There's nothing new beneath the sun !"—and so—
From mouth to mouth the proverb onward passes,
The cuckoo note of moralising asses,
Who scarcely know, for all their solemn braying,
The sterling import of the wise man's saying !
'Tis not my drift, by any means, to scout it ;
Without its sacred sanction,—who can doubt it ?
But still, the very soundest observation
We ought to take—with proper limitation.
In every age, our nature still is nature,
Yet holds to view variety of feature ;
And though, in truth, it ever is the same,
Yet, justly, claims diversity of name.
Had David's son lived with us now-a-days,
He had been frequent with his " lack-a-days !"
At many a thing, at least, in semblance, new,
Which every now and then, presents a view
Of varied man, in many changing phases,
Which, sometimes laughter,—often sorrow raises.
But whether one or other it will please
In some dull hours, the graphic pen to seize,
And try to give a little sketchy picture
(Whether in hues of praise or shade of stricture)

Of passing times and persons,—to divert
One's spleen :—to bygone times we may revert
For subjects too ;—and even to the future
We may advance,—remembering—" *Ne sutor
Ultra crepidam !*"—This scrap of Latin means
(A note for all sweet misses in their teens)
That when a son of Crispin needs must take
The measure of some pretty foot, to make
A pair of boots or shoes, he ought to guard,
Lest, in the very millionth of a yard,
He shall exceed the model of his last,
And have the boots or shoes upon him cast.
In such affairs, without express permission,
He never ought to go beyond commission.
Now, in the meantime, some may ask the theme ·
Of these same " Random Rhymes ;"—'tis just a whim
(Doubtless scarce worth the Scotch coin called a boddle !)
That finds unfurnished lodgings in my noddle,
And there intends to tarry, for a time,
To spin a line or two of angling rhyme,
With which to catch, perchance, some oddish fish
To furnish matter for a little dish
Of laughable absurdity :—should I fail
To hook up some one—" very like a whale !"
I must harpoon him with a hand unerring,
And strike the " fall" as dead as any herring !
Although one likes to give a random rap
To any happing *outre* sort of chap
That strikes the fancy, by his comicalities,
As one of nature's rather queer realities ; .
Yet quizzing shall not be my only aim,
For this were surely somewhat of a shame ;
All have their weak sides,—we must, therefore, take

N

A little care lest we should cause them shake
To splitting, at the follies of another,
Who, in this point, is nothing less than brother
To all of us :—it is our common lot
To have our failings ; who, I pray, should not
Have his, and why not his forgiveness too ?
At very best, 'tis little that we do
Aright ; yet true it is that charity,
On mutual grounds,—is somwhat of a rarity !
Oh ! gently, gently let us ever scan
The many failings of poor erring man !
Where is the sin that brings not in its train,
The vengeance of retributory pain ?
Who, save sad self, may ever, partly tell
The terrors of the heart's tumultuous swell
When chafed to tossing by the bitter blast
Born of the clouds and darkness of the past ?
When conscience executes its stern behest
On points that seemed to us, long, long, at rest,—
It glares, a raging lion in our way,—
E'en when we deemed him cheated of his prey
By timely flight ;—alas ! 'tis only then
We meet the monster—in his very den !
Then be the archer's shaft with caution sent,
Lest it should wound, where, haply, his intent
Had been to spare ;—for who would, gladly, break
The bruised reed !—Who would not rather make
It raise its drooping head, and wish the dew
Of heaven might make its beauty bloom anew ?
In secret, oft the bitter tear will flow
For woes the front were studious not to show
Before the cold—perhaps the flouting gaze
Of fellow-man ! the stifled sigh betrays

At times the strife within the bosom's core,
And if some one would venture to explore
Its hidden cause,—with laboured ease we try
To seem so very calm !—although the eye,
That *will* speak out, in spite of every curb,
Blabs of some thoughts that inwardly disturb,
Like the volcano's deeply smouldering wrath,
Ere yet it bursts upon its fiery path :—
Calm is the sky above ; around are thrown
Both sights and sounds which quiet for its own
Adopts :—the distant city's busy hum
Like music of the far-off wave will come
Upon the listening ear ;—and then we mark
The silent shrub-grown portal of the dark
Pavilion of devouring flame ;—the rock—
(That shows the scathing of the tempest shock)
The noteless eyry of the soaring cloud,
Whose downy pinion covers, as a shroud,
The kingly glory of the mountain-head
(Like the shorn honour of the crownless dead !)—
The drowsy humming of the humble bees ;
The low-breathed whispers of the rustling trees ;—
And flocks of peaceful sheep ; and simple pipe
Of gentle shepherd ; tempting cluster ripe
Of tender vine ;—and awe-inspiring gloom
(Scarce second to the horror of the tomb !)
Of the deep forest—mute as marshalled host
When every breathless warrior at his post

*   *   *   *   *   *

These " Random Rhymes " were never completed ; and
what Mr. Ramsay's intentions were the writer has not discovered.

MORNING: A FRAGMENT.

How sweetly, now, a virgin blush
Aurora's cheek began to flush !
The rose was bathed in di'mond dew
That lent fresh lustre to its hue ;
Night had resigned her every gem—
That doffed her starry diadem ;
Whilst, riding in her car of light,
Fair harbinger of day or night,
Venus showered her silver beam
On hill and dale and steaming stream.
From the still vales the mists arose
Where, through the night they sought repose,
To wanton round the mountain's brow
Crowned with the everlasting snow,
And there to hail the Prince of day,
Basking in his orient ray.
The winds were chained in troubled sleep
To some lone cavern of the deep ;
(Pillowed on the rock they lay,
The billows sang their lullaby)
Whence issuing, o'er the chilly wave
Charged with the sailor's doom they rave ;
With heavy moan along the surge,
Foreboding death they chant his dirge,
Rousing the spirit of the storm.

*   *   *   *   *

ON HEARING A LARK SINGING IN A CAGE IN LONDON.

Sweet bird! it well may touch the heart
    Thy lively lay to hear,
Since thou and freedom dear must part
    To please a listless ear!

Though clear and careless seems thy note
    For one thus held in thrall,
What wonder if it had, methought,
    Some sadness in its fall!

A withered turf—a water glass—
    A cage—but ill supply—
The teeming field—the dewy grass—
    The temple of the sky!

No more thou build'st thy little bower,
    As wont in days gone by,
When Spring unveils the virgin flower
    To make the zephyrs sigh!

A captive midst the dull turmoil
    Of crowds to lucre given,
No more thou'lt cheer the peasant's toil,
    And lead his thoughts to Heaven!

GORDON'S HOSPITAL.

Is it not a most strange and unaccountable circumstance, that the very *grave* of the most distinguished of the benefactors of Bon-Accord is not so much as *known* at this comparatively short period after his death? The most important sources of information respecting the life of Robert Gordon being now sealed for ever, it were idle to indulge in fanciful conjecture on the subject; we shall, therefore, confine our notice to a record of the few facts which we are able to furnish from our own knowledge, or to gather from other quarters.

Robert Gordon is supposed to have been born about the year 1665. His father, Arthur Gordon, was an advocate of some repute in Edinburgh, and ninth son of Robert Gordon of Straloch, the eminent geographer and antiquary. It is probable that the subject of this memoir received an education suitable to his situation and prospects in life. His father is said to have left him a patrimony of £1100 —a considerable sum in those days. This patrimony, it would appear, he had squandered away during a youth spent in thoughtless extravagance on the Continent. He afterwards carried on business as a merchant in Dantzic, where he realised a considerable fortune. He subsequently returned to Aberdeen, where he spent the remainder of his days. As if to atone for the extravagance of his youth, his habits, in the decline of life, were parsimonious in the extreme. His usual fare was of the coarsest quality, and, in quantity, barely sufficient to satisfy the demands of nature. His wardrobe was scanty, and but seldom renewed ; and the furniture of his solitary chamber was of the homeliest description. Several stories about his penurious way of living have been handed down, some of which it may amuse our readers to relate.

In the various shifts which he made in the matter of "what he should eat, and what he should drink, and wherewithal he should be clothed," Robert Gordon displayed a share of ingenious pinching which might well vie with the achievements of the most celebrated misers. Milk was a luxury in which he did not always indulge; as a substitute he used the water in which his pitiful allowance of butter had been squeezed. It is said that the dealers in butter and oatmeal in the markets regarded him as a rather "ugly customer," from finding that his *tastings* of their saleables were too much on the principle of "cut and come again !" He had discovered the secret of deriving warmth from coals without consuming them as fuel ; for, although the grate in his cheerless chamber was always filled with them, yet they were never wastefully kindled, but merely kept in their own place as a matter of propriety. Their calorific virtue he derived from carrying a *birn* of them on his back, and thus pacing about his room, at a brisk rate, until he had walked himself into a comfortable glow! If any one happened to call on business at night, when artificial light was necessary, a single shabby candle lent its feeble ray on the occasion ; but, as soon as business was despatched, even this "darkness visible" was denied ; for Robert Gordon used coolly to remark, that "one could see to speak in the dark!" His dress displayed a struggle between his pinching propensities and some ambition to appear in a habit suitable to his rank as a gentleman. Gloves he allowed himself ; but he knew that they would last all the longer for being never put on, and so always carried them in his hand. No brush ever touched his shoes, and *jet* was out of the question ; yet he was careful to wipe them on the grass! His upper garment, a sort of gown, or cloak, might indeed, at one time, have been "fitting for his wear ;" but when, in the course of long service, it had become so notoriously and obtrusively thread-bare, as to provoke the remarks and remonstrances of his friends, he promised to get a new one if they would only suggest how the old one might be usefully employed. He was advised to lay it as a coverlet on his bed, which was by no means overloaded with bed-clothes ; the hint met his approbation, and he forthwith purchased a new gown. In the matter of personal purity, he was not particular to a shade. Soap he did not consider indispensable in the arrangements of his toilet, or a comb as a *sine qua non*, and—

    " Sure his linen was not very clean !"

Although Robert Gordon thus "pinched both back and belly too," yet he had no ascetic objections to good living, when the feast was not at his own expense. Owing to his station as a gentleman, his intelligence, the idea of his great wealth, and perhaps too, in pity of his self-imposed system of starvation, he was a frequent and a willing guest at the tables of many of the more respectable Aberdonians. These golden opportunities he took special care to improve ; not content with the more dainty viands of his host, it is said that he used to find his way into the kitchen, and there cultivate an intimacy with the plainer dishes appropriated for the menials. It would appear that he had studied the gastronomic maxims of Ritt-master Dugald Dalgetty, of *Gustavus* memory, and that he had, when living at free quarters, a steady eye to the *provant*. It is said that a surfeit, occasioned by thus overeating himself, at the house of a friend, was the cause of his death. This event took place in January 1732. He was honoured with a public funeral, his body lying in state in the Hall of Marischal College, where every one who was inclined to view it, received the refreshments usually presented on such occasons.   His remains were then interred, with great pomp, *somewhere in Drum's Aisle*, but in what particular spot is not known. We believe that the place of his interment is now published for the first time.   We have good authority for our assertion.   There is in the Hospital an original half-length portrait of the founder, from which the painting in the hall, by Mossman, was taken.   In his person Mr. Gordon was rather tall, of a gentlemanly appearance, with an intelligent countenance, and a calm, expressive eye.   He appears to have been a man of more than ordinary shrewdness, of considerable information, and of a cultivated taste.   As the founder of Gordon's Hospital, his memory is justly entitled to the veneration of all who are alive to the feelings of gratitude inspired by such a benevolent design, or who can appreciate the worth of one, who, whatever may have been the eccentricities of his character, was capable of forming and maturing a scheme for the lasting benefit of friendless youth.

It is impossible now to ascertain how or when Mr. Gordon formed the benevolent design of founding his hospital.   In the preamble of the deed of mortification, dated three years before his death (1729), he says that he had intended thus to dis-

pose of his substance "for several years bygone."
Some have ascribed his self-imposed penurious life
to his laudable desire to accomplish this benevolent
purpose. It is not unlikely that this may have
been one of the determining causes ; but mankind
generally act from mixed motives. The parsimony
of his latter years may have been at first adopted
to atone, in some measure, for the thoughtless extravagance of his youth. His design of founding
the hospital may have been formed when his
fortune, accumulated beyond his exigencies, had
warranted the hope of its becoming ultimately
adequate to the charitable disposal of it afterwards
made ; same excusable vanity, too, may have inclined him to an act which should convey his name
with honour to succeeding generations ; while the
nature of the design itself must certainly oblige us
to believe that it was partly inspired by principles
of genuine benevolence. His parsimonious mode
of life, arising at first from various motives, may
have been afterwards confirmed by custom into a
habit which maintained its sway independently of
its original causes. The preamble of the deed of
mortification runs thus :—

" For as much as I have deliberately and seriously
(for these several years bygone) intended and resolved, and
am now come to a full and final resolution and determination, to make a pious Mortification of my whole substance and effects presently pertaining, resting, and owing

to me, or which shall happen to pertain and be resting to me at the time of my decease; and that towards the erection of an Hospital, and for maintenance, aliment, entertainment, and education of young boys *whose parents are poor and indigent*, and not able to maintain them at school, and put them to trades and employments. Which resolution purely proceeds from the zeal I bear and carry to the glory and honour of God; and that the true principles of our holy and Christian religion may be the more effectually propagated in young ones; and that the knowledge of letters and of lawful employments and callings may flourish and be advanced in all succeeding generations."

The sum originally bequeathed for the Hospital was £10,000 sterling. The executors appointed are—

" The Provost, Bailies, and the remanent members of the Town Council of the burgh of Aberdeen, and the *four* Ministers of the Gospel in the said burgh of Aberdeen, commonly called the Town's four Ministers of the old and new Churches who exercise the pastoral charge there, and to their *successors* in their *respective offices*."

Does not the last clause of this sentence determine the question relative to the election of the clerical governors which arose out of the recent division of the town into parishes? Are not the ministers of the East, West, North, and Greyfriars' Churches alone properly eligible as Governors? The Deed next ordains that—

" This Hospital shall be called, in all succeeding

generations, Robert Gordon's Hospital, founded by his appointment for entertaining and educating indigent male children and male grand-children of decayed merchants and brethren of guild of the burgh of Aberdeen, of the name of *Gordon*, in the first place, and of the name of *Menzies* in the second place (the nearest relations of the *Mortifier* of the names of *Gordon* and *Menzies* being always preferred to any others), and the male children of any relations of the Mortifier, that are of any other name, in the third place, to be preferred to others; and then the male children or male grand-children of any other merchants and brethren of guild of the said burgh."

The Hospital, then, is *chiefly* intended for behoof of the sons and grandsons of *burgesses of guild.* The Deed, however, afterwards runs thus :—

" *And in case* it shall happen that there be not so many boys (as before specified) as the said Hospital can contain, *then and in that case*, I appoint and ordain the said Patrons and Governors to elect and choose so many boys of the sons and grand-sons of tradesmen of the said burgh of Aberdeen, being freemen and burgesses thereof; and failing these, so many boys as have been born and educated in the said burgh, and are the sons or grandsons of persons who are, or have been *residenters* in the said burgh of Aberdeen, who are indigent and cannot maintain themselves, as the said Hospital and revenue thereof can conveniently contain and admit of."

The proper objects of the Institution, then, are the children or grand-children of the *indigent* alone, who are required by the Deed to bring certificates of their indigent circumstances from the minister and kirk-session of the bounds where they reside—

" And the consciences of the Governors are *strictly* charged not to choose any but such as are proper objects of the charity."

It is scarcely necessary, after this, to remark that the Governors ought not, in any instance, to be swayed by motives of private partiality or convenience in the election of boys, lest they should incur the reproach of frustrating the benevolent views of the founder. For many years, owing to the great number of burgesses of guild made at a *certain period*, no sons or grandsons of trades burgesses could be admitted into the Hospital. This was the more to be regretted, as the hardship of the case fell most heavily on those who were least able to bear it.

The Deed of Mortification next directs how the money shall be laid out on the building of the Hospital :—

" And the house, and other accommodation for the said Hospital, shall be erected, built, and finished out of the annual rents and profits of the said sum of Ten Thousand Pounds Sterling money, or such sum or sums as are hereby mortified by me, and shall be recovered and made effectual, of my effects, after my decease, upon any fit place within the said burgh of Aberdeen, where the Patrons or Governors shall think fit, or upon the piece of ground called the Blackfriars, lying upon the north side of the Schoolhill of the said burgh of Aberdeen, to be feued for that purpose, or to be purchased, if it can be done legally; but the principal or capital stock, is still to remain entire; and no children to be entered or received into the said Hospital, until such time as the annual rents of the said capital stock have defrayed and discharged the whole expense of the building, and the price bestowed in purchasing the ground where the said Hospital is to be built, and year and day thereafter at least."

The spot where the Hospital is built was Mr. Gordon's favourite walk during his lifetime, a circumstance which may account for his pointing it out as the site of the building. His plan of allowing the surplus of the money which remained, after defraying the expense of the house, to accumulate until sufficient for maintaining the boys, does not appear to be very judicious. It would have been better to have allowed the original sum to have accumulated until fully adequate to all necessary expenses, and then to have commenced the building. As it was, the building lay vacant for a good many years, and, of course, required to be kept up, at some expense, while no immediate advantage was derived from it. The original Hospital was built in 1732, after a plan by Mr. William Adam, of Edinburgh. The expense of the erection was £3300. It was not open for the reception of boys until 1750. It is a singular fact, that the first inmates of Gordon's Hospital were part of the King's troops under the Duke of Cumberland. The Hospital was fortified, and received the name of Fort Cumberland. The old kitchen was converted into a stable. In various places of the old back-wall the remains of loop-holes were to be seen not many years ago. Some of the rooms of the house bore faint traces of the numbers with which they had been distinguished at this period. Government allowed the Governors the sum of £300 for the use of the Hospital.

The management and administration of the affairs of Gordon's Hospital are vested in the Provost, Bailies, Town-Council, and four Ministers of Aberdeen, for the time being, each of them having a separate vote in all matters relating to the Hospital and its members. The Provost is the ordinary Preses of their meetings. None are allowed to enter upon office before having taken a solemn oath, *de fideli*, as follows :—" I, A. B., do solemnly swear and promise before God, that to the best of my knowledge and power, I shall carry and demean myself faithfully and honestly in all matters which concern the election of the officers or children, or any thing else belonging to Robert Gordon's Hospital, founded and erected for the maintaining and educating the male children and grand-children of decayed merchants and brethren of Guild of the burgh of Aberdeen; and if I know any going about at any time to defraud or prejudge the said pious work, I shall obstruct it to my power, and reveal it to the Governors." The old Governors remain in office till the third Monday of November yearly. The new Governors meet the old, on that day, in the Hall of the Hospital, and, after having the above oath administered to them by the old Preses, they enter immediately on their office. On the occasion of a change of Governors, the old Preses is required to exhort the new Governors to the faithful discharge of their important duties. Some one of the ministers, too, who chance to be present, is required to give the masters, boys, and servants, suitable admonitions. This praiseworthy practice is not, however, now observed.

The Governors have a discretionary power of making by-laws and rules for the better administration of the Hospital, provided they interfere not with the fundamental laws of the Institution, or with the original regulations of the Deed of Mortification, except when just grounds appear for altering these. In the latter case, such alterations must be concluded and agreed upon by three-fourths of the whole members, to meet for that purpose, after the same has been under their consideration in two several sederunts, the one at the distance of at least a month after the other, and be approved by the Preses, and these alterations no ways infringing upon the fundamental articles of the Hospital—viz.

That the same is for the maintenance and instruction in the principles of the Protestant faith, and education in learning, of the various classes of boys heretofore enumerated ; that the Hospital shall always be called by the Founder's name, or in conjunction with others who shall bequeath sums to a certain amount ; and that the right of managing the affairs of the Hospital shall be vested in the Patrons and Governors before mentioned ; and that no part of the funds of the Hospital shall be otherwise appropriated than the deed provides. All these are fundamental statutes of the Institution, over which the Governors have no discretionary power of alteration. With regard to the management of the *funds* of the Hospital, the Governors have power to take up the principal sums, to re-employ them, to carry on the buildings and all necessary repairs, and contract for everything for that purpose. In placing their funds out at loan, the Governors are, however, laid under certain restrictions. It is appointed that no money belonging to the Hospital be laid out or employed, but by warrant of an act by the Patrons and Governors, voted by way of balloting, and that either for purchasing lands, or upon real security of land, reputed free of incumbrances, or to the town of Aberdeen, upon the public security, or to any two or more *responsal* persons bound conjunctly and severally, *providing* the sum lent to these two or more persons do not exceed five hundred pounds sterling.

Much praise is due to the Governors of Gordon's Hospital for the prudent management of its funds. They are chiefly invested in lands which yield an increasing revenue. At one period, we believe, a great portion of the funds was in considerable jeopardy. A proposal was made for vesting a large sum in the hands of the Town's Treasurer. We have been informed that one of the clerical Governors, the Rev. Hugh Hay, minister of the East Kirk, was the person (to the honour of his memory be it recorded) who resolutely opposed this reckless scheme. The firmness of his conduct on this occasion is the more to be admired, when we reflect that he was a very young man, and that he held the office of a Governor for scarcely one year. All meetings of the Governors for transaction of Hospital business, are usually held within the hall of the Hospital. There are four great quarterly meetings —viz. on the third Mondays of November, February, May, and August. Besides these, there are three other meetings, for the election of boys, the visitation of the schools, the auditing of the accounts, and any contingent business. These meetings are all called by the officer of the eldest Bailie, who may be required to make a judicial declaration, in presence of the meeting, of his having warned the Governors to attend. It is ordained that whatever shall be concluded upon by a plurality of voices of the Governors, at these meetings, shall stand in full force, and be a final act and deed, there being always present at these meetings no less than *eleven*, who, with the Provost, are declared a *quorum ;* and, in absence of the Provost, the eldest Bailie of Aberdeen ; and, in his absence, the next eldest Bailie to him ; and, in the absence of the Bailies, any other chosen Preses by the meeting, for that occasion. The Preses and Governors must sign all acts passed at their meetings. In the case of an equality of votes, the Preses has the casting vote.

The deed next provides for the election of four auditors of accounts in the following manner :— The new Governors choose, out of their own number, on the third Monday of November, four auditors of the Treasurer's and all other accounts belonging to the Hospital, who, or any *two* of them, jointly and met together, shall peruse and consider the Treasurer's quarterly accounts, the fourth day after the end of each quarter, or sooner if they can with conveniency ; and the Treasurer and auditors shall deliver to the body of the Governors assembled, at their quarterly meeting, their accounts of the last three months past fairly written in a book, containing all the sums, less or more, paid during that space, with their report subscribed, which shall be read publicly, and there either comptrolled or allowed ; the allowances thereof shall be made under the hand of the Clerk of the Hospital, and subscribed by the Preses and other Governors present ; which book of accounts of three months, so allowed, shall lie open for the space of eight days thereafter upon the table, so that if any of the Governors, or those who may have given donations, or their heirs (but none else), have a desire to peruse them, they may ; and if they find any oversight or fault therein, the discoverers thereof are charged, on conscience, to reveal it to the Governors, who shall take care to correct and amend it. The third Monday of November, yearly, the auditors shall deliver to the body of the Governors assembled, the whole preceding year's accompts, where they shall be comptrolled or allowed, every man as is expressed in the quarterly accompts. The election of auditors shall be by plurality of the suffrages of the Governors, or their quorum, and they shall give their oaths *de fideli* in presence foresaid ; and if any of them shall happen to die, or not accept, the Governors shall, within *ten* days, elect one in his place. And for making the auditing of the accounts more expeditious, it is expressly provided, that before the Treasurer pay any particular accounts of merchants, tradesmen, or others, excepting the stated and settled provision for the diet of those in the Hospital, which is to be regulated by the Governors, the said accounts shall be laid, at least, before two of the auditors met together, who shall visit the work, consider the account, and report their opinion thereanent to the Governors, who are to approve or restrict, as they shall see cause, and shall give warrant to the Treasurer for payment of such a sum, in satisfaction thereof, as they shall see just.

The deed next provides for the election of the Clerk of the Hospital. He is chosen by the Governors, and continues in office during their pleasure only. His office is fairly and faithfully to keep in order all the evidents and other papers whatsoever belonging to the Hospital, and to attend the Governors at their meetings, to draw all orders and resolutions made by them, and to keep a clear and distinct record or digest of all their proceedings, marking down upon the margin of each sederunt the material thing transacted that day, and to make up an alphabetical index pointing to the particular sederunt or statute where every matter concerning the Hospital is treated of. He shall, likewise, have the sole benefit of drawing and composing of all manner of evidents, securities, and writings, which shall be made betwixt the Hospital and any person.

" It being also expressly provided, That, in case it shall please God, that any of the boys, one, or more, shall at any time, after their departure out of the said Hospital, attain or succeed to any considerable fortune or stock in the world, that each boy attaining to such a condition shall be *obliged to pay back* to the Hospital what was laid out and expended on them during the time they were in the Hospital, and putting them to a trade, or otherwise ; and the Governors are hereby *re-quired* to *pursue* for, uplift, and receive the same from them, according to the following rule, viz.—If they acquire and succeed to two thousand merks Scots money, of free stock, they are to pay back one half; and if they acquire and succeed to four thousand merks money foresaid, of free stock, then they are to pay back the *haill* that was bestowed on them."

In the appendix to the deed we find this clause referred to, with the following *addendum :*—

" I hereby declare, and will and ordain, that such sums to be recovered, shall be added to the capital stock of the said mortification."

It might reasonably be expected that feelings of gratitude would induce those who were brought up in the Hospital to endeavour to make some return to an institution which had been the means of enabling them to acquire a competency in life. It will be seen, however, by the above extract, that the matter is not left to their better option, but that it is their imperative *obligation.* The Governors are empowered to *pursue* for reimbursement of the expenses of the maintenance in the Hospital of such as may afterwards acquire or succeed to certain specific sums. Such strong measures have never been resorted to by the Governors, although instances, not a few, have occurred which might have justified such procedure. Of all those who have been educated in Gordon's Hospital, a considerable number have risen to comparative affluence in the world, and yet, *to their shame be it told*, only a few of its *adopted sons* have had the common gratitude to make a return for the benefits they there received. A good many years ago, a person, whose name we forbear to mention, died in Leith, worth £60,000 ; and, although he made bequests to almost every charitable institution in Aberdeen, yet to Gordon's Hospital, where he was brought up, he *left not one farthing.* What can be the cause of such unnatural conduct ? Are those who *get up* in the world ashamed to bequeath anything to the Institution, lest they should thereby betray the lowliness of their origin ? This were surely one of those cases—

"Where 'tis a shame to be ashamed t' appear !"

We suspect, however, that there is too much of this discreditable feeling among those whose circumstances in the world are such as to contrast rather strongly with the poor and friendless condition of a " *Sillerton laddie.*" Nay, there are some so utterly destitute of common sense and common gratitude, that they are offended, forsooth ! if you make even slight allusion to the circumstance of their having been brought up in the Hospital ! If they feel the obligation irksome, let them forthwith partly rid themselves of it by paying back to the

Institution the expenses of their education. But, even when they shall have found grace enough to do this, let them still remember that they owe that institution a debt of gratitude which they can *never* repay. We envy not the contemptible creatures who allow the better feelings of the soul to be stifled by *poor pride*—of all kinds of pride the most pitiful. In making these remarks, we mean nothing *personal;* but, if any should choose to take offence at their truth and appropriateness to their own particular cases, they are very welcome to do so. They need not whine about *feelings, etc.,* until they have shown that they really do possess feelings entitled to respect. We suppose they would readily boast of their having been brought up in Gordon's Hospital if they could derive any advantage by the boast ; but as long as they are *ashamed* of the circumstance, we would just hint, for their special edification, that they have more credit by the Hospital than the Hospital has by them !

If there is no legal claim, there certainly is a moral one ; yet up to this date *twelve* old scholars only have shown their respect to the wishes and request of Robert Gordon, by repaying the cost of their education to the Hospital.

TO DESPAIR.

BEGONE ! begone ! Not I thy prey !
Haste, on thy gloomy wings away !
Well, well I know thy shadowy form
In mantle woven of the storm !
The cloud and darkness in thy train,
Thy girdle—of the captive's chain !
Thy crest—to mark thy dire dominion,
Is borrowed of the tempest's pinion !
A garland since thou needs must wear,
The mildew doth the weed prepare
That battens on some nameless mound
Far, far from consecrated ground !
And ever, in thy luckless hand
Seems more than fabled wizard's wand,
And still about thy shaken finger
Some evil omen seems to linger.
The furrows on thy brow have all
The dankness of the dungeon wall ;
Thy breath—the treasury of sighs !
Oh ! save me from those spectral eyes !
For never on their eyelids sere
Distils the dew-drop of a tear !
Turn not on me their fixed stare,
That mocks the lightning's lurid glare,
Destruction's fascination there !

Forbear, forbear that sidelong glance
That seems, in kindness, cast askance,
As if thou knewest, but too well,
Mishap thy tongue were loath to tell !
Nay, nay, I cannot, will not brook
The mystery of thy boding look !
Thy tongue, to prayer still a stranger,
In hope of mercy, dread of danger ;
Self-blasting curse, it skilleth well,
The current dialect of hell !
From song of gladness turned, thine ear
Finds music in the shriek of fear,
The stifled moan of agony,
Expiring nature's feeble cry,
And still it deems the sweetest note
The rattle in the speechless throat !
Fell tyrant of the broken heart
That feels same untold, hopeless smart !
Foul trafficker in human blood
With coin of chalice, steel, or flood ;
Tempting the wretch, with ready rope,
To barter life for atheist's hope !
In fiendish form 'tis thine to crouch
By the lost sinner's dying couch ;
And if thy clutching hand thou stay—
'Tis only to enhance thy prey !
Why should thy presence oft be found
In this, at best, but weary round ?
By pillow of unconscious sleep,
Thy unseen vigil wilt thou keep—
And wilt thou dash my better dreaming,
Jealous of bliss—though but in seeming ?
And when the breezy hill I climb,

To share the raptures of the prime,
Wilt thou turn the morning's gladness
To midnight silence,—midnight sadness?
And when, at eve, I wend my way
Where the clear brook delights to stray,
A-listening to its pleasing chime,
All heedless of the passing time;
E'en *there* thou haunt'st my secret track,
I catch thee hovering at my back!
Go! wander, by thy gloomy self,
Thy page some foul-begotten elf!
And if thou wilt that some there be
To bear thee fitting company;
The worm—corruption's darling daughter,
The vulture—parasite of slaughter,
The raven—glutted from the gibbet,
Thy fellowship I'll not prohibit!

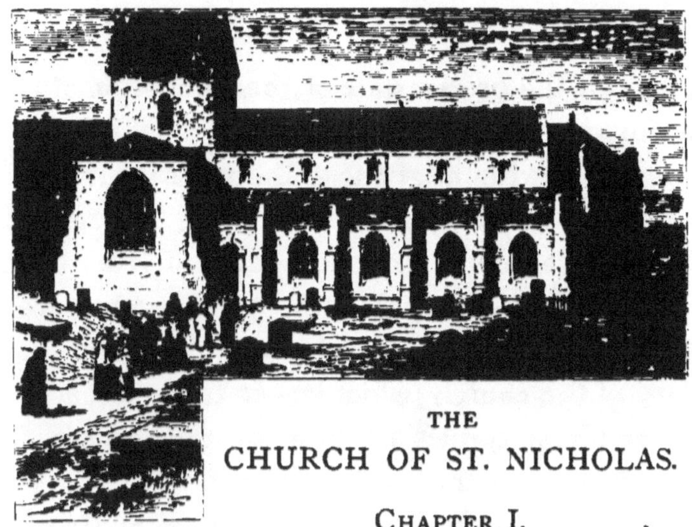

CHURCH OF ST. NICHOLAS.

CHAPTER I.

WE do verily believe there are citizens, not a few, who know not what this means. Yet, by this name was known, for many generations, a building in our churchyard, which our forefathers loved and cherished as the very apple of the eye. All that now remains of it are the north aisle, which has been so long profaned by an abominable heating apparatus; the square bell-tower, with its supporting piers and arches; and the quaint steeple, a comparatively modern addition to the former, of some four hundred years' standing!

Unquestionably, these are the most ancient ecclesiastical remains in the district. In the tower still hangs the bell "Lawrence," more familiarly "Lowrie," which was placed there five years before a stone of the cathedral of St. Machar was laid in

1357.   Of the precise date of the foundation of this ancient church there is no record.   The Parson of Rothiemay (without giving authority) says it began to be built in the year 1090, during the reign of Malcolm Canmore ; and he speaks of it as being in his day in good repair, although *then* (the seventeenth century) six hundred years old.   The chartulary of the church (which *ought* to be among the city archives) throws no light on the subject, for the oldest entry therein is under date 1342.   The citizens of old used to speak of this fabric proudly and affectionately, as their " mother church."   The church of St. Nicholas, of which the Bishop was Vicar, is expressly mentioned in a Bull of Pope Adrian IV.; and there is no ground for the belief that the establishment, then and there referred to, was other than the fabric of which some fragments remain in our day.

Doubtless a very considerable period elapsed between the foundation and completion of the original building.   War, pestilence, famine, and lack of means, were all serious drags on the progress of such works.   That such incidents had obstructive influence in the case referred to is apparent from traces of the transitional style in the fabric.   There is reason to believe that the original building commenced with the nave, which occupied the site of the present West Church, increased by fifteen feet in length westward, but diminished, in the side aisles, by several feet. The arches of this nave were round-headed, like those still supporting the tower, but their piers were *probably* of somewhat older type. The original church had a transept, yet no choir with side aisles, as latterly, but merely a chancel, rather more in length than either limb of the original transept. When that which was called the old East Church was taken down in 1837, to make way for the present preaching hall, the foundations of the ancient chancel were, for the first time, discovered. The eastern end was round—Byzantine—a peculiarity (in connection with other considerations), decisive of its reference to the early part of the twelfth century. Parties familiar with the details of Durham Cathedral (built by Canmore), have traced a similarity of style even in the few remains of our church, which has been referred to the same period. Taking, then, into account a variety of considerations, purposely omitted in this popular notice, we should be disposed to ascribe the commencement of the original church to the time of Canmore, and its completion, in the main, to that of Malcolm IV. At the time when the old East Church was taken down, two stones, of the same material as the ancient fabric, were discovered (by the writer) in the stairs which then led up from the aisle to the ringing-chamber. They had evidently formed one in some part of the ancient church:—

The stones are still to be seen at the north entrance into Drum's Aisle, built into the wall in a
most careless and ignorant manner. The letters
are of the most ancient form ; and their preservation has been owing to the incrustation of successive coats of whitewash, before the stones were
taken from the wreck of the old church to form steps
to the belfry. The material of which the ancient
church was built was old red sandstone, probably
quarried from the rocks at Stonehaven. Some of it,
which has never been exposed to the weather, is as
sound as ever.

The ancient church, then, consisted of a nave
with side aisles, a chancel, and a transept, the inter-
section of which was surmounted by a squat square

tower (which still remains), surmounted by a cape-house, like that of Kirkwall Cathedral.

Thus remained the ancient church for between three and four hundred years, when our citizens, increased in numbers and wealth, and probably jealous of the rising glories of the Cathedral in Old Aberdeen, determined to take down the old chancel; to build a stately choir with side aisles; and to crown the square tower with a lofty steeple. In short, nothing would serve them but a handsome minster, for celebration of the full choral service, with a suitable contingent of singing-men and cherubical boys, and a grand organ to boot. This project seems to have been the great local question of the day, and was prosecuted with singular zeal and liberality. Contributions of salmon, stones, lead, victual, etc. etc., were profusely poured in; and the very backslidings of the frail were " turned to commodity," on Falstaff's principle, by fines for behoof of "St. Nicholas' Wark." All this commenced about the middle of the fifteenth century, the movement being greatly encouraged by Bishop Spence, an active and public-spirited prelate.

Let us now suppose ourselves in Drum's Aisle, looking towards the north. The first thing we notice is, that it was originally intended that the roof of the space inclosed by the ancient arches should be of stone and groined; but that this intention had been abandoned, for what reason it is now impossible to say. The arches, with their piers of clustered columns, are evidently Anglo-Norman. There is a remarkable peculiarity on the eastern side. The piers have there been strengthened by masonry, evidently of the fifteenth century. On that side, too, there is a crack in the tower, which has been there for centuries, without being the cause of any instability in a fabric which has become a very rock of concrete. The probability is, that these anomalies had been caused by the removal of the old chancel, and the supra-imposition of the new steeple. It was, therefore, not without some apprehension, that in 1837 the buttressing afforded by the old East Church was removed ; but the old tower and steeple stood firm (to the disappointment of certain parties), and the erection of the new church has rendered both more stable than ever.

Along with the old choir, the southern limb of the transept was renewed in 1837. It was twenty feet longer than the north limb, having been to that extent prolonged by Provost Leith (who was there buried) about the middle of the fourteenth century. About two centuries later the great window was repaired at the expense of the Drum family, who have a place of burial there, with an altar tomb, bearing the effigy of the brother of the laird, who was killed at Harlaw in 1411, and who married the widow, his sister-in-law. The window of the north aisle was repaired, towards the beginning of the sixteenth century, by Collieson of Auchlunies, who had a tomb there, the arch of which now spans a doorway! The frame of the window, however, is original, belonging to the Early Pointed style, as may be seen on the inside. There are two side windows in this aisle, both Norman ; and the sharp pitch of the original roof may also be here traced. In this aisle too (called Collieson's) was the altar tomb of Sir Robert Davidson, Provost of Aberdeen, slain at Harlaw. His effigy lay in an arched recess, where the abominable boiler was placed in 1811, and which was close by the altar of St. Anne. The writer of this (then a boy) recollects the finding of his grave stone (in excellent preservation), with the inscription around the border. At the suggestion of the sexton, Peter Kerr, this ancient memorial was placed, face downwards, for better preservation in the place where it was originally ; and there it will be found when some new arrangement shall be made for supplementing the fervours of the pulpit by the calorific virtues of " Wallsend." Peter Kerr was one who took pleasure in the very stones of the old church, and had profound respect for the memory of the gallant Provost, he himself having in his youth " followed to the field some martial lord," in capacity of drummer.

Sir Robert's effigy now lies in the sill of the window near the stair leading to the Grammar

School gallery in the West Church. Provost Collieson and his lady occupy each a sill on the same side. The noses of the whole look as though they had been long on the grindstone—a peculiarity inflicted by the graveboards which used to be carelessly tossed into the original receptacles of the effigies. Thus much, off-hand, must suffice for the present.

CHAPTER II.

As we have already remarked, this ancient church originally consisted of a nave with side isles, the site of which is now partly occupied by the West Church; a transept, popularly known as Drum's Aisle; and a chancel, subsequently enlarged into a choir, latterly known as the old East Kirk, which was, in 1837, superseded by the present church.

The circumstance of the church having been dedicated to St. Nicholas, who was the patron saint of mariners, seems to favour the opinion that the commercial relations of the community of Aberdeen had attained some importance at a very early period. Indeed, the idea of so extensive an undertaking implied no little ambition and commensurate ability for its execution. From authentic documents, which have happily survived the consequences of " chance and change," it would appear that the church was in a very flourishing condition during the thirteenth, fourteenth, and fifteenth centuries. In the year 1277, Richard Cementarius founded in it the chantry of St. John the Evangelist, for the celebration of masses for himself, his relatives, and friends, and all the departed faithful. During the prevalence of the Romish faith it was customary for those whose circumstances enabled them to indulge in the more costly observances of religious zeal, to dedicate chantries with shrines to favourite saints, within the venerated precincts of some distinguished church, for the purpose of securing services believed to be promotive of their eternal peace. Of such endowments, with suitable appointments, there were no fewer than thirty-one in the church which St. Nicholas was supposed to regard with peculiar favour. To this church, indeed, the zeal of our remote ancestors would seem to have paid most loving and liberal tribute. It was amply furnished with all the paraphernalia and " properties" requisite for the pomp and circumstance of the Romish ritual. Many and massive were its chalices, and censers, and crucifixes of pure silver, besides " four cruets and ane littel shippe" of the same precious metal. Then there was ample store of sacred vestments—copes, and chasubles and tunicles of fine cloth, of gold and velvet ; and frontals for the altar of red damask, etc., etc. Nor was there wanting a goodly array of "brazen work"—eighteen brazen chandeliers ; two great chandeliers of the high altar with the sacrament chandelier ; "the great chandelier of brass, with the image ;" a laver, a font, and holy-water vat—all of brass ; with many other decorments which imparted impressiveness to the services of the church.

The nave was a stately and extensive building, 116 feet long by 66 feet wide. The roof was supported by eight piers on each side, spanned by round arches. It had thirty-three windows, great and small, and three doors. Of the latter, one was in the Marriage Porch, situated about the middle of the south side. A rude, but not uninteresting sketch of the building may be seen in Gordon's account of Aberdeen, published by the Spalding Club. The floor and walls were covered with many monuments of the dead, most of which have shared the fate of the memories they were fondly but vainly intended to perpetuate. A few more distinguished names have triumphed over the destruction of the frail memorials of their rank or worth. It is to be observed that there were originally no seats or galleries for a congregation in the nave, or indeed in any other part of the church, which was more especially a house of prayer and praise, worshippers either standing or kneeling.

The transept is some twenty-four feet broad by nearly one hundred feet in length. The height of its originally sharp-pointed roof must have been sixty feet. In the western side of its southern limb is the oldest sepulchral monument about Aberdeen.

It is a mural tablet to the memory of Provost Leith, 1352. It is greatly decayed, the only words which may, with difficulty, be traced being *honorabilis vir*. On it are represented a priest, with singing boys, in the act of celebrating a post-obit at an altar, for the soul of the departed. It is curious to notice how the crucifix and altar have been erased by the zeal of some reformer, the marks of the chisel being distinctly visible. Two fine sepulchral effigies belonging to the Drum family lie in the north-east corner; but their original place was under an arch in the opposite corner, where the family grave is situated. The burial-places in the northern limb have already been noticed. When the south transept was partially removed, before being rebuilt in 1837, several square boles were discovered in the ancient wall, in all of which were greatly-decayed human bones, and, in one of them, a silver cross very much oxidised. What became of it is best known to the party by whom it seems to have been considered as lawful plunder.

The circumstances which led to the building of the choir have already been partially noticed. In correspondence with the nave, it had a centre and two side aisles, and terminated in a semi-hexagonal apse, where stood the high altar. In this, and in some other points, the influence of the French style of Gothic was plainly discernible. The piers and arches resembled those of the Cathedral in Old Aberdeen. The latter were pointed, and formed five bays. The roof was ceiled, waggon-wise, and in this, as in every other respect, exactly resembled the coeval roof of the chapel of King's College. When the seats and galleries were all removed it was only then that the fabric was seen in all its harmonious proportions and impressive solemnity. Three wide steps, embracing the whole breadth of the central aisle, led to the entrance of the apse, the breadth of which was spanned by a pointed arch some forty feet high. The highest point of the ceiling must have been some sixty feet above the lowest part of the floor. The apse was twenty-two feet broad at the great arch, eighteen feet deep, and thirty-six feet high. The body of the choir was eighty-six feet long and sixty-four wide. Thus, when the old choir was completed, the whole length of the church was nearly 250 feet — a stately and extensive building, and, as a parochial church, unmatched in the kingdom.

It has been already mentioned that, when the old East Church was taken down in 1837, the foundations of the original chancel were discovered; the Byzantine character of its eastern extremity indicating its great antiquity. At the same time it was found that the tops of the north and south side walls were covered by a large quantity of human bones. Were those relics which had been dislodged when the foundations of the choir were dug? When that choir was taken down several stone coffins were discovered, supposed to be of the thirteenth century, and of which one *ought* to be in the Museum of Marischal College.

A suitable conclusion to this part of our notice is the following quaint inscription, of date 1672, which was placed on the wall of the old nave, and is fortunately preserved in Monteith's *Theatre of Mortality*:—

> " St. Nicholas' stately structure here doth stand,
>   No paroch church can match't in all the land;
>   Our architectors, most worthy of renown,
>   Did build this church for to decore the town ;
>   And that God's worship might be in it raist :
>   Should not their virtuous paines be highly praist
>   Who such a splendid fabric did erect?
>   No Momus eye can blame its architect.
>   With all the ornaments fit to decore
>   A Temple, where our God we should adore
>   In sp'rit and truth ; with fear and trembling we
>   Should worship him within his sanctuarie.
>   It hath, of real and of casual rent,
>   Enough it to maintain, if rightly spent;
>   Then, let its masters in succeeding ages
>   Bestow its rents, and not be sacrilegious.
>   And since we praise those who this work did found,
>   And raised it up even from the gravely ground.
>   Let all succeeding ages mind that we
>   Deserve some praise by our posteritie.

CHAPTER III.

AN adjunct of the ancient choir was the crypt at the east end, forming a chapel dedicated to. the Virgin Mary, as our Lady of Pity. It was connected with the former by two flights of steps, one at the east end of each of the said aisles. It was intended for the accommodation, during the performance of mass, of the aged, sick, and infirm, who could thus, with less fatigue, participate in the service. For many years this chapel was degraded into a cellar for all sorts of odds and ends. There were deposited the *stocks*, which had doubtless, in their day, done ecclesiastical duty, but now exchanged for more refined, but not less tyrannical instruments of priestly domination. There, too, was kept the hideous gibbet ; and, when the building was taken down in 1837, upturned the suit of irons for which, in 1776, Morrison (murderer of his wife) had been measured. At one time this chapel was used as a plumber's shop; at another time it was redolent of the savoury streams of the soup kitchen for the poor, and that, too, on Sunday, it being then deemed no sin to furnish the cold and hungry with a good dinner even on that day, although malice, slander, and swindling would seem now, as in olden times, quite consonant with envenomed Sabbatical observance. In the same place are said to have been found the last fragments of the organ which woke the echoes of the ancient church, leading and aiding the service of worshippers, which would seem less objectionable than a case where a congregation is all but struck dumb by a squalling and expensive choir. The crypt is now converted into a vestibule, chapel, and vestry, and is fitted up with much of the carved work which adorned the old East and West Churches, particularly the former. When that venerable structure was doomed to wanton destruction by Provost James Blaikie and the Rev. Mr. Foote, it was resolved that every fragment of the carved work should be strictly preserved. Nevertheless, a good deal of it was *sold* and converted into articles of household furniture. The only remnant of the canopy of the choir (a counterpart of that in King's College Chapel, and probably the work of the same artificer, John Findon) was cut up, partly to adorn a set of book-shelves, partly to form a sideboard; several chiffoniers were constructed out of carved panels emblazoned with the armorial bearings of "gentle blood;" a similar panel does, or did do, duty as a fire-screen in an aristocratic mansion not twenty miles from Aberdeen; but perish the thought!—that there should be any truth in the report that part of the plenishing of a sanctuary is actually degraded into a coal-box, and that, too, under the very eye of the pastorate! In the front of the lower western gallery, which Presbyterianism had thrust into the old choir, was an ancient terminal figure, with hands and arms arrayed in the usual attitude of devotion. What was our horror, several years afterwards, to find an object, which had long excited our reverent admiration, stowed away in the corner of the garret of a gentleman—ay! a professed archæologist, from which durance vile it seemed to pray, although in vain, for deliverance!

The square tower has already been referred to as part of the original fabric. At a less remote period it was crowned by the steeple. The most remarkable tenant of the tower is old "Lowrie," which has given warning (as it still does) of the flight of time for more than five hundred years. He and his sister Maria (the 6th bell) were both presented to the church by Provost William Leith, in ecclesiastical expiation of his slaughter, in a quarrel, of a Bailie Catanach at Barkmill, where for many years a cairn marked the spot where the rash deed was perpetrated. Lowrie is 4 ft. 1 in,

across the mouth, weighs about 26 cwts., and sounds
F.   He was head of the house until the arrival of
the new bells, of which the largest, the tenor, weighs
about 32 cwts.   The cultivation of change-ringing
has been here retarded by various causes.   A little
is still done in that way; but, until greater proficiency is attained, parties who remember the ring-
ing of the fine old bells will regret the absence of
their random measures, when, on occasions of rejoicing, they declaimed away, at the very top of
their bent, in a transport of jubilation.

A tolerable volume might be filled with narra-
tion of matters connected with our ancient church.
At present attention shall be confined to one—

THE TRADITION OF THE RAT.

Those who attended the Mathematical School
previously to 1837 (how *long* is more *their* business
than concerns the too forwardly curious!) will recollect the boyish interest excited by the appearance,
on a string-course of the old choir, and in the angle
formed by the gable of the church and the south
side of the apse, of the figure of a quadruped,
which was pronounced to be a " rotten," and which
certainly looked as like that as anything else.
But why such a disgusting varmint in close conti-
guity with the sanctuary of the church ? Why was
it placed there ? How long it was ere reply to this

query took the following shape it is impossible to say; but the story current among the "subferulary" community and the public in general, was this :— That many years ago, during the prevalence of Romanism, the pyx, which contained the host, was missing one morning; and it turned out that an old woman had been noticed lingering about the church at the previous vespers, whereby suspicion fell upon her—that she had been tempted by the Enemy to steal the little round box, which was made of silver. An investigation and trial, under the not very scrupulous authority of the church, were gone into; and the result was, that the old woman was pronounced to be either a sacrilegious thief, or, what was much worse, a witch, and so was condemned to death. But before the sentence could be carried into execution the pyx was found at the entrance into a rat hole, the occupant of which, after his kind, showing a strange predilection for treasure not its own, and of no use to it, just like a good many of the rational creation! Of course the poor woman's innocence was thus proved; and although a witch was lost, yet, what was as good, a miracle (no doubt) was found.

Although reared, *a teneris usque unguibus*, under the shadow of the old church, and in daily view of the "rotten," it never attracted the writer's notice until the story became current in 1837. Then, indeed, it was plainly seen, and the puzzle was—how it came there.   An attentive scanning of the church showed in the immediate neighbourhood two beautifully cut chalices, crowning buttresses belonging to the apse, where stood the high altar, and where their position was thus most appropriate, as indicating one of the elements of the eucharistic mystery.   One of them stood above the " rotten."   It immediately occurred that the other element must also be symbolised in similar manner, and that what was supposed to be a representation of the sacrilegious vermin was, in reality, a rude figuration of what was intended to represent the Paschal Lamb.   To test this conjecture it occurred that, if it was well founded, the pyx, as correlative symbol, would be placed in the corresponding position on the other side of the apse, under the other chalice. Inspection at once showed that this was the case ; the whole matter afforded its own explanation ; and still, the legend of the " rotten" was just as good as others of greater pretension !—Care was taken to have those two curious objects removed to what was *considered* safe keeping ; but—well, we shall only say that, " if this should meet the eye" of any one who knows of the old stones in question, he will do well to hand them in to the writer, when, if he is not " handsomely rewarded," at least " no questions will be asked." .

CHAPTER IV.

IN describing, generally, the various parts of which the Ancient Church was composed, we have seen that the choir (where now stands the East Church) was substituted for the original chancel in the latter half of the fifteenth century. The erection was prosecuted with great zeal by the citizens. Of course St. Mary's Chapel was first built. It has a groined roof, the ribs resting on corbels, with quaint faces thereon, which are curious, and would show better were their masks of whitening washed off. The architects and master-masons of the building were John Gray and Richard Ancram; the former having of salary twenty-five merks, the latter of twenty merks per annum. The stones were imported from Caussie in Moray; the lime came from Dysart; and the lead for the roof was purchased in England in exchange for a quantity of salmon. But, notwithstanding the liberality and zeal of the citizens, the work proceeded but slowly. The death of Bishop Spens in 1480 seems to have been a great discouragement. His successor, Robert Blacader, appears to have given great offence by withdrawing certain benefactions which had been granted by his predecessor. On this subject there is a curious entry in the Council Register, which we quote as a specimen of the time :—" The VIIth day of November 1481. The Aldermen, Counsel, and Communite of the brugh of Abirdene, the Communite gadrit throw warning of the belman, ryply and weill avisit with ane assent, nane sayande the contra, has deliverit and ordinyt because that Robert elect, affirmat of Abirdon, has schavine hym unkindly in the restricion of the second tend of Abirdene quhilk is gevine by his predecessor bishop Thomas Spens, whom God assolze, to the biging of the quere of Abirdene, the forsaid Aldermen, Counsel, and Communite has decretit, deliverit, and ordinyt, that nane neighbour duelland within the said brugh, sall mak na f'mas (*fermas*—customs payable to the bishop) to the said Robert elect, na zet to nane of his factoris on his behalf. And whatever he be that dois in contrar of this act, sall tyne his fredom, and his tak sal waik, and incontinent be disponit at the will and sycht of the Aldermen, Counsel, and Communite of the said brugh, but ony faworis."

It would seem, however, that the Bishop had afterwards regained the good-will of the citizens. He was succeeded, in 1484, by Bishop Elphinstone. This illustrious prelate, the munificent benefactor of Aberdeen, prosecuted the building of the choir with as much diligence as the other great works which he projected and executed would allow. The structure was not finished, however, until 1507, when thirty-four stalls were ordered to be constructed in it for the Ecclesiastical College. John Findon contracted with the Magistrates for the execution of this branch of the work, for which he was to receive £120 (Scots), besides a bonus at their discretion. In the following year, 1508, some thirty years after the commencement of the building, it was consecrated by Bishop Elphinstone. On this occasion the Magistrates provided a sumptuous entertainment for the Bishop and his attendants ; afterwards presenting to him a propine of two puncheons of claret, with wax and sweetmeats to the amount of £16 : 3 : 8.

The ceiling, which was exactly the same as that in the chapel of King's College, was finished in 1515, as appears from the following inscription in black letter :—

Ad Laudem. Dibi. Nicholai. In. Anno. Prepositure Honorabilis Uiri Johannis Mar hoc celamen factum fuit tempore Patricii Leslie Magistri fabrice hujus ecclesie Anno Mcccccxb.

That is :—In honour of St. Nicholas, in the year of the Provostship of an honourable man, John Mar, this ceiling was made, Patrick Leslie being master of the work of this church, 1515.

The above inscription ran continuously in one line along the margin of the ceiling, on the north inner wall above the windows of the clerestory, immediately above the spring of the arch of the ceiling. About the middle of the inscription was an escutcheon with Mar's armorial bearings—viz., two boar's heads in chief, separated from a heart in base, by a chevron ; the escutcheon being flanked by his initials J. M. This inscription was removed to the west end of the modern church.

In the church thus finished there continued to be duly celebrated, for nearly half-a-century, the impressive services of a cathedral. But a great change was on the eve of consummation. Already had the principles of the Reformation been more or less publicly advocated, and the Romanist clergy began to take alarm, and to be anxious to provide against the coming storm. The people of Aberdeen, however, with characteristic caution, did not recognise the change with the same enthusiasm with which it was hailed in the south. It would seem, too, that many of the clergy saw and acknowledged that there was much room for improvement in some of their ecclesiastical brethren ; for a number of them memorialised Bishop Gordon on the subject, earnestly exhorting him, in respect of impending trouble, to do his best to reform the moral conduct of his clergy.*   Although there is some

* In one of the volumes of the Aberdeen City Register a copy of a round robin, sent in by the clergy of the diocese to their spiritual head, affords curious evidence of the lax ecclesiastical morality of the period. It is not certain whether the "Janet Knowles," or another, is the then "cause of stumbling" pointed at.

obscurity about the character of this bishop, yet there can be no doubt as to the document addressed to him by his clergy, in which he is earnestly advised to dismiss a certain female from his intimacy, in order that his good advice might have the more weight! Contemporary scandal imputed to the bishop the fatherhood of several children by this woman (Janet Knowles), and that he had provided for them out of the sale of the church lands in the Spital. This, if true, was a sad falling away, indeed, from the character and conduct of the great and good Elphinstone, whose life was a model of Christian purity.

During the memorable era of the Reformation, the early promoters of the Protestant faith carried their abhorrence of what they deemed the spiritual wickedness of the times against those high places which had been its cherished dwelling for many generations. In the height of their destructive zeal they levelled with the ground many venerable and beautiful edifices, rich in the gathered tributes of well-meaning devotees ; they defaced the images of saints which had been regarded with popular reverence for centuries, and broke down the carved work of shrines at which had been made the votive offerings of their remote forefathers. But, as already remarked, the introduction of Protestantism in Aberdeen was not attended with so much of those violent outrages which accompanied it in the southern dis-

tricts. Indeed, it would appear that those who in
that quarter had formed themselves into a band
styling themselves the " Congregation," thought it
incumbent on them to visit Aberdeen for the purpose of stimulating the supineness of its people.
Accordingly, a roaring rabble, from the south, bent
on mischief and plunder, invaded the "braif" town,
and were proceeding forthwith to assail the church
and steeple of St. Nicholas.   But, due notice having
been got of their intentions, the magistrates prudently prepared themselves for a visitation of which
they well foreknew the nature.   The sacred vessels
and appointments of the church, and certain records,
including the Council Register, had been carefully
removed to a place of safety.   When the mob
showed a fixed determination to destroy the church
—a feat not to be easily accomplished however—
the citizens, after regarding them with ill-suppressed
indignation, broke out upon and peremptorily
warned them off, as they would not allow their
mother church to be interfered with.   Baulked of
their purpose, the mob proceeded against the various religious houses, which seem to have been given
up to their fury, the hapless inmates being left to
provide for safety as best they could.   One of the
Trinity Friars was killed in the act of defending
what had been to him a home, and a refuge to
many a poor wanderer.   Ultimately, all that remained of church furniture, much of which had

disappeared, was sold *pro bono publico.* The prestige and splendour of the ancient church vanished like a dream. Protestantism gradually worked its way; but it was not until it had assumed the form of an intolerant Presbyterianism that it emulated, or even exceeded in rigour the discipline of anti-reformation times. In the rancour of ecclesiastical zeal, the mild graces of the message of peace and love were utterly neglected.

The ancient church was now altered to suit the change of faith and worship. It was divided into two kirks by partitioning off the nave and choir from the transept. At first there were no seats in either, the people either standing or sitting on chairs or stools which they brought with them. By and by corporations or individuals constructed permanent seats for their own accommodation. In the old church (as the nave was then called) the magistrates fitted up a gallery for King James VI., who frequently attended worship there.

CHAPTER V.

WE have seen that after the establishment of Protestantism the church was divided into two places of worship, of which the western was called the Old, and the eastern the New Church. In the former were only six galleries, and fewer seats than in the other. In consequence of its great age it had become rather infirm, with a corresponding loss of confidence in its stability. Notwithstanding the destructive zeal of the so-called Reformers, it retained not a little of its ancient ornamentation, chiefly in carved wood-work. We are told that on solemn occasions it was lighted up by eight double brazen chandeliers, suspended from the roof ; and that, in the centre of it, was also hung by an iron chain, a globe, " which answered for a meridian line,"—an astronomical fancy of which we discern not the mystery. The walls were ornamented with texts of Scripture painted upon them, according to the usage of the time.

It contained a good many monuments of distinguished citizens. One of these was that of Provost Alexander Chalmers of Murthill, of date 1413. The stone which bore this inscription was missing for many years, when it turned up imbedded in a wall which was taken down with the old East Kirk in 1837. It is now built into the wall of Collison's aisle, at the north-east corner. Another stone indicated the tomb of Gilbert Menzies of Pitfodels, and his spouse, Marjory Liddel—date 1433. The effigies of this ancient couple were removed, probably about the time when the church became hopelessly ruinous, to the churchyard of Maryculter, where they still lie, exposed to the variations of the weather. Is it not a pity that they should be "left out in the cold," when one would think they might find suitable protection within the walls of the institution of Blairs, which the last laird of Pitfodels left for behoof of the church of which he and his ancient line were steady adherents for so many generations? Another monument was that of Provost Fyfe—date 1436. Sir Robert Davidson's monument (1411) has been already mentioned. When the present West Church was being built, his grave was accidentally laid open, when his remains were discovered. On his head had been placed a crimson velvet cap, which was in tolerable preservation. It disappeared, and was said to have found its way into the museum of a nominal virtuoso in London; but in reality something like a resetter of stolen goods. A Thomas Branch had a monument in the nave—date 1574; Sir Paul Menzies' of Kinmundy bore date 1657; Town-Clerk Kennedy's, date 15—; Alexander Davidson of Cairnbrogie, advocate, 1666; and his son, Alexander Davidson of Newton, advocate, 1685; Dr. Duncan Liddell's, 1613. He had reposed underneath a stone in the floor of the old church, on which was fixed a beautiful incised brass. On its removal, probably when the new church was built, the brass was tossed aside into the Pity Vault, and was not discovered there until many years afterwards, when it was affixed to the wall of the present church, where it is now to be seen.

Liddell was a great benefactor of Marischal College; and the neglect with which his memorial—apart from its merit as a curious work of art—was treated, proves a degree of ungrateful vandalism altogether unpardonable. How futile all attempts to give endurance to memories, even under circumstances the most favourable! But it little matters to those whose place here shall know them no more *for ever.*

This venerable pile, after standing the brunt of elemental strife. and the bad usage of senseless zealots, for more than six centuries, began to give way. About the beginning of last century, during the performance of divine service, some plaster fell, and a groan seemed to issue from part of the old walls. The congregation became panic-stricken, and a hasty "skailing" was the consequence. The church was abandoned, and the congregation accommodated in the College Kirk. The old church seems to have been not thought worthy of reparation, or perchance there were some parties in the Council lying perdue for a job—a thing which is never thought of in *our* days, such is the potency of the alterative and restorative elixir of Reform, which some, however, seem to think has now become as dead as ditch water. Be this as it may, the building was dealt with as a broken ship by a set of felonious wreckers. The lead was stripped from the roof. The rains descended, and the winds blew and beat upon the poor old house, and at length, after a tough struggle, it fell—like Samson, carrying devastation in its fall. Many ancient monuments, and curious features of the fabric, were utterly destroyed ; and the materials appropriated to the paving of the new church and the erection of houses in the Correction Wynd, etc., where the " disjecta membra" of the red sandstone may still be recognised in contrast with the granite.

In such ruin lay the church until 1751, when the Town-Council resolved to build a new church, partly induced, no doubt, by their having received from the noted architect, Gibbs, a plan of the building, the more prized that it was a present. Gibbs was a native of Aberdeen, the son of a builder who occupied what was called the White House, in the Links. Both were Romanists and Jacobites, the son being a devoted adherent of the fortunes of the Earl of Mar. He built various churches in London, of which St. Martin's-in-the-Fields is a lasting monument of his genius and taste. He also built the Radcliffe Library, and other fabrics which are justly admired. The master-mason of the new church was James Wyllie of Edinburgh, whose name appears on a little slab of white marble inserted into the wall of the church, on the north side of the western window, very near the top. Tradition reports him to have been a very handsome young fellow, who so turned the heads of the young ladies of the town that they actually followed him, admiringly, in his favourite walks ; the fair of our day seem to reserve any approach to such homage for young and good-looking (more or less) preachers. The master wrights were Archibald Chessels and James Heriot of Edinburgh. The church cost altogether about £6000, the whole being defrayed from the particular funds belonging to the church ; and *no part of the charge was either imposed upon the inhabitants, or contributed by them.** Golden age! We trust the surplus treasure has been guarded with dragon jealousy, and that it is still available. Then, no mention shall be made of voluntary subscriptions compulsorily exacted — or exorbitant seat-rents—or cunningly-devised bazaars—or frigid soirees — or grinding taxation, like that which threatens us for the lumbering, useless congeries of stone and lime called the new municipal buildings.

Many there are who know not, that to a wild building mania was attributed the bankruptcy of the Corporation in 1817, when the town was sub-

* To move for a return of the monies received as revenue from seat-rents, and to set off this sum against the amount paid as stipend to the different city clergymen now representing the old parish of St. Nicholas, is a fashionable bit of clap-trap with some *reformed* representatives of the people. These gentlemen are far above taking any notice of the value of the fishings in the Bay of Nigg—the revenues of the glebe lands of Fittie—or the present money product of the thousand and one confiscations made of Holy Mother Church's funds.

jected to the disgrace of disfranchisement. If our citizens will not be taught by experience resistance to such projects, undertaken and prosecuted by parties who risk not a penny in the reckless venture, well may it be said, as of the Galatians—O! foolish Aberdonians! who hath bewitched you!

A SUMMER EVENING WALK WITH LUCY.

> " Dulce ridentem Lalagen amabo,
>   Dulce loquentem ! "

COME ! and let us, free from care,
Taste a bliss which none may share !
Bliss—which freshens every sense—
Dew of love and innocence !
From the city let us hie,
Far from ken of common eye,
To the deep-retired green-wood,
(Sweet retreat of solitude !)
Where the wanton evening breeze
Toys with the yielding trees ;—
Where the thrush, from hidden spray,
Pours its varied roundelay,
While the cuckoo's simple note
Ever and anon doth float,
O'er russet heath and bright'ning fields
Where the lark its bower builds ;—
O ! the transports of its song
Shed the welkin blue along !—
Let us seek the spreading moor,
Where the sheep their pasture poor
Nibble, midst the furze and broom,
Flaunting in their scented bloom !

Sweet to mark the puny lamb
Toddling to its bleating dam !
Sweet to see it suck its fill
While the mother stands so still !—
Sweet to hear the lively linnet
Tell the tale of love that's in it !
Sweet to hear its callow brood
Faintly chirping for their food ;
While the mother every wile
Tries—our footsteps to beguile,—
Flutters in a false alarm
Where she apprehends no harm !
Come along ! and list, with me,
Th' humming of belated bee ;
Sweet to hear it, all alive,
Booming to the busy hive !
Would I were some wand'ring bee,
Could I find sweet flowers—like thee !
List—the beetle's drowsy horn !
List—the land-rail midst the corn !
Let the ravished hearing mark
Music—in the watch-dog's bark !
Music—in the lengthened lowe
Of the home-returning cow !
Music—in the shrill huzza
Of the youngling rustic's play !
How the eye exults to roam
O'er wide heaven's cloudless dome,
Gazing on the setting sun
As he rests on mountain dun.
Down he is !—but we shall soon
Find companion in the moon,—
See ! she peers above the ocean—

Serene—amid its deep commotion!
Bootless though her friendly ray
To our loving—ling'ring way,
While we see her calmly roll,
Oh !—'tis healing to the soul !
Feebly though a star or two
Twinkle in the depth of blue,—
One flashes in the west above—
Enough ! enough !—the star of love !
Come !—and let our mutual glance
Nature's every charm enhance !
More than all her charms I spy
In the glances of that eye !
As they dart from thee to me—
Signs which none may feel save we!
How I love to hear thy tongue
All these pleasant sounds among !
Wrapt in a delicious dream—
Heedless of it should I seem ;
Chide me !—I will not complain !
Since I hear thee speak again !
Nought a rapture can impart
Like words glowing from the heart,
Save it be—the conscious flutter
Of the love—it may not utter,
When it glistens in the eye—
Thrills the blood—and wakes the sigh !
What these sights—these sounds to me ?—
What were life—if wanting thee ?—

*　　*　　*　　*　　*

Ah ! there is—there is a balm
In this hour of eve—so calm !
On its downy wing it bears

Sweet oblivion of the cares—
Toils—and fears—and woes of life—
Toils—and fears—and woes so rife !
If a foretaste e'er be given
Of the unknown bliss of Heaven :—
If the blessed e'er be sent
To our earth—on mercy bent—
Prompting good—or warding ill
With a power—strong though still :
If a chosen time there be,
For the parting soul to flee
From its prison-house of clay
To the realms of nightless day :—
Heaven-caught feeling whispers reason—.
" This—this must be the hallow'd season ! "

GRAMMAR SCHOOL REMINISCENCES.

THE MAY PLAY.

To the cherished associations investing this most ancient, well-conducted, and useful seminary, no little violence has occasionally been done by the tamperings of pretentious innovation. But, while some new arrangements may claim approval on the score of manifest utility, yet the undeniable results of others seem to be gradually awakening, in the public mind, the conviction that mere change is not always synonymous with improvement. We must be permitted to regret the removal of the school from a locality where it had flourished for some six centuries, a memorial of royal munificence, of which it proved itself not unworthy, by the fruits of the labours of many an able and zealous teacher in succeeding generations. It was certainly in operation towards the close of the thirteenth

century, years not a few, before the foundation of
Winchester and of Eton, and long before grammar
schools were rather common in England. It became famous for many eminent masters, whose
qualifications it was customary to test by rigorous
examination. Among the more ancient we find
the names of Cargill, Reid, and Wedderburn ; in
later times we may note Dr. James Dun, who was
either master or rector for the long period of
seventy-two years ; his son-in-law, Beattie, the
poet ; and Dr. Melvin, of our own day. We
humbly think that an effort might have well been
made in favour of a reasonable sacrifice to the old
genius loci, even on the score of its demonstrated
convenience for the eastern, as well as for the
western, quarters of the city. Where there is the
will there is the way. Might it not have been
possible to acquire the present Gordon's Hospital
for the purposes of a grammar school, and other
public seminaries ; transferring the former to the
site of the new Grammar School, a situation
most desirable, for various reasons, for such an
institution?— But enough of such matters which
are but incidentally connected with our present
object, and regarding which we have no wish to
provoke controversy or to dogmatise.

To those, whose recollections are more or less
synchronal with our own, the return of the merry
month of May must evoke recollection of the holi-

day enjoyment of its first three days, a standing privilege of the Grammar School boys, in commemoration of the foundation of the school, which has been recently abandoned. A still older school tradition places somewhere near the top of Harriet Street; while the oldest was probably part of the monastic buildings of the Black Friars, which stood somewhere near the site of Gordon's Hospital.

Of all the play-days, the first three days of May were the most delightful. They were a kind of *gude send.* We even thought more of them, for all their shortness, than of the *Simmer Play*, or the *Christmas Play.* These we looked on as our own, by right of common use and wont. They were the same at *all* schools; but the *May Play* was the peculiar glory of *our* school. We could enjoy the privileged pleasure of sauntering about the streets, and cracking boyish jokes at the expense of some less favoured comrades who were creeping unwillingly to some other school. Or, we would gaze at the prints and story-books in the booksellers' windows; and feast our eyes, if not our appetites, with the tempting cates in the confectioner's. Then, we had no long task to mar the enjoyment of those holidays. Besides, they came on us in the sweet prime of the year, when everything around us was glad. We seemed to share the joys of Nature's own holidays.

A party of some half-dozen of us, perhaps, meet

by accident in the street. The day is bright and
breezy ; how to spend it is settled in general council. The question of ways and means is matter of
inquiry. Our consolidated funds are rather limited,
but are considered on the whole sufficient. After
due deliberation, " the Rocks!" (at Nigg) is the
word. So, off we go, ever and anon capering along
the streets at a speed which seems rather superflu-
ous in those who have the whole day at their com-
mandment, as Falstaff says. Crossing the *Plainstanes*, we fail not, of malice prepense, to count the
fishwives, careless of a broadside of Billingsgate
from the clamorous crew. The declivity of Marischal Street naturally leads us in a sort of gallop
to the quay, where we hail our old friend, *Jupiter*,
take a sham shy at his target of gingerbread, thereby
incurring his ready and fervent, but by no means
refined malison. Arrived at the Lime Sheds, which
we pass, enveloped, like our " pius *Æneas*," in a
white cloud, we encounter that formidable person-
age, *Water Kelpie*, whom, of course, we cannot pass
without a word of recognition. The natural consequences are—a chase—a half-brick thundering
after us—a volley of articulation not to be recorded
—smithy danders, and various other missiles in
rapid succession. But we are too nimble for the
enemy, and "We care not who sees our backs."
So we *cut* through *Middle Third*, and scarcely think
ourselves safe until we reach the *Boil House*, where

we meet *Eelie Betty* in hermaphrodite apparel— politely beg a Sunday of her jacket, and are by her treated with silent contempt.

We then endeavour to work our passage across the ferry, two of us hanging on to one oar, to the amusement, perhaps the annoyance, of the boat- man, who taunts us with the observation that he "wants nane o' our wark." Landed, away we scour to the rocks, laughing, speaking all at once, slapping each other, and playing all sorts of tricks. Here we spend the livelong day, alike insensible to the cravings of hunger, and careless of strict paren- tal injunction to "come hame in time." The hours pass swiftly along. We cram ourselves with dilse, tangles, and badderlocks (active our digestion), hunt for young crabs, fish for sæthes, collect shells, set off flists of gunpowder by means of a spectacle eye, perform various gymnastic feats, bathe in the sea, and so forth, until the lengthening shadows and declining sun admonish us of home. Wearied with play and exhausted by hunger, which neither buoyant spirits can stave off, nor our scanty provant of bap or biscuit appease, we slink homewards, when, perhaps, we narrowly escape a rencontre with "the Maister" (Nicol), whose well-known form is readily recognised by the *hat*—perched in a most authoritative attitude on the top of his deeply- powdered head—the *cane* stuck under his left arm, both hands thrust into his breeches pockets—while his snow-white stockings display to advantage the shapely limb, and the peremptory gesticulation of the foot which stamps the law to all the juvenile subjects of his most absolute government! At length we reach our respective homes, where some cold collation and a hearty scolding, with sundry cuffs, perhaps, by way of clincher, are our inevitable portion. These we endeavour to take as coolly as possible, and soon, in slumbers light, seek forgetfulness of the transactions of the day.

To those who delight thus to live over again such days of buoyant spirits and exuberant health, is it not matter of thankfulness to feel—that the petrifying influence of weary years of incessant yet often fruitless toil—that the heart-sickness arising from the frequent experience of reasonable hopes blighted in the bud—that the disgust naturally consequent on concourse unavoidable with the proud, the false, the fickle, the ungrateful, and the vain— that all the soul-searing effects of a chequered life have still left their hearts impressible by renewed familiarity with the long-remembered sports and haunts of their youth? In the outward man Old Time may have wrought much regretful change. More years ago than they care to confess even to themselves, light was their step as their hearts ; their locks were of brightest chestnut, their eyes beamed with courage and with hope. Now—fast are they falling into the sear and yellow leaf, years are silvering o'er what care may have left of once sunny locks, while " those that look out of the windows are darkened" indeed. But, let Time do his worst ; they grumble not at his ravages—'tis the common lot. His chilling influence cannot quite quench the fire of youth. If years have robbed them of many external enjoyments, they have learnt to seek, not in vain, enjoyments within themselves.

" THE VISITATION."

Time has been when this heading must have suggested to many a reader feelings which he may now, perhaps, have some difficulty in re-awakening. Men long accustomed to the world, in its most worldly sense, may be somewhat apt to forget that the rising race have a world of their own too, and just as rife with enterprise, anxiety, and care, in its own way, as that in which your reverend seigniors fret their hour.

With all the youthful disciples of our public schools, "The Visitation" was a very great day indeed. More especially used this to be the case with the Grammar School at the period to which our reminiscences extend, but of which the distance we care not much to confess—a silence in which a remnant of condisciples will mayhap approvingly acquiesce. Be this as it may, in our day the Visitation of the Grammar School was an occasion marked by a solemnity bordering on the awful. Its advent was looked forward to with much anxious forecast of its eventualities, for at least three months previous to its actual arrival. As it approached, the anxiety felt by youthful aspirants to scholastic distinction increased to rather painful intensity. In the two junior classes, what keen competition to secure a seat within the honoured bounds of the first four " factions," before the places were stopped— when fixed the fate of all remained ! In the higher classes, what hoarding of " phrases !" what collation of " idioms !" what rivalship in daily " trial versions !" The day before the Visitation was a half-holiday, but most falsely so called, for its afternoon was one of painful preparation, and no trifling perturbation of spirit. No use *now* to count the hours to the great day—it came with to-morrow's sun ! In vain the endeavour to beguile the moments of aching suspense by the ruling of version paper, the mending of pens, and the revisal of neglected lessons. All this brushing up of arms only served to keep up the anxiety connected with the approaching contest. Then there was such rigorous ablution of the person—that of Saturday was nothing to it ! No wonder ; had we not to pass muster before " authorities "—civic, clerical, and academic ! At length the appointed hour of meeting approached. How many smartly arrayed, rosy little fellows, did that morning behold trudging rather pensively from all quarters towards the Schoolhill, bending under load unwonted of dictionaries, and grammars, and phrase books, that nothing might be wanting in such munitions of scholastic war. Manifold their conjecturing as to "the version"—serious the speculation as to the chances of individual failure or success. Some, with a modesty which became their idleness as much as their youth, would declare that they did not expect "a book." Others, whose experience had sought consolation under disappointment by reference to cases of neglected desert, ventured an opinion that they ought to get prizes; but they had their doubts about getting fair play. They had no friends—not they—in the Council. But the actual hour of meeting disperses the little groups of such speculators; each takes his seat in the "public school;" the catalogue is called amid silence as universal as unwonted, and all is tiptoe expectation for the arrival of the visitors. The whole school has undergone a lustration which carries something solemn with it, from its very rarity. The floors have actually been dusted over with clean sand, which gives additional impressiveness to the authoritative tread of the "Masters," as they pace to and fro. And is not the Rector, arrayed in his gown, so grand?—just like a professor!—an indication of pomp and circumstance to be seen on such occasions only—a demonstration which impresses the " Eelieytes" with ideas of the dignity of " the seminary" which have ne'er before entered their little craniums, although, with the upper classes, it is rather the butt of daring witticism. But bold indeed are they who would hazard even a suppressed titter, whatever the provocation, at such a crisis ; for the hour is come, and the men ! It is heralded by the measured tread of the town serjeants, glimpses of whose red coats are caught through the windows, like flashes of lightning !

What solemn courtesy in the greetings between masters and visitors, the former positively appearing bareheaded, which shows us boys that there *are* greater men in the world even than they, albeit that may avail us nought in sub-ferulary hour !

The " dask" is completely filled with visitors, the Provost presiding—but precentor-wise, to the " knock !" The " dask" assumes in our eyes new importance—*miratur novos frondes*—and looks as though it were intended for better things than " burrie," and all sorts of madcap pranks. Then the Rector delivers a speech—a Latin one ! It sounds like a trial version. The great " version" is then given out. It is something about the Romans, or the Greeks, or the Carthaginians ; Epaminondas ; Turnus, king of the Rutuli ; or at least Hamilcar— all familiar acquaintances of ours. Perhaps it is a plaguy passage from modern history—a thing by no means agreeable to our classical tastes; or it may smack somewhat of the marvellously philosophical, beginning with—"A certain author relates," followed by the qualification, "but I know not whether it be true," which is merely a trap for young grammarians; for it is of no earthly consequence whether the relation be true or not. Ah! the careful pen-scraping, distinctly audible in the hush of that awful hour! Is it not the commencement of a struggle on which is hung the chance, not of a "book" merely, but, tentatively, of a "buss?" The dictation ended, the competitors are left to their fate. Unassisted, they must fight it out. Some get through the business rather rapidly. On the painful labours of others, the shadows of that shortish day rather ominously fall—and the latest at length leave the school, and *cetera divis.* Each has done his best, and a Porson could do no more.

In our day the prize-books were given on the night of the day on which they were won. During the whole evening the Schoolhill was in an uproar. It swarmed with groups of scholars comparing notes about their versions. Here and there might be seen a "colleginer" laying down the law grammatical to a "buroch" of eager, inquiring juniors; squibs and crackers flew about in all directions; bells and knockers were compelled to vigorous exercise of their calling; shutters were exposed to wanton assault and battery. Old folks wondered what things would come to ; that finishers of the law would have more work was quite clear !

The row at length was extinguished on the appearance, about ten o'clock, of the municipal authorities, in darkling procession, guided by the leading lights of the sergeants, two and two abreast (although not " trumpeters !"), each bearing a lantern radiant with a couple of candles. Again, is the " dask" crowded with the honourable, the reverend, the learned. The well-powdered head of the Town-Clerk towers amid the full blaze of " fours in the pound !" He unrolls the scroll of fate. The names of the successful competitors are announced by him rather with the voice of one having authority than of a mere scribe. Each fortunate rogue bustles up in front, and receives (with a *rax*) from the Provost's own hand the much prized book— the honour acknowledged by a bow, bespeaking more gratefulness than gracefulness. Many, of course, are disappointed, but they soon forget their sorrow in the pastimes of the holiday week. So much of sketchy reminiscence of " auld langsyne." Who is insensible to the feelings which such retrospection suggests ?—

> " Be it a weakness, it deserves some praise,
>   We love the play-place of our early days ;
>   The scene is touching, and the heart is stone
>   That feels not at that sight, and feels at none.

The wall on which we tried our graving skill—
The very name we carved subsisting still ;
The bench on which we sat, while deep employed,
Though mangled, hacked, and hewed, yet not destroyed—
The little ones, unbuttoned, glowing hot
Playing our games, and on the very spot,
As happy as we once—
The pleasing spectacle at once excites
Such recollection of our own delights,
That, viewing it, we seem almost to obtain
Our innocent, sweet, simple years again.
This fond attachment to the well-known place,
Whence first we started into life's long race,
Maintains its hold with such unfailing sway,
We feel it e'en in age and at our latest day."

AN OLD ABERDONIAN.

SKETCHED FROM LIFE.

FORTH from his mansion—just at ten o'clock—
Struts the learned Banker, like a turkey cock,
Burly and big : behold him sail along,
Wit in his wink, and wisdom on his tongue !
Through Silver Street he steers for Golden Square,
Soon Diamond Street proclaims his presence there !
Then Union Street must feel, in all its stones,
The heavy burden of his beef and bones !
Here—let us mark him as—with look profound
And solemn gait, he clears the granite ground
Right to the Bank—the scene of all his labour,
Where Willie G— was once his drouthy neighbour ;
Famed Greece and Rome may, jointly, claim his nose ;
His cheek is red—the cause you may suppose ;
His mouth is but a so so perforation,
Through which to dole the frequent long oration !
His eye—though never meant to face a battle—
Would grace a calf, or some such other cattle.
Now for his dress :—Unbutton'd, his surtout
Exposes fully to convenient view
A goodly corporation, *a priori*,
To balance matters, a posteriori.
The knowing cocking of his glossy castor
Proclaims to all the sapience of its master ;

'Tis smartly worn *agee*, in guise so *jemmy*,
And looks as if 'twould say—" How d'ye do, demme."
If hats like heads could speak, 'twould say, moreover,
" O ! what a precious noddle I do cover !"
At times, you know, he has a social trick
In seeking chumship with a walking stick ;
Athwart his shoulder when, anon, it lies,
He grasps it—like a trooper, falchion-wise,
And seems about to charge, with all his chivalry,
On all who dare to show the slightest devilry.
But—if a pendant posture rather please—
The cane inclines just forty-five degrees
To terra firma ; you then would lay a wager
Its owner was a rather uppish gauger ;
Meet him, the silent greeting of his eye
And measured bow announce him who but I ?
Or if he choose to play the waggish shaver,
A nod and wink, say, " dang it ! no palaver ;"
Talk of the times—he shakes his head, and then
What does he ? why, he shaketh it again !
His finger laid, right gently, on his nose,
Conveys to all how very much he knows ;
And, eke could tell ; but catch him, if you can !
He knows—ay does he !—yes !—he knows his man !
Behold him at the window of the Bank,
Just where the coalmen used to sit in rank
And file, to catch a lucky job, or else
To cram with *partans, badderlocks*, and *delse!*
Ah ! how august appears the Banker's mien,
Through the transparent window often seen ;
With what an air he takes a pinch of snuff,
Of which his noddle needs a quantum suff,
To clear the murky vapours of his brain,

And send them, dropping, through his nasal drain ;
Forth from his vest he takes the polished box,
Then gives the lid some peremptory knocks ;
A moment pauses—with an upward look
In solemn musing—just as if he took
Time to consider what he was about—
With all great men 'tis usual, no doubt—
Then from the fragrant dust he takes a doze,
The thumb taps on the brink, the snuff up goes
Into the very garret of his gnomon ;
At brown rappee the Banker yields to no man :
And if a few stray grains the deed betray,
These same few grains he deftly puffs away,
Hast thou e'er seen him at a sale of books ?
How very, very knowing were his looks ;
How solemnly he said, " a penny more !"
How gravely turned the purchased volume o'er :
" A rare edition this, I know it well,
If known by others, it would surely sell
For ten times more—but half-a-crown is plenty
For such a work-—prized but by *cognoscenti.*"
Off to his library with it he'll steal,
As magpies sometimes silver spoons conceal.
In sooth, he is a man of various knowledge,
His very clerks must now be bred at college :
In parts and learning he may truly pass
For a Scotch cousin of Sir Hudibras
Macenas, he of teachers, fiddlers, painters,
Professors, parsons, lecturers, precentors.
But to conclude, lest we should overstrain,
His whole deportment says, in language plain,
" Such men as I, you know, are rather rare,
So, if you please, you'll just as well take care."

ABERDONIANA.

THE OLD EAST KIRK—NOTABLES AND NOTABILIA.

So fertile is this subject, that the task of preferential selection is rather perplexing. The congregation, as a whole, was somewhat peculiar. It was mainly composed of respectable burghal families of the middle class, with a considerable portion of artizans, and a sufficiently marked garnishing of citizens of the better class, the representatives of old families whose members had frequented this church for many generations. They were all more or less known to each other. Seldom were they found wandering into other churches. On Communion occasions Dr. Ross's personal piety and the fervour of his addresses attracted a large number of communicants from other congregations— the services beginning at 9 A.M., and continuing until 4 P.M.; as many as thirteen tables and nearly 3000 communicants have been known to participate in the solemnity. On those occasions the collections of money at the door were exceedingly liberal, and

were privately and delicately distributed among
members of the congregation who had seen better
days. In those days no individual members presumed to dictate to their fellow-worshippers in
church matters, nor did the ministers aim at lord-
ing it over God's heritage. Among all there was
a deep conviction of the importance of the one
thing needful ; and the mutual knowledge of each
other prevalent in the congregation was not favourable to the cultivation of individual simulation or
dissimulation.

We have already noticed the grave earnestness
with which all parts of the services were conducted.
In that of praise the congregation had not the advantage of much artistic skill in their leader; nevertheless, precentor Cowie got on reasonably well.
He taught a venture school, which was frequented
by sailors not a few ; and he rather plumed himself on his elocutionary powers, which he would
display, evidently with much self-satisfaction, in the
winter afternoons, when he "read out the line" by
the light of a couple of candles, which, with the like
number twinkling on the pulpit, were all that
served to make darkness visible in the venerable
kirk. About the year 1812, however, or thereby,
an impulse was given to the psalmody in all the
churches, by the appointment of Mr. John Knott
to the precentorship of the West Church. He was
an Englishman, from Newcastle, and, if we mistake

not, had been by trade a baker. He was a respectable and very gentlemanly, stoutish man, of nearly middle height (age thirty or forty), with a fine fresh complexion, beautifully-curling fair hair, and an easy roll in his gait—in fact—an Englishman all over. He had a powerful mellow voice (tenor), and a very animated — somewhat declamatory manner in singing. He introduced several new tunes, but all of the best classical style. The tune which got him his appointment was St. Stephen's, at that time new to the Aberdonians. This fine tune he sang alone (of course) with triumphant effect. He became at once immensely popular both as a precentor and teacher of music. He had a psalmody class of some 200, whom he taught in the western gallery of the West Church. In addition to the other emoluments of his office, he had the proceeds of an annual concert, patronised by the Town-Council. Gradually some of his tunes found their way into the East Church, and other churches both in town and country. Mr. Knott ultimately became precentor of St. George's, Edinburgh, where he closed his career. In this city he gave an impulse to psalmody, which has been cherished ever since. We must not omit to mention that Mr. Knott was sometimes accompanied by Mrs. Knott singing a part. She had a remarkably fine and powerful voice.

Nevertheless, while William Cowie sang, the tunes

prevalent in the East Church were all of the plainer
and graver sort. Some tunes there were, indeed,
which William, although a bold singer if left to
himself, would not have dared to raise in the old
kirk. There was " Blackburn," for instance ; he
has been seen to shake his head, and look grave at
a proposal to sing *that* tune. Indeed, he was so
short-winded, that he naturally preferred those
tunes which the congregation, once started, could
sing without much of his guidance. Once, however—but only once—did we see him sorely put to
it, and that by none other than good easy Robert
Doig, who was certainly the last man in the world
to annoy William, or any one else, of malice prepense. It is to be observed that the great majority
of our Psalms are in what is called common
measure. There are two or three, however, of such
"peculiar" measure that there seems to have been
a doubt whether, like the majority, they were,
according to the old phraseology, "fit to be sung
in churches." In these cases there is always
"another of the same," in the common measure,
and this is the version which is usually given out.
Now, among these "kittle" measures is one of the
versions of the 148th Psalm, which had never been
known to be sung in the church at all. One sultry
afternoon, however, when William was reposing on
the certainty of the common version being given
out, to his utter consternation and evident tribula-

tion, Mr. Doig gave out the very "peculiar" measure, and that in the coolest manner possible, just as though there had been nothing extraordinary in the matter. He seems to have been actuated by sheer curiosity to know what sort of a tune suited the kittle measure ; or, in short, whether it was singable at all ! William, however, although well knowing that not one of the congregation could join, screwed up his courage, and started the proper tune, a lively lilt, with the aggravation of a chorus—to the amazement, not to say scandal, of the dumfoundered congregation, who regarded such a wanton demonstration as provocative of nothing short of some judgment or other. We warrant you, such a trick was not tried again.

In those days we had no poor-laws or poor-house. The poor were supported partly by begging —the " blue-gowns " or king's beadsmen having licence for this vocation—and partly by a monthly pittance voluntarily contributed at " the plate," by entrant worshippers. Once a quarter there was an extraordinary collection, when, on the previous Sunday the claims of the poor were read from the pulpit in the following rather peculiar style :—

Boys in the house	40
Orphans maintained at nurses . .	25
Poor on the out-pension list . .	322
Poor on the occasional supplies . .	413
Total	800

Coffins have also been *distributed to seventeen poor people* since the last quarterly collection. A "deal" of coffins was certainly rather picturesque.

Among the notables were, of course, included the elders; and of these, Robert Stronach was rather a character. He was a wright by trade, in easy circumstances, and was proprietor of some houses in a close in Castle Street which still goes by his name, although sometimes called the "Shelly" Close, for a peculiarity which no longer distinguishes it. Robert was a tallish and rather bulky man, with a large dewlap, a brown wig, old-fashioned clothes, and a long staff, like the "broom-stick o' the witch of Endor, weel shod wi' brass." Portly was his presence when, with a jaunty air and a sort of *andante* movement, he advanced up the middle "pass" to his seat in the body. of the kirk, Saunders Matheson's father, as beadle, bobbing along before him. Robert was always primed with *politesse*, more especially to ladies, and especially at communion times, for some reason or other which might have been more easily surmised than explained. But Robert's peculiar fancy was the decoration of his houses with shells stuck on the walls with plaster in various fantastic forms. With this view it was his custom to traverse the sea-beach after storms, and pick up the shells which Ocean in his agony had vomited. These he stowed away in the capacious pockets of a blue greatcoat, which it was his comfort to wear on such occasions. His occasional competitors were schoolboys rummaging for " carn tangles," a marine delicacy suitable for no stomach but theirs, or that of an ostrich. Like one of the soldiers of the conchological Roman Emperor, Robert would return home laden with the spoils of the deep, which in due time figured, painted in various colours, on the walls of his tenements. Robert at length disappeared from his little sphere, but not until he had buried spouses twain. In the churchyard of the Aul'ton is the following characteristic epitaph on his second wife, evidently written by himself :—

" Here lies, &c.—spouse to Robert Stronach, wright, in Stronach's Close, New Aberdeen ; who desires to be laid in the same grave with her *after* his decease. They, who have lived together in love, may *innocently desire to lie together in the grave.*"

From the demurrer insinuated in the above, it is clear that Robert had no notion of anything like *suttee*, or premature interment ; while his fancy about his posthumous disposal would have been quite innocent, even had he and his spouse been the torment of each other's lives—an occurrence so rare (?) in the conjugal state.

THE OLD EAST KIRK.

In our last paper we endeavoured to recall the features of this venerable place of worship, as they appeared just before it was rudely swept away by the hand of miscalled improvement. A few particulars may here be added. On a small wooden shield, affixed (inside) to the north wall of the central aisle, was the following inscription :—" Hanc sacram ædem reficien*dum* curavit Ninianus Johnston— 1792." This gentleman was Master of Kirk Work in his day ; and the repairs which he ordered were as little creditable to his taste, as the above inscription was to his Latinity, although proficiency in this way is not to be expected of a Town Councillor. This is probably the reason why some members of that worshipful body are so fond of tampering with the system of teaching pursued at our Grammar School, a seminary which has, nevertheless, produced a very creditable array of eminent scholars. We think that, before a councillor is permitted to dogmatise on such matters, he ought to be required to furnish some proof of his " knowledge qualification "—say—not to pitch the thing too high—of his ability to decline *penna, a pen.* Something of this sort would not only be good for the school, but would prevent the councillor from making a greater fool of himself than nature intended that he should be. We recollect that that admirable teacher, Mr.

Nicol, used to propound the above inscription to his pupils as bad Latin for their correction. But this by the way.

Below the lowest eastern gallery was a seat for one person, which had formerly been a stall in the choir, for the accommodation of some tuneful Canon, but which was latterly set apart for—the hangman ! The last seatholder was Robbie Welsh, who dropped from the stage about the end of last century. The Norman arch at the west end of the church had been built up soon after the Reformation. The opposite arch was of course built up when the West Church was erected. The northern arch was built up when the present East Church was completed. The walls of the transept and the piers of the central arches were profusely covered with fine plaster, partly under the impression that this would preserve the clustered pillars from decay. They are very ancient ; and some care was taken not to obliterate the few simple decorations which their capitals present. We have already mentioned that these arches, and the central tower which they support, are the oldest parts remaining of the original church. The bizarre windows in the tower, however, are not original, but a repair executed under the auspices of an amateur architect, one Anderson, laird of Bourtie, about the year 1785 or so. The original arches (as good as ever) were Early Pointed, and seem to have included, each, two lights. In this tower were occasionally confined poor creatures, to whom the cruel ignorance of a barbarous age imputed witchcraft. In old times bells were christened and dedicated to some saint with great ceremony, and were thus considered as being endued with miraculous powers, occasionally useful in dispelling storms and defeating other pranks of the prince of the power of the air. Our system of storm-signals, with its " drums," etc., was not known in those days.

Peter Kerr, in his day, was very particular about the names of the bells. The three original bells were named *Laurence*, *Maria*, and *St. Nicholas*. About the beginning of this century, when the work of celebrating our frequent victories over Bonaparte was, perhaps, considered too hard for the original bells considering their great age, two bells were added by way of reinforcing the tintinnabulary staff, of which one was named by Peter—" Little St. Nicholas ;" the other, " St. James," in honour of the Masonic Lodge of that name, at the head of which Peter, as Master, would occasionally issue on St. John's day in all the glory of its mystic para- phernalia from the hall at the head of Mutton Brae ! The bells recently procured by the public have not, so far as we know, been named. As they were added under the auspicies of Provost Webster, perhaps the tenor might be suitably named St. John ; while the D *flat*, in respect of there being no

St. William, its silence and somewhat hoaxy character, might be called *La Trappe.* Since the departure of the English " change " teachers, whom the beverages of our country did not suit so well as those of their native land, there has not been much of change-ringing, a want not much felt, as few of our citizens know " change-ringing" even when they hear it.   However, we must, meantime, *hotter* on the best way we can.

At the period to which we refer, the East Kirk was a collegiate charge, the pastors being Dr. Ross and Mr. Robert Doig, who preached alternately. Dr. Ross was the son of a most respectable teacher of a school in Aberdeen, and was distinguished as a pupil of Principal Campbell.   He was for some time private tutor to the boy Byron, who spoke of him in terms of affection and respect.   The good man would often speak regretfully of his pupil's wayward manhood, but, inspired as he was by that charity which thinketh no evil, he would still indulge hope of the poet's reformation.   Ross was originally a candidate for Trinity Chapel, along with Doig and a Mr. Cowie, who ultimately became a distinguished minister of the Congregational denomination in Montrose.   The popular choice, or rather the partial fancy of a forward and pretentious clique, turned the scale in favour of Mr. Doig, a jolly fresh-looking man, with a powerful voice, and a rather orthodox drawl.   But Mr.

Robert had another advantage which his partizans knew not of. He had borrowed a sermon of Cowie's, and, of course by the merest accident, he preached it as his trial sermon for Trinity Chapel! Both Ross and Cowie were rejected; but the East Kirk folks were soon after unanimous in petitioning the Council for the former, and the patrons had the good sense to grant the prayer of the petition. A more fortunate appointment never was made. Ross at once showed how deeply his heart was in his profession. The congregation rapidly increased, until every seat in the old church was crammed. His pulpit ministrations, thoroughly scriptural and always practical, were delivered with a fervid unction, which brought them at once home to the hearts of his hearers, and effectually alarmed the too just fears of the most callous of his flock. His manner was such as Cowper has so beautifully and strikingly traced of the preacher, such as St. Paul himself, were he on earth, would approve. Our readers will do well to refer not only to this noble passage, but to all the leading poems of, perhaps, the greatest of uninspired bards, whose works will live when time and improved taste shall have consigned to merited and ever-during oblivion the fantastic trashy rhymes of self-complacent poetasters, panderers to false taste—perhaps to prurient imaginations; patronised by mercenary trafficking publishers, and puffed by the prostitution of hireling critics.

Dr. Ross possessed not the advantage of a commanding figure; but his countenance and manner were highly impressive from the unmistakable evidence they afforded of the permanence and strength of his religious convictions, and of the truly earnest interest which he took in the spiritual welfare of his flock. And, above all, his life and conversation were a practical illustration and enforcement of his preaching. As long as health and strength permitted, his feet were frequent at the bedsides of the poor, the sick, the disconsolate, and the dying. Possessed of ample private means, his charities were as liberal as unostentatious. His devotion to his duties, and his simple tastes, left him little time or inclination for social festivities; yet was he "given to hospitality" in a plain genial way, while his table and house were ever open to honest fellow-labourers of all denominations. Although always rather serious, he was the reverse of being gloomy or ascetic, but was distinguished by a serene cheerfulness, the inseparable blessing of a conscience void of offence towards God and man.

The worthy Dr. Ross, to whose memory we have paid a tribute, how inadequate soever, continued to "run his godly race" with unfailing acceptance, when his faith was tried by a signal chastisement of divine love, in the form of the premature death of his only son, a young man of varied accomplishment and most amiable character, between whom and his father there subsisted the deepest affection, consecrated by the sincere piety common to both. The son had just attained his majority ; had completed a successful career at college ; was prosecuting his theological studies, was devoting much attention to literature, more especially to the languages of the East ; and was returning from a continental tour, buoyant with health and hope, and ardent for the renewal of his duties as assistant teacher of Greek in Marischal College ;—when an accidental fall from the top of a Belgian *diligence* inflicted an injury which confined him to a couch which in a few months proved his death-bed. A trying situation this for one so young, animated by the prospect of that legitimate distinction which crowns a life of unpretending usefulness ; but the youth had been educated in another school than that of the mere learning and wisdom of this world, of which it has been said that it sometimes only " increaseth sorrow." Hence the sweet serenity, the uniform cheerfulness, the humble but unflagging hope of his numbered days. How deeply the spirit of the father was wounded it is needless to say. While the son's fate was but too certain, although the parent's heart was still unwilling to anticipate the worst while life yet trembled in the scale, what a touching thing it was to mark the struggling animation with which the worthy pastor discharged his usual duties, and the profound sympathy with which the hearts of his conscious and devoted flock throbbed responsive to the conflict of feeling which would sometimes all but overcome their beloved minister. But, when all was over, when dust had returned to dust, and Spirit to Spirit, the result of the conflict between parental affection and an inspiration holier still, became apparent in the text selected by the worthy Doctor for his first sermon after his son's death—"What I do thou knowest not now, but thou shalt know hereafter."—For some time the Doctor continued to preach, but aided by Mr., afterwards Dr. Black. Indeed, for a good many years, his delicate health obliged him to seek such aid. All his assistants became useful ministers. The first, now Dr. Paterson of Montrose, is still alive, a marvel at his great age. Others were—Mr. John Bower, Mr. Francis Grant, Mr. Robert Simpson.* But the "harvest" was at hand, and the " angel reapers " were in readiness. On the morning of a beautiful

---

* The venerable Dr. Paterson, at ninety-one years of age, is still an able and loved labourer in his Master's vineyard at Montrose. Mr. Bower, son of Byron's early teacher, died in his manse at Maryculter in December 1866. The fine chastened diction, antique eloquence in delivery, and guileless simplicity of character of Mr. Bower, will long be had in remembrance. Mr. Grant predeceased him ; and the worthy Free Church minister of Kintore, Dr. Robert Simpson, died there in the autumn of 1870.

Sabbath, as the Doctor, seated in his study, was ·looking over the notes of the discourse he hoped to preach in the course of an hour, he was suddenly wanted. Signless passed his spirit in a moment! The first intimation of his release was given by Mr. Black, who preached from the appropriate text :— "This day a prince and a great man is fallen in Israel." Never was there deeper lamentation for a pastor. The congregation felt as sheep without a shepherd. Though thirty years and more have rolled away since his removal, his memory is still fondly and gratefully cherished, and, let us add, without offence, his place is still open for occupation. Let those who read the unpretending record, in our churchyard, of this good man's birth and death, bethink them of what manner of spirit animated the little dust below, and rest assured that it is better to have one's name recorded in a certain book written by no mortal hand, than inscribed in the proudest page of history—too often fallacious and false, and perishable, at its very best.

We have left no room at present for the old kirk's other minister, Mr. Doig—(*other* indeed!)— and various matters of interest, for which the venerable fabric's name may serve as index.

Since the times above referred to, a great change has taken place in the character of all time-honoured seasons, and particularly of the present.

Then, we had no temperance demonstrations, because we had less of habitual and brutal drunkenness. We had few or none of pretentious lecturings and quacking lecturers, because people were more in the way of *studying good* books than of *skimming* over *trashy* ones. We had less of sloppy journalism, draggle-tailed magazinism, and maudlin, hysterical novelism. We had something decent in the way of the legitimate drama, instead of childish pantomimes, which are not half so funny as were the performances of the old " Tumlers" in our links, with their " Tailor from Brentford," and tight-rope dancing, etc. We had no " routing" preachers in our streets, emulating the clangour of the tolbooth bell, because some had more sense, and others more modesty. We had few Sunday lectures, because quiet folks thought it better to cultivate fireside devotion, along with their little ones, than to trail out to preachings, very suitable, as they are, for the assignations of lads and lasses ! So, in regard to our present season : Christmas was really a holiday then, but now it is merely an ordinary day, except with the peculiar few. New Year's Day is now chiefly remarkable as a day of dissipation among the populace, particularly among the young, and we lament to say, many of them mere girls ! When we think of such things, we are more inclined to grave reflection than to imitate the thoughtless cackle of journalistic jubilation. To say no more of these and of other sources of serious reflection, is there not, with many, sufficient personal motive to pensiveness at such seasons as the present? What would not some give for the buoyancy of spirit, the exuberance of health, the innocence, the candour, and the truth which marked those years, to them, alas! for ever fled, when they looked forward to Christmas and New Year's Day as seasons of delight unalloyed, as annual jubilees of the heart! Does even external nature now wear to them the same aspect with which she beamed on the halcyon days of their boyhood? Don't they think even the sun less joyously bright—the moon less serenely fair;—spring less hopefully fraught with promise;—summer less voluptuously redolent of sweets;—and even winter less magnificently dread in its gloom of cloud and storm? Where be now the innocent gambols of Christmas of olden times—the *guisards*, with their quaint simple song, —" Be soothing, be soothing?"   Are we, forsooth, become too learned—too scientific for observances in which, old-fashioned though they be, heart calleth unto heart? Have we been gainers by the change, or are we to a great extent mere dabblers in science, and praters in literature, thinking more of sound than of sense, of shadow than of substance, of conventional sentiment than of natural feeling, of formal profession of creed than of the eloquent religion of a pure heart and holy life ? Knowledge may be power, but certainly it is not *goodness.* Unless improvement of the understanding and amelioration of the heart keep pace with the diffusion of knowledge, better remain in a state of comparative ignorance. Unless thus it be, we shall find, by fatal experience, that he that increaseth knowledge only increaseth sorrow ; and that where ignorance is bliss, it must be folly to be wise.

RANDOM NOTES OF LOCAL ANTIQUITIES, ETC.

I.

There was found, some years ago, at a considerable depth below the surface of Clarence Street, a hoard of small silver coins of Edward III. of England, and of one of our Alexanders. Many years ago, when St. Nicholas Street was being laid out, a similar hoard of precisely the same coins was found in a spot, which must have been not far from what is now the new Lemon Tree Hotel. It was supposed to have belonged to the Bead House in the neighbourhood. Under what circumstances such hoards were deposited, it is impossible to say. Apparently, they were concealed during times of trouble with those whom local memoranda designate " our auld innemies the Inglis."

It is somewhat remarkable that all the diggings in the site of our city have failed to disclose any very ancient relics, such as primeval stone coffins, clay urns, etc. The nearest point where any of the latter have been found is the Spittal Churchyard. But even those were of doubtful character, and *might* have been fragments of coarse pottery used in the old hospital, an institution of the twelfth century.

The oldest urban relic we have seen is the head of an iron spear, much decayed, which was found in all but contact with a boar's tusk imbedded in moss, in Littlejohn Street, while digging a foundation for some works of the Messrs. Blaikie. Old people, within the last forty years, recollected moss having been found in laying out Longacre and George Street. A gentleman, who died recently at the age of eighty-three, used to tell of his having in youth shot wild ducks on the marshy ground whereon now stand John Street, St. Andrew Street, etc. In fact, here was situated *the* loch, occasionally mentioned by Spalding, as the popular resort of what he calls "sea maws." Indeed, all the lower portions of the present site of the city seem to have been covered with water, leaving the eminences dry, and probably occupied by some tribe or tribes of primeval settlers.

In the course of ages, the surface has undergone great changes from the decay and demolition of old tenements, and the erection of new. Most of the very old houses were of wood, or turf, and were liable to frequent conflagration. They must have been marvellously ill-aired, filthy, and unhealthy; and, doubtless, greatly contributed to foster the plague, which seems to have been a deadly sort of *typhus gravior.* Even the best stone houses, belonging to royalty, steel-clad barons, or the dignified clergy, were gloomy, gousty, dirty "jambs," where the occupants were more solicitous about the protection of life than the comforts of living.

II.

On the west side of the Guestrow stood, and still stand, some old houses. Originally, there were no houses between the Guestrow and Broad Street, which was anciently called the *Braid-gate* of the *Gallow-gate.* To understand the topography of these localities, it must be borne in mind that the ancient quay-head was what is now the Shorebrae, a sort of jutty, the interior of which was filled up with the earth dug out of St. Catherine's Hill on the north, thus leaving the gap where some of the Messrs. Pirie's warehouses were recently situated. From this ascended the Shiprow, with houses only along the west side. It wound around the bottom of St. Catherine's Hill, until it reached where now stands the Queen's Hotel, when its main line passed along Rotten, now Union Row, into Guestrow; one branch diverged eastward into the Narrow Wynd, leading into Castle Street, and another

turned westward into the Netherkirkgate, by what
is now called St. Catherine's Wynd. St. Catherine's
Hill was so called from a Nunnery, the only one
in Aberdeen, which stood thereon, and which was
founded towards the end of the thirteenth century
by the then Constable of Aberdeen, and dedicated
to St. Catherine. It was a small house, and had a
chapel attached to it. It was demolished about
the Reforming times; and it is not unlikely that
some of its fragments are to be found in buildings
in the vicinity. In the Shiprow there is a door
leading to a rudely vaulted cellar, which has evidently been part of a small Early Pointed window,
probably of the nuns' chapel. From this hill there
was an extensive and pleasant prospect; and it was
much resorted to, as long as it stood, by ancient
females for fresh air and social gossip, while they
busily walloped away at the " shank." The hill
was cleared away to make room for Union Street,
Adelphi Court, etc. While undergoing this process
there were discovered the ruins of a small house (the
writer saw it), over which, tradition said, part of the
hill (all gravel) had been turned, because the plague
was in it. It stood on the site now occupied by
the premises of Mr. Black, wine-merchant. In
digging out the ruins, a gold ring, probably of the
time of Charles I., was found. It was engraved
with cabalistic characters, and was, doubtless, considered a potent charm against evil.

Some have thought that the Guestrow was so called from being occupied by the dwellings of leading citizens, who entertained strangers as "guests." But the true meaning is apparent from a Latin charter of the fifteenth century, where the street is mentioned as "*vicus lemurum*," the street of spirits—*ghaist* street; probably from the backs of the houses overlooking the churchyard of St. Nicholas at no great distance, and then not concealed by intervening buildings. It must have been the north side of the cemetery which was chiefly visible; and this was always held unlucky and fear-inspiring—a remnant of Celtic superstition.

Boethius tells us that the English garrison who were massacred by the citizens in the times of Wallace and Bruce, were, by permission of the clergy, buried "*ad posticam Divi Nicholai*,"—near the back entrance of St. Nicholas Church; and he adds that a commemorative monument was to be seen at the time he wrote. What Boethius says must often be taken *cum grano;* but his above statement, if imaginative, would be a "rousing whid" with a vengeance. Certain it is, however, that in the days when Sexton James Kerr (Peter's son) "rang," a large quantity of greatly decayed human bones were found, huddled into a trench, at the place mentioned by the elegant, if occasionally inventive, biographer of the Bishops of Aberdeen.

III.

There is an old house to which entry is from a close in the Guestrow, while one side looks into Barnet's Close, in which some forty years ago the local Society of Friends used to hold their religious meetings. It was bequeathed to them for this purpose by a Mary Bannerman who married a Leslie of Findrassie, a quaker. Mary was buried in the garden attached to the house, and her tomb, composed of granite slabs, is still to be seen at what must have been the western extremity of the garden, the end of it cropping out from underneath the foundation of an outhouse. The nearest way to it is from an entry near the bottom of Barnet's Close. Some years ago the old house referred to was gutted in order to its being fitted up for a brass-foundry. At one part of the ceiling was found a considerable quantity of sheet copper. It appears that the house had been occupied, in 1746, as the Duke of Cumberland's mint, for making what was called siege-money, which consisted of square pieces of copper stamped with the head of royalty. In the wall of the same house was found the skeleton of a female child, much decayed. In the cellarage of the old house adjacent, eastward to the former, was found the remains of a cask of red wine, which had oozed out and stained the gravel in which the cask had been buried. In the entrance to what is now a pauper lodging-house was found the skeleton of a man, at a considerable depth below the surface. These premises had once belonged to the Jaffrays of Kingswells, a noted quaker family. The interments referred to were probably caused by the rigorous persecution of the quakers, who were even denied the rites of Christian burial.

IV.

We have mentioned that the Shiprow branched off, eastward, into the Narrow Wynd, of which the south side was removed in order to complete the south side of Union Street, ultimately terminating with the Athenæum Buildings. The north side of Narrow Wynd stood many years after the south one had been removed, until the new Municipal Buildings were projected. The shops in this row, although neither roomy nor convenient, were much sought after, and yielded the Corporation a considerable revenue. In one of them, which was occupied by the Messrs. Angus, booksellers, there was a sort of newsroom, where several well-known citizens used to while away an hour or two, interchanging political and local gossip. There might be seen the elephantine form of Fiscal Low, with ponderous but shapely limbs—fattest and kindliest of men. In not a few cases did his merciful nature attemper the murderous severity of the laws in his day. That tall splay-footed figure in top-boots, queue, and head bepowdered into rivalry with the driven snow, while not a speck is to be seen on any part of his vestments, is the Town-Clerk. He looks awfully authoritative; but softish is his horn. He is a favourite butt of his waggish familiars; yet hath he far more gumption than it is his good fortune to get credit for. The paunchy little man in pigtail, powdered poll, sorely pitted face, and keen eyes, who heaves and pitches along on right tip-toe, is Kennedy our annalist, an enthusiastic and laborious, if not quite trustworthy digger into local antiquities. Another antiquarian appears in the long-remembered form of Professor Stuart, conspicuous for a club queue, economical black straw hat, and cork leg. The tall, handsome, frank-looking young man is familiarly known as Sandy Bannerman, a noted reformer, arrant wag, and addicted to practical jokes.

The brothers Angus were both characters; the elder taciturn and peevish: the younger, brusque, outspoken, and the object of his brother's perpetual objurgation.

Their next door neighbours were the " Missey Tamsons," booksellers in a small way. They were both rather curt and deformed, but one of them was well read, very intelligent, and famous for smart repartee. They kept a brace of lap-dogs, barking imps, the terror of infantile customers yearning after *Riggy-med-easy, Jack the Giant Killer*, and

the other useful information of that primitive
time.

Westward of the Anguses' shop was that of
Johnny Moir, a grocer in pig-tail, white neckcloth,
and Hessian boots with dangling tassels—a very
gentleman compared with the bareheaded, coatless,
and be-aproned countermen of our day. The haber-
dashers and other shopkeepers in this row were all
respectable men. They professed no " great bar-
gains," " tremendous sacrifices," and all the other
romancing trickeries of modern trade. They might
be seen occasionally taking a turn in front of their
shops, and indulging in social crack with a friend.
At their counters many of them wore their hats,
taking things easy—not stooping to " competition,"
dining at two o'clock, and, in the afternoon, indulging in a game of bowls in the green at Gordon's
Hospital. A rubber of whist, the lug of a Finnan
haddie, or a partan tae, and a temperate tumbler of
toddy, concluded the day. Were those worthy
burghers, who laid the foundation of the handsome
style in which some of their descendants live and
move, now to look in upon us, they might, perhaps,
consider some of Dr. Cumming's finality notions
not so very whimsical.

v.

When the foundation of the most westerly house
of Union Buildings was being dug there were dis-

covered the remains of an ancient mill-course, probably the oldest in Aberdeen. The mill-burn ran between Guestrow and Broad Street, from the Loch which was dammed up at the south end by an embankment, of which the top was a road, connected with the Vennel (since taken into St. Paul's Street), and continued along Crooked Lane (bounding the property of the Black Friars), and so onward, crossing the steps of Gilcomston, to an ancient windmill, which seems to have stood somewhere in the neighbourhood of the brewery (built in 1767). The mill referred to seems to have stood near where Union Chapel is now situated.

The remains of its "lead" were many feet below the present surface, and were black and charred, as if from the effects of fire. In this neighbourhood seems to have lain the most ancient part of the city, straggling from the Green, along Shiprow, the south side of Exchequer Row, and so onwards to the Castle, which stood (for many a year ruinous) on the site now occupied by the barracks. Within the defences was a small chapel dedicated to St. Ninian, the oldest missionary of the Christian faith, whose influence extended coastwise to our northern district. Mention is made of this chapel in documents of the latter half of the thirteenth century, but of its foundation no record has yet been discovered. Was it one of the very early chapels planted along our eastern coast, like those at Cowie,

Portlethen, Finan, Nig, Old Machar, etc.? or was it merely coeval with the original erection, or with a subsequent restoration of the Castle? Within this stronghold, in ancient times, were sometimes held the courts of the justiciar. Occasionally they were held in the open air, between the Castle and Heading Hills. This locality, too, was sometimes the scene of the infliction of the last penalty of the law. Here witches were burned. Within the parade enclosure, where now stands the powder magazine, was a small astronomical observatory (afterwards removed to Marischal College), which was superintended by Dr. Andrew Mackay, who wrote a book, once rather noted, on the longitude, and a system of navigation, still in some estimation. He was born in Aberdeen, and was the son of a dancing-master, who taught in the house with the " tympany," not far from the bottom of the south side of Long Acre, then a highly respectable quarter. Mackay taught navigation, and was an unsuccessful candidate for the professorship of mathematics in King's College, when it was bestowed on Mr. Duncan, formerly the greatly esteemed and truly estimable master of the Public Mathematical School. Mackay's claims were supported by the then Duke (Alexander) of Gordon, who was an amateur astronomer in a small way. Mackay afterwards became mathematical examiner at the Trinity House. In his favourite department of practical science he showed highly commendable ability. He was of a kindly and obliging turn, and much beloved by his "salt" pupils, whose gratitude was not unfrequently testified by votive libations of grog, occasionally ending in somewhat "fresh departures." He was a little, bustling, bandy-legged man, with eyes of jet and a countenance of much intelligence and animation. *Vide* his *vera effigies* which adorns his work on the *Sliding Gunter.*

VI.

In Part V. of these Random Notes we endeavoured, in our rambling flighty way, to conjure from the vasty deep of the past, a few of our more noted ex-citizens—notable not more by social position than by a certain grotesquely distinctive individuality of character. Such singularities were, in the times referred to, rather numerous. In our day there seems a general complaint of the decay of such eccentricity. "We have no originals now," sighs the sexagenarian, as he compares the contemporaries of his spring-time with the humdrum generation of his autumnal years. Such regrets are not altogether groundless ; but how come they ? The impression which prompts them is probably in part produced by the distance, in point of time, from which we now survey the beings whom we used to see and hear, when what is now our past was our present. The matter-of-fact business of observation has been exchanged for the reproductive exercise of memory, aided by the constructiveness of conception, and rendered more or less vivid by the light of imagination. In this way does " distance lend enchantment " to our visions of the past. Moreover, as regards a certain class, doubtless the tender mercies of parochial authorities, and the comprehensive sympathies of lunatic asylums have made a solitude of those " innocents " whose aphelion from the sun of reason was of cometary eccentricity, and who wandered " here-awa, there-awa," the objects of general sympathy and kindly treatment, except by a thoughtless fry of urchins, more bent on fun than mischief. Then, have we not our hydropathic institutions, where certain eccentricities, traceable to infatuation rather than to fatuity, are reduced to the orbit of due regularity by the proper adjustment of the relative forces of vitals and victuals, and a steady reliance on the *vis medicatrix naturæ.*

Still, all these considerations, whatever their weight, will not wholly account for the absence, in our day, of that picturesque individuality of character which is thought and alleged to have been the more common the farther you recede from the present. The causes are probably various, and are to be sought for in the great changes which have passed over all our social relations, more especially in commerce and trade, politics, religion, and what is called education. More especially is the influence

of the latter assimilative in the matter referred to.
The systems of education now in vogue seem to
have for their main object to cram young noddles
with a perplexing and mind-crushing multiplicity
of mere smatterings of knowledge, by. processes
most grindingly mechanical, whereby parental
vanity is gratified, and the teacher's purse comfort-
ably lined. Schools there are which are as much
factories as any cotton-mill in the country, where
the condition of the poor little scholars is as pitiable
as was that of the poor little "white slaves," of
whom we used formerly to hear so much. But we
must resist the temptation to launch into this subject at present. Suffice it to say that the tendencies of the present educational system are to
stunt, and not to promote, the development of the
natural character ; that they proceed on the fatal
error of confounding *education* with mere *instruction*.
Thinking people, who understand this and other
important considerations involved in the subject,
are not surprised at the unsatisfactory results, notwithstanding all the fuss about the matter in Parliamentary debates, in educational committees of
which perhaps not one member ever taught half-
an-hour in his life ; and in the pottering reports of
pedantic inspectors, a kind of scholastic gaugers
who sometimes prove a crook in the lot of the poor
schoolmaster, while they, lucky fellows, have a jolly
and roving life of it, jaunting about the country,

.mayhap relieving the great anxieties of duty by the angler's gentle craft, and a modicum of those little social amenities of which the relish is so greatly enhanced by plenty of fresh air and moderate exercise. But *revenons a nos moutons.*

VII.

Contemporary with the notables already sketched was Mr. Robert Troup, grocer, etc. etc., in that shop now 44 Castle Street. Of a surety ROBBIE TROUP, as he was generally called, was a marked original. Any lawful morning in the course of the year you may see him on his way to the Firhill Well, to gulp his tumbler or two of its sulpho-*iron-eery* water. His person is more remarkable for rotundity than height. From underneath his hat peeps a wig — a reddish-brown, sober, seceder-looking wig. His face speaks for itself in no dead language. There is no mistaking its lumpish cheeks, snub nose, chatty-like mouth, and double chin. It is round, fat, greasy, upturned, and usually clad in an easy, careless, good-humoured smile. It gives broad hints of beef-steaks, double Glo'ster, and London stout. The rest of his person seems in equally good keeping. His paunch is tunnish ; his limbs dumpy and stumpy. He usually wears a blue coat with gilt buttons, a swan-down vest, knee-breeches, grey stockings, and shoes. In walking he makes up for the shortness of his steps by their frequency, waddling along at a bustling pace, and ever and anon twirling his watch chain. In his inward man were various marked features, of which the most prominent was his utter antipathy to anything like order and regularity in the management of his business. To all remonstrances on this head, to all endeavours to methodise his affairs, Robbie uniformly presented a front of flint. Easy on most other matters, on this he was inexorable. Manifold were the proofs of this in his shop, where you might see, in sweet confusion, cheeses, and hams, and candles, boxes of tea, weights and measures; soap, barley, tobacco, funnels—and what not? The same peculiarity distinguished his advertisements, which consisted of an enumeration of sundries huddled together on a system of the oddest disarrangement. They usually began with—" To the curious in sauces," and ended with—" A single gill of wine to the afflicted, 6d.!" So the rich and poor here met together. If Robbie began with the house of feasting, he landed in the house of mourning; if he pampered the epicure, he compassionated the sick. In the body of the advertisement were set forth—" treacle and train-oil ;" "soft soap and Malaga raisins ;" " Spanish juice and sperm oil ;" and other equally bizarre concatenations. In the depths of his cellars underneath Marischal Street Bridge were goods of every kind, but of the contents Robbie was as ignorant as he was of those of the womb of futurity. When occasion required he used to make stepping-stones of double Glo'sters.

Behind his counter Robbie had an inexhaustible fund of small talk for all his customers and all occasions. He was particularly facetious with servant lasses, with whom he used to crack many a sly joke, but not like that "foolish jesting which is not convenient;" for Robbie was a stanch religious professor, a stickler for sound doctrine, and a pillar (of the Saxon type) of the "Tarnties." He showed a good deal of policy in this badinage. He thus gained time with his customers, who, owing to the hugger-mugger state of his shop, could seldom obtain what they wanted as soon as they wished.

Robbie's confused and unbusiness habits led him into another peculiarity—a knack of telling white lies about his goods. These had always an excellent character, whether they deserved it or not. They were all the best and cheapest in their way ever offered for sale. It was in vain to say this was musty, or that was stale; the fault, Robbie assured you, lay in yourself, and not in the articles. A servant girl chanced one day, in Robbie's absence, to ask for some pearl barley—the very best. The shopman told her that what they then had was good, but not of the best quality. The girl was going away when she was met by Robbie, who inquired, in his usual jocular way, what she wanted. She informed him how matters stood. " Barley!

my lassie," said he, "we've the best in the town; it's as fite as thae bonny teeth o' yours!" This assurance, backed by such a compliment, was irresistible. The barley was sold. When the girl went away, the shopman remonstrated on the score of conscience. "Tut! tut! man," said Robbie, "ye hae a foolish conscience."

Robbie was a married man, but had no family. His wife was an original in her way, rather a termagant, and kept the upper hand of him. She used to scold him before his customers when fortified, as was suspected, by Dutch courage. Sometimes she became hysterically demonstrative, the fit passing off in an explosive belch, when Robbie would gently remove her from the shop, meekly exclaiming— "Enough said, my dear!—Enough said!"

VIII.

The history of our present Town House is rather interesting, although not generally known. In the earliest times of Aberdeen there seems to have been no Town Hall. Such an institution is the concomitant of a community in which commerce and trade have been, to a certain extent, developed, with the establishment of guilds in both. It is probable that the meetings of our earliest municipal authorities were held in the castle; while the burghal prison is said to have been situated in Virginia Street, a little to the west of Marischal

Street. In the seventeenth century not a vestige of its ruins had remained ; but tradition said that it stood somewhere about the south end of the garden attached to a house belonging to the Earl Marischal, who founded Marischal College, and which stood on the south side of Castle Street, on the site, nearly, of the Union Bank. Immediately westward was a huge old house called Pitfodels' Lodging, a town residence of the Menzies family, and probably of the Reids before their day ; the last Reid, a lady, having been married to a Menzies about 1439, he thus became laird of Pitfodels. On the probable site of the original prison there is a large and deep well of oblong form, brimful of beautiful cool water, which never fails. It is evidently of great antiquity. On the premises (now occupied as a brewery) are some ancient vaults, in one of which were found human bones. Did these belong to some hapless captive ; or were they the remains of some victim of feudal vengeance and oppression, who had miserably perished unseen by any eye save His who sees all things ? The old Menzieses were a grasping homicidal race. They bore absolute sway in Aberdeen for upwards of one hundred and fifty years, engrossing all public offices, buying up for an old song much of the town's landed property, and even stooping to the meanness of farming the public hand-bell ! But a day of retribution came. Where are they now ?

It is only the memory of the just which is blessed ; for, assuredly, sooner or later, " the name of the wicked shall rot." How well it is for all, especially public men, who " consider this !"

As the town increased in importance the citizens aspired to a new tolbooth, as it was called, worthy of the advanced state of things. But this could not be done without Royal authority. On their petition, accordingly, Robert II., about the end of the fifteenth century, granted charter permission for the erection of a tolbooth in any part of Castle Street, except within the limits whereon the public market was held. The building was of two floors, the lower one occupied with such shops as they had nearly four hundred years ago. They were, and still are, stone vaults, with walls of great thickness. The length of this part of the building extended westward as far as the present Council Chamber. The upper floor was of course of the same length, and comprised one room or hall, where municipal justice was administered, and burghal meetings were held. Such meetings were thus said to be convened within the *laigh tolbooth.* There are some curious arches worthy of the examination of such of our local architects as have souls above mere masonry and house-carpentry. Preserve those relics. The Royal heads are casts from those on the Cross. The arch over the present bench in the Police Court is original work, and seems to have spanned the communication between the high and the laigh tolbooth. The former consisted of a square tower, battlemented, which was divided into several dungeon-like rooms, all stone vaulted, some of which were used for confining prisoners, and others for keeping tollage which had been collected in kind. Hence the names of the "wool room," the "fish room." The original tower was extended at a comparatively modern date by additions, and the whole was then occupied as a prison. The entrance to the old tower was on the east side, and was discovered when arrangements were made for erecting the North of Scotland Bank. It was low and round-headed, and stood some thirty feet above the level of the street, whence it was reached by a double flight of stairs, one leading from the north and the other from the south, thus forming an angle with the door at the apex. Down this steep stair culprits were conducted by the hangman, when proceeding to be "justified" on the gallows, which was occasionally erected in Castle Street, where the Duke of Gordon's monument now stands. Tradition says that, early in last century, while a wild Highlander, Alaster M'Alaster, was being thus conducted, he suddenly leaped from the stair down among the surrounding crowd, through which, brandishing a dirk, he soon made his way, obtained temporary concealment, and was never more heard of.

About the middle of last century great alterations were made on the original tolbooth in the
time of Provost Robertson of Glasgowego, an intelligent and public-spirited, and also a very honest,
man. In old times there seems to have been attached to the west end of the tolbooth a wooden
too-fall, for the accommodation of the Town Clerk
and the Chamberlain. But, at the period of improvement referred to, the old fabric was raised by
an additional floor, containing the present hall ; an
addition was made on the west end, and the whole
was faced up as we now see it. The entrance was
changed from the east to the west ; and a new entrance to the prison tower was made in its south
side, which was reached by a double flight of stairs,
leading to a sort of hall, in which were doors which
led into the prison, the court room, and the stair-
case which rose to the battlements. All these
arrangements were radically changed in 1819, when
the tower was newly faced as we see it, and the
prison and new Court House were built; but the
old Town House, with its hall, was spared. This
room has seen the freedom of the city conferred on
Dr. Johnson, Sir Robert Peel, and many other distinguished historical personages. It is a very handsome hall, and contains some curious things, which,
it is to be hoped, will be carefully preserved—
such as the splendid crystal chandeliers; the view
of the town above the fireplace, by Mossman ; the

chimney marbles ; and the Provost's chair, which, like its fellow in the hall of Gordon's Hospital, was captured, along with a Spanish vessel, at a period which we are not prepared to state offhand.*

IX.

In ancient times it would seem that there had been no houses between Huxter and Exchequer Rows, the intervening space having formed the western portion of Castle Street, its boundary being St. Catherine's Hill. The former Row was so called as having been remarkable for the booths of huxters. It extended from Broad Street, eastward,. in a line with the north side of Castle Street. At that portion of the Row nearly in the rear of the present North of Scotland Bank was situated the printing-office of Edward Raban, the earliest Aberdeen printer, some of whose quaint productions are in the libraries of King's and Marischal Colleges, and are found, though rarely, in the collections of book-

* "Our present Town House" will have vanished ere these sheets are printed ; its demolition, commenced on the 21st January 1871, is now all but complete. Some of its "curious things" are, with praiseworthy care, replaced in the New Town House. Mossman's painting again hangs over the fireplace, the grand old Belgian crystal chandeliers again glorify the room, the Provost's chair is being repaired, for the Dean of Guild's use doubtless ; but the "marbles" and the "very handsome hall" are gone.

hunters. The building was occupied by successive town's printers, as they were called, for many years after Raban's time. From this office issued the first number of the *Aberdeen Journal* in 1746; but its career was cut short by a party of rebels who took offence at the loyalty of the printer, James Chalmers, the first of the three who have borne that name. So sudden was the on-fall of the Highland host, that the printer was fain to "absquatulate" by a window at the risk of life and limb. We have been told by one who had seen the remains of the house in his boyhood, that, although greatly decayed, it bore the impress of former consequence, some of the walls having been covered with leather, on which might have been still traced the faint vestiges of gilded decoration. The printing-office was afterwards removed to the upper floor of a building (originally a silk-mill) in the rear of the Town House, which was reached by a long and rather steep outer stair. It was in this office that the first Bishop Skinner (Tullochgorum's son) met Robert Burns.

From the Huxter Row diverged Luxembourg Close, running nearly in the line of the west side of King Street down to the fields lying about North Street. In this close is *said* to have been seen, some seventy years ago, a very rude and ancient tenement, which tradition assigned as the rendez-vous of the citizens who suddenly attacked and routed the English garrison who held the castle in the fourteenth century. To adopt a favourite phrase of a late well-known citizen—"Such is the report," but it requires consideration.

The tolbooth, which was built in the end of the fifteenth and beginning of the sixteenth century, stood in advance of the Row, making with the latter a narrow lane, which was afterwards prolonged towards Broad Street, when the houses in Narrow Wynd, lately taken down, were built. A *row* in old times seems to have been built only on one side.

Many must of course recollect the original position of the Cross, erected in 1686, by John Montgomery, the Old Rayne mason. Whether John planned it is problematical, although not impossible. "Master mason" in those days was synonymous with "architect" in ours. Whoever planned it showed better taste than those who recently renovated it. In the original Cross were arcades (not arches), each of which was relieved by an oblong panel, giving an appearance of lightness and elevation, which was altogether lost when, subsequently, the arcades were transformed into open arches of a squat and dwarfy character. It ought to have been placed, too, where it might have been seen from King Street as well as Union Street, without prevention of a better place for the Duke's statue.

The original Cross seems to have been in the

form of the emblem of our faith, but destroyed or greatly injured at the Reformation. It was sometimes called the Flesh Cross, probably from the proximity of butchers' stalls. There was another cross at the east end of Castle Street, called the Fish Cross, which seems to have disappeared at an early period ; for the fishwives who used to congregate there latterly mustered at the other Cross. They were in great wrath against Provost Robertson of Glasgowego, when, about the middle of last century, they were obliged to make room for the *Plainstanes.* They declared that the next of his whimsies would be to plant the street " wi' gillieflowers." The fishwives, however, made good their quarters on the steps of and around the Plainstanes in that golden age of *real finans,* and *partans* at three ha'pence a pair all so sweetly fresh. The fishwives, however, were not the only huxters squatting at the *Plainstanes.* But what boots it *now* to write of little rosy *Betty Osely* (Oswald), poor bodie, with her wheel of fortune, London candy, and snaps ; or of *Thumb John,* an old campaigner, with his cap and its fateful polyhedron, and his vixen spouse ; or of *Gibbery John* with his hazardous dice ;—all so tempting for the younker with his " Friday's bawbee." Nor were the more refined attractions of literature wanting so long as *Joseph* sat within the corner of his covered stall, presiding over his little array of old magazines, stray volumes of Shakespeare, the Pilgrim's Progress, and such like, his wooden leg projecting in front.

The *Plainstanes* were originally intended to be used, and were used, as an exchange for the city merchants. There they might have been seen of a fine morning in powdered periwigs and velvet morning gowns, stately pacing, more like lords than mere merchants. In latter times the place was the favourite promenade of all sorts of lounging loafers, and specially of proudly-strutting recruiting sergeants. On the occasions of George III.'s birthday (June 4th), the Plainstanes were occupied in the evening by a party of soldiers from the garrison drawn up facing the Town Hall, in which the members of Council and a party of friends were drinking his Majesty's health and other loyal toasts. As each toast was being drunk, it was accompanied by a volley of musketry, on signal of a white handkerchief displayed at a window of the hall. One of the Town Sergeants, Robert Cantley, used to act as toast-master. On one occasion, Robert, mistaking the Provost's enunciation of "all the king's allies," proposed " all the kings alive !"

X.

We have already mentioned that there were originally no houses between the north side of Huxter and the south side of Exchequer Row.

The latter was so named from an ancient house in which was carried on the business of the Scottish Exchequer, including that of the Mint. This house stood between Stronach's and Burnet's Closes. Part of it was taken down not many years ago to make room for the house built by the late Mr. P. Williamson. Whether it was the first Exchequer House seems doubtful, as it was more like the buildings of the seventeenth century than the large castellated-like mansions of an earlier date. The latter belonged only to the nobility and gentry, or to the dignified clergy, or to the Knights' Templars. They were, in fact, town fortresses, so constructed as to resist those sudden onfalls of the vindictive or the marauding, which were so frequent in the reigns of weak monarchs, or in times of popular disturbance, when the arm of the law was in great measure paralysed. It is questionable whether any one of those more important buildings now remains. One there was within the last thirty years, which stood on the north side of Upper Kirkgate, the entrance being from the Burn Close. The title-deeds, extending to the earlier years of the fifteenth century, showed that the house had belonged to the Knights' Templars. It had been a large massive building of one floor above the ground-floor (as almost all those houses were), and at one time had been connected with a room underneath, which opened the " PORT " of the

Upper Kirkgate. It was in this room that Rutherford was confined, and from which he dates some of his *Letters.*

The old Exchequer was at one time purchased by Mr. Leslie of Berryden. In the room where meetings of the Court were presumably held was a very fine carving, in oak, of the Royal Arms of Scotland, which he presented to Marischal College, where it is still to be seen in splendid preservation. It would be curious to speculate as to how many people in Aberdeen know this, or the far more important fact that the Museum in question, which owes its present admirable arrangement to the scientific care of Professor Nicol, is always open (under very indulgent regulation) to the public.

Outside, over the entrance of the old house we write of, were the Royal Arms cut in sandstone. This the curious will perhaps find in the ruins of the grotto at Berryden. It formed one of the gimcracks with which the retired merchant garnished what he meant for a little paradise wherein to while away his few remaining days. It is still a pleasant spot, although its tranquillity is now disturbed by the thunder of the train and the shriek of the steam-whistle. No such sounds Tartarean disturbed the musings of the youthful OUTRAM, who, when attending College, was domesticated in this neighbourhood.

All the houses forming the south side of

Exchequer Row, and stretching eastward so as to form the south side of Castle Street, seem to have been very old, and occupied by important persons. The circumstance of the locality being under the more immediate protection of the Castle may have, perhaps, rendered it a favourite situation for building. Immediately eastward of the Exchequer stood what is called the Bursar's House—so called by Dr. Guild's express injunction, that neither " it nor the rents thereof should be perverted to any other use" than the " entertaining of poor boys who are craftsmen's sons, as bursars in the new College of Aberdeen, who are of good ingynes, etc." It appears that Guild occupied this house himself. He speaks of it as the fore-house, implying the co-existence of a back-house, and mentions the " brew-house or victual-house, with the room above, on the other side of the close," remains of which seem to be still standing, although altogether altered from their original purpose. But it is questionable whether the house, or at least part of it, is not much older than Guild's time. He seems to have acquired it by heritage,—this is very likely, as he was wealthy, and appears to have been rather vain, to have renovated and fitted it up in the best style of his day. At all events, in the seventeenth century, it was considered suitable for the temporary accommodation of Charles II., when that monarch's varying fortunes landed him for a short time in Aberdeen.

X

Tradition mentions two curious circumstances of his sojourn in the Bursar's House. It is said that he was one day served with a dish of fried "sauties" (the true flounder), of which he seemed particularly fond. Apparently he had not been very familiar with the dainty, for he is said to have eaten only one side, and then to have demanded more. But there were no more. So the cook turned over those partially discussed, and his most sacred Majesty ate the other sides, and was satisfied.

The other tradition is but too characteristic of, although not very creditable to, this graceless sovereign. It seems it was at a window of this house that he was seen laughing and gallivanting with one of those worthless randies to whose society he was so partial, and from some of whom certain nobles have the misfortune to trace their descent. Of course all right-minded folks, and more especially the Presbyterians, were scandalised by such light behaviour ; and a minister of the name of Douglas was appointed to deal with the king, which he did, but as much like a man of the world as a minister, for he cautioned the "most sacred" to adjust the window-screens more carefully in future.

 This Douglas seems to have been a canny, time-serving carle, who contrived, in all the troubles of his time, to take care of "number one." His hard-winking, to say the least, at the "ramsch" sovereign's folly, was not forgotten, although the more important

services of devoted loyalists were not remembered.
Howsoever, Douglas was at length laid underneath
a large black marble stone, still in fine preservation,
at the south-west corner (outside) of Dunbar's Aisle,
on which is a long account in Latin of his mental,
moral, and religious excellencies, in accordance
with the prevailing, but vulgar fashion of the time.

Close by his grave is that of Thomas French,
master-mason of the Bridge of Dee, 1530; as appears by an inscription on the wall of the aisle.

MEMORANDUM

RESPECTING SOME ANCIENT INSCRIPTIONS

IN SCOTLAND.*

TOWARDS the end of January 1846 my attention was directed to an inscription on a portion of
what was once the Cross of St. Vigean, a parish of
Forfarshire, contiguous to that of the town of
Arbroath.   Through the medium of a friend, I was
permitted to inspect a handsome lithograph of this
interesting monument of antiquity, executed, I
understand, under the auspices of the late Patrick
Chalmers, Esq., of Auldbar, a gentleman not less
skilled than zealous in archæological pursuits.   The
cross referred to is thus mentioned in the *Statistical
Account of the the Parish of St. Vigean* (1845),
written by the parochial clergyman, the Rev.
John Muir: " In the churchyard there formerly
stood a large cross over the grave of some person
of eminence, richly carved in hieroglyphical figures

* Vide *Proceedings of the Royal Irish Academy*, volume
iii. Part 3.

of the kind found on sepulchral stones in some other places of Scotland. The cross has been long ago demolished, but the stalk remains, *with characters at the base hitherto undeciphered.*"

I entirely concur in the opinion of the reverend writer, that the cross in question was monumental. Such sepulchral monuments were common about the period to which the Cross of St. Vigean seems to belong. A comparison of some of its ornaments with those of other crosses of the same kind, suggests that it was the production of the latter part of the tenth century. The peculiar and beautiful interlacery in the compartment immediately above the inscription, and on one of the *faces* of the cross, is of kindred character with that which is exhibited in similar monuments of the same era, sketches of which are given in Mr. Petrie's valuable Essay on the Ecclesiastical Architecture of Ireland. I observe that it is stated, in the *Account* of the parish already referred to, that St. Vigean lived in the latter part of the tenth century; and that he had his residence in the neighbourhood of the spot where the cross formerly stood. " His original chapel and hermitage were at Grange of Conan, where there is a small grove, and the foundations of a chapel; also a most copious fountain, which preserves his name. Three or four acres of land contiguous to these are by tradition held as belonging to the chapel."

May it not, then, be not unreasonably inferred, that this monument marked the place of St. Vigean's sepulture ?   This, of course, is merely a conjectural suggestion,—at all events the cross is evidently the monument of some person of distinction.   Of the personal history of the saint I know nothing; but I think it not improbable, that he was of Irish origin or connection.   From the similarity to like monuments in Ireland, of the cross referred to, and of others in Forfarshire, and the adjoining districts, not to mention the round towers at Abernethy and Brechin, it is evident that *Irish* missionaries were intimately connected with those parts.   The inscription, according to *my* copy of it, is as follows :—

```
cι-ꝓoγceм::
γpeuoꝑec
cccEoꝑ...
cuγ'.....
```

The above inscription appears to be partly in the old Irish, and partly in the Roman character, I take the alphabet of the former from *Armstrong's Gaelic Dictionary.*   This mixed character of the inscription is quite common in monuments belonging to a period prior to the distinctive fixation of alphabets, established in later times, particularly after the introduction of printing.   Supposing, as is not improbable, that the *aboriginal* alphabets of Britain and Ireland had been lost sight of in the darkness attendant on social convulsions, so remarkably coincident either with the extermination of the order, or the decay of the influence, of the pagan priesthood ; a renewed acquaintance with the use of letters was only to be derived from *two* sources, either from the Romans, or from the early Christian missionaries.

Hence, I believe, it comes to pass, that the *most ancient* native inscriptions in *Britain* (see *Borlase*) are in the Roman character. Subsequently, some letters were borrowed from the Greek by the Christian missionaries, owing to their acquaintance with the original language of the New Testament. In all writings and inscriptions, then, of the earlier mediæval times, we may naturally expect a mixture of Roman and Greek characters. Hence the strong similarity of the old Irish to the old Anglo-Saxon.

This premised, I proceed further to observe, that the inscription above noted seems to be only *part* of that which originally belonged to the Cross of St. Vigean. I conjecture, for reasons which will afterwards more clearly appear, that the *first* part must have been cut on the *top* of the cross above the interlacery, which is now lost. It was not unusual to divide such inscriptions into two parts. An instance of such arrangement is to be found in

Borlase's *Antiquities of Cornwall*, pp. 399, 400. Further, in monuments of the age to which the Cross of St. Vigean belongs, the *beginning* of the inscription was usually prefixed with a small cross, either so (+), or so (⊕); but this is wanting in the portion of the inscription referred to. Taking all these circumstances into account, I venture to *restore* the inscription (for it has evidently *suffered*) as follows :—

CI·ΓΟΓCEM*PU*

ΓPEUOΠEC

ECCEOΠ*PRO*

CU I*s* *A N I M A;*

that is, using Roman capitals :

C H R O S. T E M *P U*

S. D E V O R E T

E T. T E. O R. *P R O*

C U I*s* *A N I M A.*

I do not pretend to give the *original letters* or *contractions*, which time or accident seems to have effaced from the inscription. It is impossible to determine what selection the stone-cutter may have made in his drafts on the Roman and Irish alphabets. At all events, he must have so managed matters as to confine his work within the prescribed limits.

I translate the above as follows :

O ! Cross ! Time may destroy thee, too ! Pray

for his (the person *named* in the *first* part of the inscription) *soul!*

Now, there is a singularity in this inscription : the first word (*Chros*) is *Gaelic*, and the rest are *Latin.* How may this be accounted for? The *ancient* Gaelic term for a cross is *cros.* The *vocative* is formed by *aspirating* the nominative into *chros.* To write the **Latin** *crux* with the *Irish* character was *impossible.* The alphabet has no *x*, and the sound of this letter is foreign to the Gaelic language. Hence, instead of Saxenach, we have *Sassenach.* Thus there was an obvious *necessity* for using the vocative of the Gaelic word, *cros.*

I conjecture that, as was usual in such cases, the first part of the inscription contained the name of the person to whose memory the cross was erected. Thus, the part above deciphered would be a very natural sequence. It is marked by all that touching simplicity which is characteristic of inscriptions on monuments of the same era, noticed by Mr. Petrie, whose accurate and tasteful researches have thrown so much light on some of the darkest and most interesting points of Gaelic antiquities.

Of the devices, animals, etc., on the back of the cross, I shall not here speak, as my present business is with the inscriptions. Suffice it to say, that I think I could *prove* that some of these devices are borrowed from monuments still extant in Scotland, the age of which exceeds that of the cross by many centuries.

The next inscription which I shall notice is that on an ancient monument in the Church of Fordun. Fordun is a parish of Kincardineshire, the county immediately north of Forfarshire. Kincardineshire is sometimes called the Mearns, and its people, "the men of the Mearns." In the old Irish Annals they are called "*Viri na Moerne.*"* There are many interesting particulars connected with the parish of Fordun. John de Fordun, author of the *Scotichronicon,* was either a native of it, or resided there, when he wrote his History of Scotland. It was the native parish of George Wishart the Scottish Martyr; of the eccentric Lord Monboddo; and of Beattie, author of "the Minstrel." Further, it was the *locale* of the famous shrine of St. Palladius. The remains of *Paldy*-Chapel are still standing; there is still *Paldy,* or *Pady* Fair; and there is a well in the minister's garden, called St. Palladius' Well. Some will have it that the famous Saint actually lived, died, and was buried here. I am not sufficiently acquainted with our early ecclesiastical history to give any opinion on the subject; but I am disposed to agree with those who think that Pady Chapel was built, not by the Saint, but by some of his Irish disciples, who came to this part of Scotland, probably with some of his relics. His mission certainly was to

* Instance of mixture of Latin and Gaelic.

Ireland, "*ad Scotos in Christum credentes.*" The earlier Christian churches in this quarter were certainly *Columban;* but some may have been of *Ninian*, or *Palladian* origin. Even at the early period referred to the spirit of ecclesiastical rivalry seems to have been at work.—At all events, the chapel of St. Palladius was always accounted the mother church of the Mearns.

But to come to the matter in hand : the ancient monument to which I refer (some account of which was first given by the late Professor Stuart, of Marischal College, Aberdeen), was first observed upon taking down the old *church* of Fordun, some sixty years ago. " It had been placed horizontally as a base for the pulpit to rest on, and was considered of so little consequence, as to be thrown aside for many years into the old chapel of St. Palladius, hard by." This old church of Fordun was so old, that it was *new roofed* about 360 years ago. After lying neglected for a long time, the old stone attracted the attention of the parish minister, who had it cleaned, and a drawing of it taken. The material is a very coarse freestone. The dimensions, five feet one inch in length, by two feet eleven inches broad, thickness fully four inches. It is carved on one side only. The emblematical devices are three figures on horseback, a greyhound, a wild boar, a serpent, or dragon ; and the peculiar *spectacle* device

like that on other old monuments in the north of Scotland. To these I do not refer at present ; my business being with the inscription. Professor Stuart makes it probable that this monument commemorates the assassination of King Kenneth III., in the year 994. His Majesty is said, by our historians, to have been assassinated at the instigation of Finelè, "daughter," says the Professor, "of Cruchnè, Maormor of Angus." This should be the *Cruithne* (Pictish) Maormor of Angus. The royal residence was at Kincardine. In the neighbourhood are *Strath-Finella* and *Den-Finella*. In this case, history is confirmed by tradition and topographical etymology. A drawing of the fragmentary inscription will be found in the *Archæologia Scotica*, vol. ii. p. 315.

There has been another line, if not more, above what remains, and I do not pretend to be able to decipher that with certainty ; but it strikes me that it *looks* like *Kenkardin* or *Kinkardin*, the name of the royal residence. It is to be observed that the *costume* of the human figures on this monument is exactly the *same* as that of the only human figure on the Cross of St. Vigean, belonging, as I conjecture, to the same period.

The next inscription which I shall notice is that on an old monument which was found some years ago in the parish of Insch, Aberdeenshire. The dimensions of the stone are six feet by one foot eight inches. The inscription runs along the central *length* of the stone. It is —

ORATEPRO/RHIMARADVLFI: SACERDOTIS:

this is evidently :

Orate pro Anima Radulphi Sacerdotis.

The characters show the influence of Anglo-Saxonism at the period when the monument was executed. There are some grounds for believing, that it was placed over the grave of *Radulph*, Bishop of Aberdeen, who died in 1247.

I have been induced to give the above specimens of ancient inscriptions in Scotland, in the hope that they may incite the able and zealous archæologists of Ireland to direct their attention to the subject. There are other inscriptions in this country of perhaps greater interest, to which I forbear to refer; partly because I confess my entire ignorance of their nature, and partly because I believe they have already attracted the notice of members of the Royal Irish Academy, from whom, if from any, the interpretation of those inscriptions may be expected.

Between the antiquities of Ireland and those of the north of Scotland there are many points of interesting connection. The aborigines of both countries belonged to the same great family of the human race; both remained *almost* equally intact from the ambition of ancient Rome; neither had to bow the neck to the yoke of the old Saxons; both were harassed by the Danes; and while the Picts were compelled, partially, to succumb to warriors of Irish descent, it was to missionaries of Irish origin that they owed their first acquaintance with the Gospel of Peace! In both countries are still to be found many memorials of aboriginal times, which had once their resemblances in England, but which have there disappeared under "the tramplings of three conquests," and the march of modern improvement. I refer, particularly, to those remote times when Druidism bore its mystic sway. Its usages yet linger in customs of popular superstition, although oblivion has long since fallen on the meaning attached to them by a crafty, powerful, and domineering hierarchy. Many an age has passed since its oracles became dumb; but the nomenclature of its religious creed is still employed to express, by the unwitting Gael of the present day, some of the mysteries of his purer faith! We have still the mysterious " temple," with its massive " cromlech," the poetry of the solitary moor, and seldom-trodden height,—many of which have been protected by our landed proprietors,—with commendable feeling, disregarding not the protest against eviction of those *adscripta glebæ*, and refusing to abandon to

" Hands more rude than wintry winds."

relics which have braved the buffetings of countless storms.

NOTES ON THE PRESENT STATE OF CRIME.

THIS subject is still a leading topic of discussion by all the more influential organs of opinion and their numerous correspondents. It has been a theme of comment by several of the English Judges on their various circuits, and in one instance a strong representation of the necessity of penal reform was made by a Grand Jury through its Foreman, the Speaker of the House of Commons. In short, various circumstances have recently concurred to rouse the community to earnest consideration of the state of crime under its multiform relations and aspects, and to produce a universal conviction that some vital change of our penal system is indispensable to the security of society.

The system under which criminals have been disposed of during the last few years, involved a great change from that which preceded it. It was, of course, experimental, and its merits or demerits are being only now practically ascertained. That, to a considerable extent, it has proved a failure seems to be admitted even by its warmest advocates. That this has been particularly the case in England is beyond denial. A great blunder has been committed in making the terms of penal servitude awarded by the Bench convey a false meaning. It is absurd to read of a Judge solemnly expatiating on the severity of a sentence of ten years' penal servitude, when it is well known that this really means only seven years' confinement. Then, it is stated by most competent authorities, and popularly believed, that this confinement is no adequate punishment; that, in fact, it is accompanied by so little of that suffering and discomfort which are the essence of penal infliction, that it falls altogether short of the end of all punishment, the deterring from crime. Reflection and common sense seem now to have reached the conclusion, that the change from the old to the present system partook not a little of the character of a rush from one scheme to another. Without doubt, a decided change was in various respects imperative. Our penal code was in many instances cruelly severe, and the reformation of criminals was a thing scarcely thought of unless by a few considerate philanthropists. Many comparatively venial offences against property were visited by the terrible punishment justly attached to the most atrocious murder. Retrospection to those times now fills us with astonishment that the community should have so long submitted to so cruel, so unchristian a system. But the great crisis in our political relations which occurred some thirty years ago, imparted to popular opinion an authority which has made itself powerfully felt along every fibre of our social frame. This influence was beneficially manifested in the proceedings of our Criminal Courts. It was tacitly respected by the Bench : it purified and improved the selection of Juries ; and encouraged those Juries to assert their constitutional independence. Popular feeling and opinion, acting through Juries, corrected the too sanguinary character of the law. Jurors chose rather to do violence to their convictions, than perpetrate what in their estimation was a greater evil—the consigning of a fellow-creature to capital punishment for an offence adequately punished by a few months' imprisonment. Nothing could have more clearly indicated the confliction between the law and public opinion, which is, in fact, the basis of all law. But the uncertainty of punishment caused by this anomalous state of things was found to involve defeat of the very ends of punishment. The only remedy, therefore, was to reconcile the character of the criminal code with the conclusions of intelligent and humane opinion, and to aim at the prevention of crime by the increased certainty of appropriate punishment. The number of capital offences was accordingly reduced to treason, murder, and arson attended with the loss of life; of which the second is that most frequently appearing in our Criminal Courts.

A leading defect of the old system was the undue severity with which offences against property were visited, which was rendered all the more glaring when contrasted with the comparative leniency with which offences against the person were punished. This may have been owing to the statutory nature of the former class of crimes, and reform was undoubtedly most imperative in this department. But little or no attention seems to have been directed to the inquiry, whether some improvement was not required in the penal treatment of offences against the person? This inquiry, however, seems likely to be now forced upon our law reformers by the alarming prevalence of such offences, not only in the metropolis, but in almost every county of England. Scarcely a week passes without some appalling record of homicide, or of violent and cruel assault. Witness the many deliberate murders caused by revenge, jealousy, covetousness, lust, and intemperance, or wanton blood-thirstiness! What fearful disclosures of other crimes and gross immoralities are afforded by the trials of the criminals! Now there seems to be a growing and well-founded impression that in too many instances those crimes are not punished with adequate severity, and that this is a direct cause of the increasing jeopardy of human life.　It outrages the sense of justice to find, at the same assizes, a set of unfortunate creatures, convicted of theft, and doomed to years of penal servitude ; while sóme ruffian, convicted of culpable homicide, is sentenced only to some months imprisonment ! Then there are cases, not a few, of what most people would consider murder, which are softened down into culpable homicide, either through the quirkiness of counsel, or the unaccountable, and seemingly capricious doubts and difficulties insinuated by the Bench, or by some culpable carelessness in the getting up of the prosecution. So very anomalous are some of those cases, that one would think that the object of committal for trial was rather to favour the escape of the criminal scot-free, than to prosecute him to conviction ! Now, such a system seems a gross inversion of the natural order of things. Surely one's life is of more value than his purse, or even all that he has. Protection of property undoubtedly implies previous provision for the personal security of its owner. Undue leniency, in such cases as those referred to is cruelty and injustice to society. It directly encourages atrocities not merely perilous to the individual, but brutalising to society, by the revolting accounts of their perpetration, and the hideous punishment which they occasionally entail. To keep down such crimes there ought to be adequate certainty of punishment proportionate to their particular character ; while inferior courts of summary procedure might be beneficially intrusted with increased powers, not of fine, but of punishment by flogging and imprisonment, even in the more common cases of offences against the person.

There are many other matters connected with this subject which seem obviously susceptible of improvement. To these further reference is meantime postponed. There ought to be such a thorough revision of our criminal code and procedure, as to render the Court of Appeal, which some have projected, comparatively unnecessary ; for what does such a project imply but faultiness in the primary proceedings ? Trial by jury is too sacred a popular right to be tampered with, either directly or indirectly. Infallible it is not ; but what merely human institution is so ? All that can reasonably be expected of criminal law and procedure is that they shall be so framed and administered as to diminish the chances of error as much as possible.

We have already referred, in general terms, to the failure of our system of penal servitude, partly in consequence of its errors in principle, and partly through the faultiness of its administration. In the endeavour to reconcile the penal with the reformatory intention of imprisonment, failure has been the consequence in both respects. It does seem to exceed all the reasonable claims of humanity, when it is deemed a duty to support convicted criminals in a degree of personal comfort denied to those whom the chances of life have reduced to a state of honest poverty. We are assured by parties who have personally inspected our places of penal servitude, that they are less like prisons than institutions founded by the tenants themselves, to sharpen the faculties of swindlers by a good education, and to send out garotters, after an excellent course of physical training, to prey the more effectually upon the public. It is stated as a fact, that some time ago a chairman of Quarter Sessions having sentenced two prisoners to four years' penal servitude under a misapprehension, was obliged afterwards to reduce the sentence to a year's imprisonment in the House of Correction. The next day the prisoners actually sent to him to say that they were advised that, having been convicted upon two counts of the indictment, they were entitled to the longer sentence, and to entreat that it might be inflicted! In fact, the " run " of the prison is far superior to that of the House of Correction ; and, far from deterring from crime, it seems rather to encourage it, for, the more aggravated the offence, the less disagreeable the punishment!

The inmates of our penal institutions have a wholesome, nutritious, and toothsome dietary, about which they are very particular. Loud and indignant are their complaints if there is the slightest error in the quantity, quality, or cookery of their meals. Banyan days are unknown in these "stone-frigates," the daily dinner including a handsome portion of the best butcher-meat, beef and mutton being given on alternate days to prevent unpleasant monotony! There is besides a basin of savoury soup, and a sufficit of first-rate potatoes, "admirably boiled." Breakfast consists of a proper allowance of bread and restorative cocoa; and for supper there is a pint of balmy "brochan." The prisoner's bed-room is a snug little place, clean, well-aired, and pleasantly warm. There is every comfort about the bed to induce sound sleep; every week the prisoner has his refreshing bath, heated to an agreeable temperature; and he enjoys the devoted services of chaplain, doctor, and schoolmaster. If he likes to be rather reserved, attractive books are at his command; if he is gregariously inclined, he has society, rather numerous, however, than select. In short, to regard his confinement and treatment as a punishment were absurd. Then, if he feels even this confinement rather irksome, he may abridge it by a mechanical conformity with prison routine, which makes him a good prisoner, but not a whit the better man. There is no such thing as really hard labour in any of the prisons. Calico-weaving, mat-making, shoemaking, and such light occupations are the only descriptions of work performed within the prison. The prisoner is consulted, as far as the resources of the establishment permit, as to the particular trade he prefers ; and, if he chooses to be industrious, he may earn a considerable gratuity, carefully saved up for him by the Government, and amounting at the end of a long term of punishment to £20, and sometimes even £40! At Portland, where there is out-door work, some are employed in blacksmiths' shops, some at bricklayer's or mason's work, but the majority work in the quarries. In winter they work about eight and a half hours, in summer nine hours daily; but they take it very easily, five of them doing no more than is accomplished by two free labourers working for hire! This explains why criminals make so light of what is termed hard labour. Should a shower fall, they are actually marched off to sheds for protection, while the honest labourer plods on through foul and fair! At noon the latter sits down, when he works, to his poor dinner of bread and cheese, with some occasional scrap in the way of relish, and a jug of sober coffee ; while the convict is marched to quarters, where he first makes his toilet, and then sits down to his ample and savoury dinner, either in solitary enjoyment, or in a snug little mess of some half-dozen.

We have already mentioned what is the usual "run of the kitchen ;" but convicts who choose to behave so decorously as to obtain the "fruits of good living," in the only sense which they seem capable of appreciating, may obtain a standard of moral excellence which is marked by an ascending scale of " suet-dumpling, baked meat, treacle-dumpling, cheese, and beer!" These creature-comforts, the regularity of habits, the cleanliness, and the " constitutional" labour which the convicts undergo, all tend to keep him in tip-top health and good spirits, and are an agreeable and refreshing change after the irregular hand-to-mouth, feast-and-fast sort of lives which they have led previous to imprisonment. At length, when there is no real regard for social and moral amendment, even this regular and easy life palls, and the convict, unchanged in heart, sighs for enlargement, with all its roving licentiousness. In many cases he quits a prison a more depraved being than he was when he entered it. This is caused not only by the misdirection of what is intended to be reformatory treatment, but by the directly injurious consequences arising from a promiscuous intercourse among the convicts which it is impossible to prevent. It may be easily imagined that the conversation which prevails on such occasions is not of the most refined or edifying character. "Old hands" recount their criminal exploits with great gusto to groups of admiring "greenhorns," who thus learn the arts of housebreaking, lock and pocket picking, and the scientific use of the bludgeon or life-preserver. In short, such a system is neither a terror to evil-doers nor a praise and protection to such as do well. When its natural tendencies are considered, the results, as manifested by the increase and atrocity of crime, cease to be matter of wonder.

A return to our former system of transportation has been generally recommended as a ready and effectual means of getting rid of the evils of penal servitude. Transportation has not been altogether discontinued, but it is resorted to in comparatively few instances. Formerly, for many years, it was a ready outlet for criminals; and the home country had thus good riddance of them, while their labour was of great importance to our nascent colonies. By convicts all great and useful Government works were executed; and not a few of them were usefully employed by private individuals. In those days transportation was awarded for comparatively light offences, and in other cases not implying great depravity of character. Not a few convicts, therefore, betaking themselves resolutely to honest industry, attained, in process of time, much wealth and consequent consideration. They had chances of well-doing which they never could have commanded at home, where even their merited prosperity was rather unlikely than otherwise to cause their unfortunate antecedents to be overlooked. Besides, in our Australian colonies there was boundless scope for enterprise. There was society for those of a social turn; there were " fresh fields

and pastures ever new" for those who preferred
the independence, tranquillity, and ease, of comparative solitude. All went well until sad abuses
crept into the system of convict management.
Convicts were permitted the unrestricted purchase
of intoxicating liquors even from the very Government officials! A train of mischiefs followed, so
that at length the colonists, greatly increased in
settled communities, in wealth, social refinement,
and respectability, loudly protested against a continuance of the then system of transportation, as
threatening their utter ruin. Their complaints
were listened to ; the system, instead of being improved, was abolished ; and the evils of which the
colonists complained were transferred to the home-
country. But experience has shown that transportation is best suited to those colonies which are
in a state of comparative infancy. Along the west,
and particularly the northern coast of Australia,
there are vast tracts suitable for the purpose ; and
in some quarters convict labour would be thank-
fully received. It is some such improved system of
transportation which is now advocated, as a measure
beneficial both to the home country and to the
colonies.

ANCIENT CITY WELLS.

No city in the empire is supplied with better water for every domestic purpose than Aberdeen. It was not, however, until after the lapse of many centuries, the adoption of various imperfect expedients, and a world of local contention, that our citizens bethought themselves of applying to the river Dee, as the source of a never-failing supply of an element indispensable to their health and comfort. Availing myself of some curious particulars, kindly communicated by an antiquarian friend (W. D.*), I have thought it may not be deemed uninteresting to give a history of some of the earlier projects for furnishing the city with one of the prime necessaries of life.

In ancient times the wants of the community, in the respect referred to, appear to have been supplied either from draw-wells, or from the various burns which traversed the town, the waters of which then flowed in all their primitive purity.

* The sagacious, witty, kind, true-hearted William Duncan. *Next* to the last literary work Mr. Ramsay finished was that memorial notice of his friend, W. D., inserted in an earlier part of this volume. Mr. Ramsay's *last* writing was a short memoir of *another* friend, very dear to the Editor.

Before the Reformation it was customary to dedicate wells either to the Virgin or to some favourite saint. Hence, St. Mary's well, which gave name to Marywell Street of the present day ; St. John's Well, still dispensing its limpid stream in the neighbourhood of Gilcomston Church ; and the Angel Well, near Hanover Street, which was probably dedicated to St. Michael. Each of the four Monasteries formerly in the town had its well, all of which have been discovered in the course of modern improvements. That of the Trinity Friars was immediately underneath the eastern wall of the Charter-room erected by the Incorporated Trades. The Corbie Well, on the Denburn, is so called from its flowing from the base of what was anciently named the Corbie Heugh, where part of an old forest afforded shelter for a settlement of rooks. Tradition has it that the old trees were cut down to furnish timber for building the steeple of St. Nicholas. In the ancient Bead House was a large well, which recently remained in a house in Correction Wynd. It probably supplied the water required for the ceremonial of the adjacent church of St. Nicholas. The Garden Nook Well, still to be seen, was dedicated to the Virgin, and probably quenched the thirst of our "ancient forefathers" in the heat of their sports in the contiguous Play Field. Among the old draw-wells for common use was one situated in Park Street (close by No. 17), near

the corner of East North Street. This was made
in 1558, when licence was given to William Ronald-
son and his neighbours to dig a well without the
Thieves' Port, provided it were enclosed with a wall
of stone and lime. Elderly citizens recollect this
well. It was of great depth; and the water was
raised by means of a bucket, rope, and wheel. The
loch appears to have anciently supplied water for
domestic purposes. In process of time, however,
it became unfit for such uses. In 1632 the municipal authorities, " considering the great necessity
wherein the neighbours of the town stood through
want of pure and clean water to serve their houses ;
and that the most part of the water wherewith they
were served, coming only from the loch, was filthily
defiled and corrupted, not only by the gutters daily
running into the burn, but also by litsters [dyers],
and the washing of clothes, and the abusing of the
water in sundry parts, with other sorts of unclean-
ness," came to the resolution that fountains should
be erected at the public expense for a proper supply of water. For this purpose the Burgesses of
Guild agreed to be taxed ; and Thomas Garden,
convener of the trades, promised 1000 merks Scots,
for himself and in name of the trades, for the
furtherance of the work. Not a little water was at
this time required for the brewing of ale. Even
about a century earlier, there were no fewer than
150 " browsters" in the town. The scheme of 1632,

however, was never carried into execution, in consequence of the civil commotions, from which Aberdeen suffered so much for nearly half-a-century. The population was about this time nearly 9000; but towards the end of the seventeenth century it had decreased to 6000. So the citizens were forced to put up with such water as they had, supplies of which were distributed by licensed water-carriers. In 1655 William Ingram and William Steven paid 10 merks yearly for the privilege of being " burne beirers."

In 1682 another proposal to erect fountains proved as unsuccessful as that of 1632. In 1706, however, a similar project had better speed. Bailie Stewart was " ordained to buy as much lead as would be sufficient for pipes and cisterns for bringing water from Carden's Well." The work, however, went but slowly on, for, in 1708, the Town-Council, " considering the many retardments that Joseph Forester, plumber, had met with in bringing in the water, allowed him the sum of £200 Scots, with £36 of drink money to his servants." Joseph's servants, although labouring to supply the community with fair water, seem to have had no fancy for the exclusive potation of it themselves. A century earlier their labours would probably have been beguiled by a tune on the bagpipes, a sort of creature-comfort which was liberally supplied by the town piper to the workmen employed on the old south pier. James Mackie and John Burnet agreed, in 1706, to build the first fountain at Carden's well for £10 sterling.

About this time William Lindsay was appointed overseer of the new fountains, with a yearly salary of £200 Scots. He engaged to erect a statue of brass on the Castlegate Well, with four "antick faces" on the corners thereof, whence water might play *ad libitum.* This hydraulic fancy seems to have been found rather expensive ; so a wooden statue, gilded over, was erected instead of the brazen image. The new wells appear to have been the favourite rendezvous of gossips, both male and female, to the great hindrance of business. In 1710 the authorities were obliged to ordain, that "stands or casks were not to remain at the wells longer than necessary." The town sergeants were authorised to "break casks, stands, or pans, and to make use of the brass and timber thereof for their own use; they always bringing the broken pans to the clerk's chamber." The latter clause seems to have been enacted in view of the possibility of any compunctious feelings on the part of the sergeants towards condemned pans, inasmuch as it was natural for those functionaries to prefer keeping entire the forfeited utensils, seeing that they were "for their own use." At the same time persons were prohibited from washing anything at the wells ; and "all women from washing and tramping in tubs in any part of the streets of the burgh, under the penalty of £20 Scots."

The demand for water still increasing with the increase of the population, it was resolved, in 1766, to bring an additional supply from the "Gilcomston Spring," and to erect a reservoir in Broad Street for the water brought from Fountainhall, which reservoir still remains. The execution of the work was committed to Mr. Selbie, plumber, Edinburgh. Now, this project appears to have been the source of much curious contention. The building of the reservoir was being proceeded with when a droll difficulty was started by certain dwellers in the Broadgate and Gallowgate, to whom a supply of mere water appears to have been a secondary object. They addressed to the Town-Council an earnest memorial, setting forth that the said reservoir "would shut up the dial-plate on the College Kirk from public view." True, there was the College clock; but this time-measurer they charged with such "insufficiency," that its vagaries "led the neighbourhood into *sundry* errors and mistakes." It would seem that these worthy citizens were conscious that it required a steady clock, indeed, to keep *them* to time ; for they candidly confessed that "an exact clock would tend much to promote regularity and good order in their quarter, *an event very desirable.*" They prayed, therefore, that a new clock and dial-plate might be placed in front of the reservoir. Moved by this frank representation, and duly perpending the grave necessity of providing the means of enabling the fallible, but ingenuous petitioners to keep good hours, the Council resolved to put up the desiderated clock, "in a handsome and genteel manner." This looks like a considerate wish on the part of the authorities to correct the irregularities of their petitioners with as little offence as might be to their feelings. Up, then, went the clock! but, alas! for the unfortunate memorialists! In the course of two years, "regularity and good order" in *their* quarter were still found to be as "desirable an event" as ever. A dial-plate, indeed, *had* been administered in their case; but it was far too obstinate to yield to anything short of the exhibition of a bell, too! The merely "silent monitor" *without*, seems to have been as "insufficient" as that *within* them. What availed it to admonish them of the value of time through one sense only—the sense of sight— bootless o' nights, and, at any time, so liable to tantalising fits of duplexity! No, their sense of hearing must also be appealed to. They required something *striking* to make a due impression. So, "on a petition from a great number of the inhabit- ants, a striking part and a bell," were ordered to be added to the clock on the reservoir. This seems to have had the desired effect. To this wise provision may we, doubtless, ascribe the "regularity and good order" which have ever since characterised the worthy "nichtbours" in this quarter! Of elder denizens of the gossipdom, old Time has spared a remnant to enjoy well-earned ease, and a crack about days of yore, amid the tasteful amenities of suburban retirement. We may remark, by the way, that the College folks seem never to have complained of the "insufficiency" of their clock ; their habitual discipline probably making amends for the free and easy system pursued by their horologe. Among other objectors to the reservoir —a staid old lady complained that it "obstructed her lights"—but whether of her domicile or understanding appeareth not ; while a certain merchant took out an "interdict" against the unhappy building—reasons not stated.

Nevertheless the reservoir was completed, and did its duty ; when, in the course of some twenty years, "the letting out of its water" again symbolised "the beginning of strife." In 1791 eighty citizens memorialised the Town-Council, to the effect that the water of the reservoir was "strongly impregnated with tar, in consequence of the improper mode of repairing the seams and rents in its bottom, by which great disgust was occasioned, and pernicious consequences might arise, both to the *health* of the citizens, and the *public cisterns and pipes.*" Here was a monstre grievance, and most disinterestedly was it urged. Not for themselves alone were the memorialists concerned, their sympathies embraced the "cisterns and pipes."

Could either, albeit of mould so leaden, be expected passively to act as the harbourers, or guides of *tar* water, without "great disgust!" The overseer of the reservoir was denounced as a poisoner ; placards were posted on the building itself, bearing—"Tar water sold here!" No faith had the citizens in the doctrines of good Bishop Berkeley, who was at the trouble to write a treatise to prove that tar water was as sovereign a panacea as Parr's Life Pills are now attested to be. An explanation was demanded of the overseer. That he was sorely puzzled appears from the fact that he gave in a "long answer." When the cistern was nearly empty not a rent appeared, but when it was full there was a "continual dropping." Despairing of finding out the mystery, he *did* tar the bottom of the cistern. The worthy man ultimately discovered that it was the weight of the water, when the cistern was full, that set the rent a-gaping, which of course closed when the utensil was nearly empty! The cistern was at length repaired without tar, and the citizens, cisterns, and pipes were satisfied!

So much for old wells, and for some of the old frets of our forefathers. What was once cause of irritation to them, is now a source of amusement to us. We, too, shall have our turn. Our ancestors, mayhap, will be avenged of our pleasantry at their expense in the jokes cracked by a future generation on the squabbles of our own day.

THE FIRST OF APRIL 1813

WILL long be remembered as one of the most disastrous days of Bon-Accord, in consequence of the melancholy shipwreck of the *Oscar* on the fatal Greyhope, a rock at the Girdleness, situated a little to the south of the entrance of the harbour. For some time previous the weather had been remarkably propitious, and everything was fraught with the promise of uninterrupted spring. Early on the morning of the 1st of April the *Oscar* had left the harbour in company with four other whale-fishing vessels, and all were riding at anchor in a sea as smooth as glass, which proved but too deceitfully calm. About five o'clock in the morning, however, the sky began to lower, and exhibited to the experienced eye of the seaman certain presages of impending storm. The *Oscar* accordingly weighed anchor and stood out to sea. Unfortunately she had not on board her full complement of crew, and was obliged to stand into the bay for the absent hands, who had been spending their time in all the reckless jollity in which the sailor delights to revel on the eve of departure on a long voyage.

By this time the storm of the morning had lulled a little, as if on purpose to facilitate the securing of its devoted victims. All the crew were safely shipped on board the *Oscar*, now far in-shore, amid a heavy sea, a stormy flood-tide setting in, and a fatal calm. Suddenly a hurricane burst from the north-east, accompanied with thick snow. The situation of the *Oscar* was now perilous in the extreme, and the spectators on shore trembled for her fate. About half-past eleven A.M., after dragging her anchor, she drove ashore on the rock called the *Greyhope*. Her destruction now appeared inevitable. A tremendous surf broke over her, ever and anon dashing her against the rock with such resistless force that the noise of the concussion was distinctly audible at a considerable distance, striking terror and dismay into the crowd that covered the pier, in defiance of the violence of the tempest, which threatened destruction to all that opposed its career. A more heart-rending scene cannot well be conceived. Forty-four hapless individuals were perishing in sight of their nearest and dearest relatives and friends, who could only send them, across the raging deep, their heart-felt yet unavailing sympathy. Some of the crew attempted to form a bridge to the nearest rocks by cutting away the main-mast, but it unfortunately fell alongside the ship, instead of towards the shore as they had fondly anticipated. Soon after the fore and mizen masts gave way, when many who had clung to them for a chance of safety were swept into the tumultuous waves. Every desperate effort of the sailors to save their lives was fruitless.

All that now remained above water of the once trim *Oscar* was the forecastle, on which five men, one of them Captain Innes, were distinctly seen, making signals for that assistance which all longed to give, but found it impossible to afford. After clinging to the wreck for some time, they were at length compelled to share the fate of their unfortunate companions. Of the whole crew only the first mate and one of the seamen were, with the utmost difficulty, saved. The loss sustained by the owners was estimated at £10,000. The *Oscar* had been recently repaired, and was completely equipped for the voyage.

This catastrophe excited the deepest sympathy for the surviving relatives of the sufferers, and the sum of £1200 and upwards was speedily raised and distributed among them, according to their various situations.

The bodies of Captain Innes and thirty-seven of the crew were afterwards cast on shore; and it was a melancholy sight to see the crowds of weeping relatives eagerly endeavouring, often with difficulty, to recognise the storm-disfigured countenances of the departed objects of their affection. In this sad employment they were much comforted

by the unremitting and unwearied kindness of the
late worthy Dr. Cruden of Nigg, who was equally
zealous in ministering to the temporal necessities
of the wretched, and pouring the balm of spiritual
consolation into the wounded soul.

Soon after the complete destruction of the
Oscar, the storm, which had raged with such unexpected violence, suddenly abated its fury, as if
satisfied with having executed the mysterious
behest of heaven. The sky resumed its wonted
serenity, the wind was hushed to repose, and no
vestige of the recent wrath of the elements remained, save the deep swell of the hollow-murmur-
ing wave, and the desolation which the untimely
visit of winter had left behind.

Fair dawned the morning of that fatal day,
  Bright with false promise of returning spring,
When o'er the wave they winged their joyous way,
  To spoil the icy ocean of its king.

Light was the sailor's heart, as best beseems
  The heart that meets the terrors of the wave ;
No idle fears, no sentimental dreams
  Be his whose pathway soon may prove his grave !

The sailor revels in the freshening gale,
  The sounding surge is music to the Tar,
Else could he brace the tempest-tatter'd sail,
  Or brave such ocean-fields as Trafalgar ?

Yet there is terror in that cloud that steals,
  Low, crouching, from the ocean's utmost verge ;
Still seems the sea-fowl, as aloft it wheels,
  To scream the mariner's prophetic dirge.

Ah, were it only *seeming!* for now forth
   From the dark citadel of cloud and storm
Rush the dread legions of the ruthless north,
   Heaven's mystery of judgment to perform !

Bootless the cunning of the pilot's hand
   To baulk the fury of the raging blast ;
Bootless the strife to reach or shun the strand,
   Yon rock proclaims the hour of safety past !

And must they yield, unaided, to their fate,
   Sweet home in sight, and all its nameless charms !—
Despair usurp the too fond breasts where late,
   Heaved the deep tumult of true love's alarms?

Are prayers of kindred, friendship, woman's love,
   Lost 'mid the uproar of the maddening waters?'
Is there no Father in the heavens above
   To soothe the sorrows of his sons and daughters?

There is :—yet clouds and darkness oft surround
   His throne though radiant with eternal light ;
Even though unsought, in mercy is he found,
   And love directs the terrors of his might !

Where erst were heard the timbrel and the dance,
   The voice of weeping steals upon the ear !
And thoughts of late departed joys enhance
   The grief that longs to share the lonely bier.

The parent's house is childless in a day ;
   The child must learn to seek the " orphan's aid ; "
The wife !—she now implores the " widow's stay ; "
   Oh ! may he cheer the more than widowed maid.

Oft as the voices of the winds and waves
   Shall wildly mingle in unearthly glee,
Some hearts will wander to the moundless graves
   Of those who sleep beneath the deep, deep sea.

THE SICK CHAMBER.

". It is better to go to the house of mourning than to the
house of feasting."—SOLOMON.

SINCE better to the house of woe,
Than that of feasting, ye may go;
Then, ponder well that sufferer's part,
When aching head makes fainting heart;
When dearest boon he may obtain
Is respite brief from tossing pain,
And the couch where he doth languish
Seems the chosen bed of anguish.
E'en from the cheerful eye of day
Despondingly he turns away;
And sounds, which joyous else appear,
Strike doleful on his watchful ear—
Still listening to the plodding clock,
And startled at the fancied knock!—
Even in the passing wind
Dreary omen he will find;
And should the voice of midnight hour
Give warning from some churchyard tower—
Loud swelling on the fitful blast—
Despair propounds—was that thy last?—
'Tis ciphered in the flickering taper,
That life is but a fleeting vapour;

There's that, in leech's guarded look,
Few, from his lips, can calmly brook !
And then around come trooping fast
The phantom memories of the past ;
And, hovering around his bed,
The sick man sees the long-lost dead—
With looks so sad—so passionless,
So shadowy all, so fashionless !
Ah ! then, how stricken conscience bleeds,
At memory of wayward deeds ;—
Of many an hour to folly given,
Despite a still forbearing Heaven ;
Of time misspent—of talent wasted—
Of pleasure's cup too deeply tasted—
Of grace despised—neglected prayer !—
Oh ! what a load of guilt is there !—
Meanwhile, the pulse's fluttering play,
Scarce warrants hope of added day,
While muttering lip, and filming eye,
Announce the time of farewell nigh,
And words, which may not be repeated,
Bespeak a brain too fiercely heated :—
The scarcely-breathing watcher's foot
Falls softly as the snow-flake mute,
For, in that chamber's gathering gloom
Seems growing kindred with the tomb,
And, brooding there, he well may ween
A presence—awful though unseen !
In such dark hour, from purpose fell !
Prevailing Spirit ! guard us well ;
For, dread to all, howe'er they die,
Is nature's parting agony !
Oh ! gently, in that hour of dread,

Deal ye who tend the lone sick-bed ;
The contrite tear be gently dried ;
Be pity's dearest art still plied ;
Still words of hope and peace be spoken,
Still ministered some soothing token ;—
Perchance some old familiar flower
Of youthful love's remembered bower ;
There's solace in its balmy breath,
For spirit drooping nigh to death,
And hint of love without decay,
Enshrined in one long passed away,
(For seraphs linger not in clay !)—
Still o'er the sick devoutly bending,
Affection's prayer with his lie blending,
That, even at nature's parting hour,
Be felt sweet mercy's purchased power ;
That faith, the quenchless lamp of Heaven,
Be to the pilgrim-spirit given,
Sure guide along the shadowed way,
Till mingling with eternal day !

TO MY FRIEND.

AND have I found a friend—tho' few there be
Worthy that name my heart bestows on thee?
Tho' some might flutter in my brighter day,
With *its*—alas!—*their* flight they winged away!
At fortune's gloom, if friendship's *show* is flown,—
Yet friendship's *self*—in thee I call mine own!
Fain would my wish some meet return impart!
If thou wilt have it—take my wounded heart!
Poor is the gift—'tis true;—tho' poor it be—
'Twill boast a worth—in being dear to thee!
And never, never may such heart be thine
As needs the sympathy—I crave—for mine!
Still as these simple lines shall meet thine eye,
Oh! let them win the comment of a sigh
For him who penned them, when to native dust
Is given his fragile frame—as soon it must!
Think—that I loved thee!—if my spirit may—
When 'scaped the prison of this mortal clay,—
Breathe one fond wish—let this an earnest be—
My fervent prayer shall oft be breathed for thee!
Nor deem my presence as for ever fled
When low in grave is laid my weary head!
In pensive mood if thou shalt, haply, steal
Where *thou* wilt need no marble to reveal

The lonely spot where unawakened lie
The tongue's prompt greeting !—welcome of the eye !
The ready smile !—the look !—which only love
Like thine might read !—all force of speech above !
Perchance even *then* my spirit shall be near,
To thine !—be, therefore, checked the starting tear,
Or—if a single droplet needs must flow—
Bright let it fall !—nor dimmed by shade of woe !
My soul shall seek thee—if it ever may !—
Unseen companion of thy earthly way !
When fortune smiles,—thy joy shall reach to me,
If aught of gladness I may share with thee !
And if thou prove the lot of all that live,—
I'll soothe thy grief—if aid be mine to give !
And when at last shall come the solemn hour
When death asserts its universal power,
And thou must pace, alone, its dreary vale—
O ! were it mine—the very first to hail
Thy stranger spirit with a brother's kiss—
A welcome denizen of realms of bliss !

MY GRAVE.

FAR from the city's ceaseless hum,
Hither let my relics come ;—
Lowly and lonely be my grave,
Fast by this streamlet's oozing wave,
Still to the gentle angler dear,
And heaven's fair face reflecting clear.
No rank luxuriance from the dead
Draw the green turf above my head,
But cowslips here and there be found,
Sweet natives of the hallowed ground,
Diffusing Nature's incense round !
Kindly sloping to the sun
When his course is nearly run
Let it catch his farewell beams,
Brief and pale, as best beseems ;
But let the melancholy yew
(Still to the cemetery true)
Defend it from his noontide ray
Debarring visitant so gay ;
And when the robin's fitful song
Is hushed the darkling boughs among,

There let the spirit of the wind
A heaven-reared tabernacle find
To warble wild a vesper hymn,
To soothe my shade at twilight dim !
Seldom let foot of man be there,
Save bending towards the house of prayer :
Few human sounds disturb the calm,
Save word of grace or solemn psalm !
Yet would I not my humble tomb,
Should wear a deep forbidding gloom,
As if there ever brooded near,
In fancy's ken, a thing of fear ;
And, viewed with superstitious awe,
Be duly shunned, and scarcely draw
The sidelong glance of passer by,
As haunt of sprite with blasting eye ;
Or noted be by some sad token,
Bearing a name in whispers spoken !
No !—still let thoughtful schoolboy stray
Far from his giddy mates at play,
My secret place of rest explore,
There con the page of classic lore :—
Thither let hoary men of age
Perform a pensive pilgrimage,
And think, as o'er my turf they bend,
It woos them to their welcome end :—
And let the woe-worn wandering one,
Blind to the ray of reason's sun,
Thither his weary way incline,
There catch a gleam of light divine :—
But, chiefly, let the friend sincere
There drop a tributary tear ;

There pause, in musing mood, and all
Our bygone hours of bliss recall ;
Delightful hours ! too fleetly flown !
By the *heart's* pulses only known !